KNIFEBOY

A NOVEL

TOD HARRISON WILLIAMS

Simon & Schuster Paperbacks
New York London Toronto Sydney

Simon & Schuster Paperbacks
1230 Avenue of the Americas
New York, NY 10020

First Simon & Schuster paperback edition August 2007

SIMON & SCHUSTER PAPERBACKS and colophon are registered trademarks
of Simon & Schuster, Inc.

For information regarding special discounts for bulk purchases,
please contact Simon & Schuster Special Sales at 1-800-456-6798
or business@simonandschuster.com

Designed by Davina Mock-Maniscalco

Manufactured in the United States of America

10   8   6   4   2   1   3   5   7   9

Library of Congress Cataloging-in-Publication Data is available.

ISBN-13: 978-1-4165-3821-9
ISBN-10:   1-4165-3821-6

FOR my mother

KNIFEBOY

The Dartmouth football office was above the locker rooms and smelled that way, normally. Except the windows were open and the spring air seeping in smelled good and fresh and made me think of trees and clouds of pollen and shit like that until a waft of air thick with the scent of burning charcoal spilled across the sill and took a seat in my lap.

There was a barbecue somewhere in the Upper Valley. I

thought about Isabelle. Maybe she was at that barbecue, drinking and cracking up at bad jokes from guys with their hands in their pants, admiring their fucking river sandals. She can be kind of a slut and a flirt when she drinks—and when she laughs it's like she's sticking a fist full of flaming sparklers in my stomach with her left hand and tickling my balls with her right.

The nausea hit me. I got up and paced around the empty office. I looked at the photos of former teams on the walls and checked out those on the empty desks. All of the secretaries and low-level coaches were gone. All of them had funny-looking kids. I was alone. Waiting.

The skin above my ass constricted when it hit the icy green leather sofa. I yanked my pants up, shifted around a bit, and closed my eyes, trying to relax. I imagined the barbecue. It was so real. I could smell perfume and beer. Lipstick. Jell-O shots. I could make out jokes, the way Isabelle doesn't listen when bored, scanning the porch for somebody she wants to impress or charm or seduce. She pets the dog—probably named Dune or Cody. And I smelled her worming away from me as I drunkenly creep toward her, watching her, wincing. Her laugh burned through me. I tasted the electric residue on my tongue like the top of a battery.

I opened my eyes and ripped off six or seven hard coughs. I almost puked. I was drooling and sick and wanted to run when I realized I was getting furious over the scent of a distant barbecue and jealous of imaginary laughter from a girl who was not my girlfriend. I had a girlfriend and wouldn't have dated Isabelle, even if she wanted to date me. She wasn't hot enough.

Nebson walked out of Zeda's office, his fists balled up, eyes red. His head looked unbelievably square, even for Nebson, whose square head was practically his trademark.

"Hey, Nubby."

"Fuckin' assholes." He blinked, eyes wet.

Clearly, Nubby had gotten passed over. He was going to be a

senior in the fall and would probably never play in a varsity game at Dartmouth.

Berkus, Nubby's offensive line coach, shuffled out after Nebson and went to his office, looking glum and guilty. I watched Zeda pick up his phone through the open door. I heard a ring in O'Mally's office, which was directly to the right of the couch I was sitting on. His door opened.

"Hauser." O'Mally had one of those classic bushy gray mustaches that jumped around when he talked. Just watching it booking all over his face could put someone in a good mood. He used to be a New York City cop. Before that he was a paratrooper in Vietnam. Now he was the defensive line coach, and I played defensive end. I smiled. "Hey, Coach."

He had a tape and my file in his hands. "You need anything before we get started? I got sodas in my office."

"No, thanks, Coach."

O'Mally sat on the edge of Zeda's desk. Zeda looked up at me, his black bull neck bulging out like walrus fat over his necktie.

"Take a seat."

I sat. Bigs, our weight-training coach, nodded at me from a chair in the corner. Bigs was huge, probably six eight. He played tackle at Williams and got drafted but only made the practice squad for some professional team. The Dolphins, I think.

I assumed that I'd get the same treatment as Nubby. Not that I was as bad as Nubby, who blew. I just wasn't much of an athlete, wasn't recruited, was undersized at six three, sucked in the weight room, and was not very enthusiastic about football. Frankly, it bored the hell out of me and I'd almost been looking for a reason to quit. I was sort of hoping for one of these deals where the coaches tell you that you're probably never going to play but they love having you on the team and appreciate the work, so, you know, it's up to you. That's what I expected. The easy out.

The only bummer about quitting was I did like that odd afternoon, when you'd be out there, jogging around in the autumn sun, sweating a little, thinking about even less, and you'd just sort of forget you existed. That was nice. Plus, Coach O'Mally wanted me to play. My friends wanted me to do it. They liked me. And sometimes, I guess, that's all it takes.

So, I was sitting there vaguely aware of Zeda's mouth moving and throat swelling, thinking about Isabelle, trying to smell charred sugar and going over my practice sales pitch in my head when Zeda said, "Hauser. What did I just say?"

"Ummmm . . . You were talking about rushing."

Zeda pursed his lips. "Is there something going on outside the window that's more important than what we're doing here?"

"No. I'm just tired. Exams. Sorry."

"Well. What I was saying is that, we don't usually like to play walk-ons, but it's happened before. Clearly you need to work on your lifting." I nodded, trying to be as attentive as possible. "But there's a difference between how a player looks on paper and how he actually plays. Your stats ain't all that impressive."

Bigs said, "Fuckin' pitiful. You are THE worst athlete I have ever seen in the weight room—female teams included."

Zeda continued, "But I've been watching your JV game tapes and some of the practice tapes here." He patted the tape on his desk. "And somehow you get it done. I think there are guys who know how to play well and there are guys who know how to win. I want to show you something. Pat, put in the tape."

Zeda passed O'Mally the tape on his desk. O'Mally stuck it in the VCR and hit play. It was the Cornell game. "Okay. Watch how you come off the line. You're the first person to move after the snap. The technique on your swim move isn't great. But look, here." The VCR was playing in slow motion. I had slipped past the right tackle and was running down the line. The tackle on the opposite side of the ball was charging toward me. Zeda pointed at the tackle. "This guy outweighs you by fifty pounds. It looks like he's going to pancake you. But watch." In the tape, you can't see it, but I remember crouching down a little when I saw the tackle and then exploding up under his helmet with my fist cocked under my shoulder. I punched him in the neck. It felt like hitting a cold turkey—a little slime, some cartilage, and a big hollow thud.

On the tape, all you could see was our bodies colliding, the flash of my fist, and his head snapping backward. I plowed forward, directly into the fullback as he received the handoff. I knocked the fullback on his ass, tattooed his chest with my cleats, and then glanced back over my shoulder to see the ball bouncing around at the quarterback's feet. One of our guys dove on it. The lineman I punched fell onto his knees, struggled to take his helmet off, and then toppled over sideways, gripping his neck. The tape cut out just as the Cornell team doctor rushed onto the field.

O'Mally made a sound with his mouth. He shut off the TV. Zeda twisted his ass around in his hard wooden chair until he faced me, his eyes wet and tired. Shitballs. I was caught.

"I think you are someone who knows how to win. That's a great quality. It will get you places on and off the field . . . That is why I want to move you up to varsity and at least get you in some late down formations. But the other part—what you showed in this clip, the ability to play mean, to bring it when they don't expect it— that is what will get you a starting spot. That's where you have a real edge. You're not an athlete like the other guys out there. You're never gonna beat 'em in the weight room or in an arm-wrestling match. But if you bring that mean-spirited shit, you will *beat* them." He repeated himself. "You will *beat* them. Do you know what I'm saying by that?"

"I think I do."

Zeda smiled. "You know. Otherwise we would have cut you in preseason with the other walk-ons."

Zeda shuffled some papers on his desk. "All right. Coach Shrier's designed a workout schedule for you. I want you to stick to it. A lot can change over a summer, but so far you've shown promise. Have a nice break." He glanced at Shrier. "Send the next guy in."

One of the place-kickers was sitting on the couch, waiting. He looked like he had an ostrich egg up his ass. A phone rang somewhere in the building. O'Mally and I stepped out into the stairwell.

"Congratulations." He patted me on the shoulder.

I looked at my feet, kind of nervous and surprised. "Thanks. I didn't expect that. I wasn't all that sure that Zeda knew my name."

"We all have different coaching styles. Zeda likes to keep his cards close to the vest. My style is more straightforward. I would have given you a heads-up during spring ball, but Zeda asked me not to and he's the boss." O'Mally crossed his arms, scratched his chin, and nodded at me. "I know you were thinking about quitting." He shrugged. "Woodsy told me. He's worried."

"Yeah. Well. The situation's a little different now."

"I thought it would be. Obviously, we all expect you to be great, and I assume that you'll be coming back. But call me if you have any doubts. Okay?"

"Okay."

"Hell. Call me anyway, just to let me know when you're coming. It'll help me sleep better."

"Will do."

O'Mally and I stood there for a second or two, feeling awkward until he said, "I hear you're working for Stuart this summer."

"Yup. He's running an office."

"Oh, shit. I'm sure that'll be a smooth-running office. You gonna try to lift together?"

I didn't tell him that Stuart's office was in Covington, Kentucky, and I'd be working outside of Detroit for most of the summer. It was too complicated to get into. Instead I said, "I don't know if he can hang with me in the weight room."

O'Mally laughed. He gripped my hand like we do before running out on the field and said, "Death from above."

I cut across the lawn, toward the street and the frat parties on the opposite side. It was dark and warm and I felt good. I saw a reddish blond figure pedaling down toward me. I got excited. Every redhead I couldn't make out from a distance could have been Isabelle. This one wasn't.

There were parties in Herrot and AD. Kids who finished finals, or failed a final, or aced one, or didn't care. AD was the fraternity that the movie *Animal House* was based on. Herrot was the hockey frat. This time I did not need to imagine the stench of rotting beer. It blanketed the lawn, oozing from the grass like hangover sweat. Someone on the AD porch recognized me. "Hauser!"

Woodsy's body was silhouetted in the light coming out of the windows. His face was dark, but I recognized him immediately. His torso was longer than his legs. He sat about a foot higher than the rest of us. He was white but he had the perfect hair texture for an Afro. It was reddish blond and formed a streamlined tuft over his head. His profile was hilarious.

I walked up under the railing. "Thanks for ratting me out."

"You're not quitting and that's final."

"We'll see. Right now I want to play."

"Yeah. What changed?"

I thought about telling Woodsy about how surprisingly well the meeting with our coaches went, but I couldn't figure out how to do it without seeming like I was bragging, so I didn't say anything.

He got up and leaned on the porch rail. "We got a game of pong later. I reserved us a table." He meant beer pong.

"Gotta work."

"Thought you were done with finals."

"With Stuart."

"Oh, yeah. Fag. You two are such homos. When you going home?"

"Day after tomorrow. My dad's coming in the afternoon, we're staying the night and then he's driving me home in the morning."

"Come out after you and Stuart fuck each other."

"Maybe."

"Come out or I swear I'll come to your room and piss on you. I'm sleeping there, tonight, by the way."

Woodsy always slept in my room and I didn't think he'd piss on me, but he'd annoy the shit out of me if I didn't come out. Woodsy stuck out his cup. "Take a swig."

"Later."

"You promise?"

I thought about it for a moment. "Okay."

"I'll be right here. I'm waiting for you."

Stuart Parsi. We called him Stuey. His shirt was off, as usual. He was simultaneously cupping his balls with one hand and scratching his nipple with the other, as usual. He had a scar on his finger (the one scratching the nipple) that looked like a booger. Stuart's roommate glanced up from a book. I nodded at him. He stuck his head back down.

"Yo, dude," I said to Stuart.

"You ready to work?"

"Yeah."

"Let's go."

I watched Stuart pull his hand out of his boxer shorts and raise it up to his nose. He sniffed.

"Stuey. I just saw you smell your balls."

"I did not."

"Like hell you didn't."

The roommate sighed.

"Grab the stuff."

I picked up my roll of knives and a notebook and stepped into the hallway. Stuart followed me, laughing. "I got ball cheese, what can I say?"

We walked down into the basement, past the study area, which was packed with students cramming for finals. Stuart had his shirt off and was wearing only his dirty boxers. Some of the people studying looked up at us and laughed. Stuart was a funny guy, always doing weird shit, like smelling his balls, or one time over spring break he unplugged his fridge "for the environment" but he'd forgotten that he had a piece of raw chicken in the freezer compartment. His entire dorm needed to be fumigated. Stuart winked and giggled at some of the girls as we walked past.

We walked through the storage space, where everyone's trunks and boxes were stacked up to the ceiling in metal cages. It was pretty tight. We stopped right in front of the boiler. There was a table set up that we'd stolen from the study area. The room was hotter than hell.

Stuart started. "Okay. You want to take it from the top?"

"Sure."

"You ring the doorbell, I open the door."

"Oh. Hello, Mrs. Smith. It's nice to meet you. How do you do?" I stuck out my hand. Stuart stuck out the one with the scar that moonlighted as a booger. We shook.

"I'm fine. I'm in a rush. Over the phone you said I don't have to buy anything, right?"

"Of course not." Smile. "I just have to go through a presentation for you and whether you buy anything or not, I get paid. Plus, I get points toward winning a scholarship."

"How long will this take?"

"Not long. Thirty minutes maybe."

Stuart broke out of character. "Dude. It'll take an hour."

"I know. Just let me go through this my way, okay?"

"Okay."

"A half hour, maybe a little more."

"Like I said, I'm in a rush."

"I'll try to be as quick as I can. Do you mind if we go to your kitchen? That's probably the easiest place to do it."

"Sure. But it's messy."

"You should see my dorm room." Stuart laughed at my joke. I motioned to the table.

We both sat. I unrolled my knives as I talked. "This is a beautiful kitchen, Mrs. Smith. It's not messy at all. Listen, I'm a little nervous about this, so do you mind if I leave my notebook open?"

"Not at all."

"Okay, before we begin, I'd just like to tell you a little about

Bladeworks knives. The company was started in 1953, by a metal manufacturer in Orion, New York . . ."

Keating, Panolini, and Woodsy were lounging in Stuart's room when we came back. Panolini high-fived me. "I hear you're playing next year."

"Maybe."

Woodsy said, "He's playing."

Stuart slapped my ass. "Good to hear."

Keating put down his beer and stared at Stuart, who was drenched in sweat. He could see through his boxers. "What the fuck you been doin'?"

Woodsy piped up. "I told you they were fucking."

"We were working next to the boiler." Stuart took a look at Woodsy and shook his head. Woodsy was reclining at Stuart's computer, sideways with his feet up on the corner of the desk. Woodsy's dirty sandals were resting on what looked like a freshly printed term paper.

Stuart glanced around the room and asked, "Where's Siwat?"

"Who's that?"

"My roommate."

Woodsy won his game. "The Indian kid?"

"He's Malaysian."

"We told him to go to the study lounge."

"This is his room. That's why we were in the fucking boiler room." Stuart was sensitive about this kind of stuff. That's also why I liked him. He was considerate.

"This is my room." Woodsy belched. "So y'all can blow me." Woodsy winced as he slid his sandals off Stuart's desk, streaking the term paper with a thick brushstroke of mud and grass. "Let's go to Delta Theta Chi."

"I thought we had a game," I said to Woodsy.

"You took too long. I played with Keating." I was relieved. I hated beer pong. Woodsy's voice changed to a sort of British retard. "Not to worry, though, since you're both heretofore and since Stuart will certainly be playing with Keating as those homosexual gentlemen always tend to do, then I'll allow you to play with me, sir. If you'd be so kind. Pray thee."

He was trying to do some sort of imitation, but it didn't work.

"Jesus, Woodsy," said Panolini. "That sounded incredibly gay."

Keating said, "Woodsy's been doing that all night. I think it has something to do with an English exam he had."

"And aced!" added Woodsy.

We all looked at him. No one needed to say a word.

These were my friends. It was always the same.

None of us were members of a fraternity. You had to be at least a sophomore to join, and we were only freshmen. We went around to the brothers' entrance anyway. It was in the parking lot, level with the basement. Someone was pissing between two cars. Woodsy was talking and leading the way. "I'm definitely pledging Delta Theta Chi. Hauser, I expect you to do the same."

"Give me a break."

"You're such a fag. You want to quit football and you don't want to join a house. What's your problem?"

"I think fraternities are gay."

"You're gay."

Woodsy banged on the parking lot door. I hung back, more or less hiding in the shadow of the Dumpster. I pulled my hat down. I couldn't stand trying to get into fraternities. It took a minute, but Scooter eventually opened the door. He leaned out with a beer in his hand, looking surprised.

"Hey. What do you want?" Of course, he knew what we wanted. He was just giving us shit.

Woodsy answered, "Open up, Scooter."

"Oh. Are you delivering a keg? I don't see the Scotty's van." He looked around behind us, pretending.

"Fuck off." Woodsy smiled. Scooter didn't like this.

"Sorry, freshmen can come in the front." Scooter grinned, and his bloated red face split like a cracked cherry.

"Dude. There's a line."

"Then get in it."

"C'mon, man. Open the door. Don't make me have to lay my goon hand down on you."

"All right." He said to us, not Woodsy, "You guys can come in. Aborwoods, go get in line."

Woodsy had another comment in development, but Panolini put a stop to the situation before he could get it out. "Woodsy, why don't you tell him why you really came here." Woodsy turned around. "To suck Armbruster's dick."

"In that case . . ." Scooter pushed the door open, allowing Woodsy to walk past. "I'm next. Okay?"

"Fuck off."

I usually found Woodsy's antics entertaining, though sometimes they got on my nerves. In this particular situation, I could see that Woodsy was really being an idiot, which irritated me in so far as I knew he wanted Scooter to like him. He just had too much pride to ask nicely. However, in the case of Woodsy versus a guy guarding a fraternity door, I would always take Woodsy's side. So I was inclined to be a dick to Scooter, who I only knew by name but kind of hated anyway. But as I walked in, he looked at me, surprised, and said, "Shit, Hauser, I didn't know you were out there."

This was weird. I nodded and said, "Yo."

He waved me through and gave me a mini–dude hug. The basement was shaped in an L, with a bar to the left as we walked in, a pong table behind it, and two more set up around the corner. It was packed with people watching the pong games and waiting for beers. The blended scent of beer, vomit, wine, and garbage was overwhelming, but no one seemed to mind, least of all the girls, all of whom were dancing in puddles of the mixture. I grabbed a beer on my way in and started looking for Isabelle. I really didn't want to see her hooking up with anybody.

It was finals. Isabelle liked to party, and there were only so many chances left to hook up before everyone went home for summer break. I was supposed to have dinner with her and my father and her mother the following night, and in my paranoia I assumed that she'd be hooking up somewhere tonight. I just didn't want to see it. And Delta Theta Chi was Isabelle's fraternity of choice. She loved the guys there. She was from Washington, D.C., she played field hockey at Dartmouth, but she always said she was attracted to lacrosse players. Delta Theta Chi was mainly lacrosse players, but they had some football players too.

Hellman was a member of Delta Theta Chi. He played lacrosse and football and was legendary at both. I tried to walk on to the lacrosse team. That was my best sport in high school, but I was from Michigan, which has a reputation in the East for bad lacrosse. The coaches didn't even let me try out. Actually, I missed the try-outs because of football, and asked the coaches if they'd just watch me in a couple practices and told them that they could cut me if they wanted to, but they said it wouldn't have been fair. Try again next year. Fuck you.

I was actually relieved. I didn't like the guys on the lacrosse team, except Hellman. He said very little, and people worshipped him. At this very moment he was sitting on the edge of the bar, saying nothing and throwing beers at people who weren't drinking. That's what the guys in Delta Theta Chi did. Someone would be there, typically a girl or some dork, not drinking. You'd hear a senior sitting on the edge of the bar say, "Drink." And the beer would already be flying through the air. Hellman wouldn't say anything. He'd just chuck his beer.

I kind of looked up to Hellman because he was a good athlete and he was cool, but he was also nice to me. He'd laugh at the shit I'd say. And one time when Bigs was screaming at me, calling me a pussy because I could only do fifty push-ups and not a hundred, Hellman said, "Why don't you do it? You fat fuck!" and walked away. Bigs was silent. Then he went bananas on me and lectured us all on Hellman's shitty attitude. Most important, Isabelle had a crush on Hellman's best friend, Brice. So Hellman was safe.

Brice was sitting next to Hellman on the bar. They were kind of a combo. Brice the chatty one, Hellman the silent one. Naturally, I had all the reason in the world to hate Brice, but I didn't. He was a hard guy to hate. He never threw any beers, and he was funny.

Also, as I mentioned before, Isabelle was not my girlfriend. My girlfriend at home, Brooke, was superhot. She was two years older than me, had jet black hair, pale blue eyes, white skin, a few freckles across her nose and cheeks, plus really nice tits that her parents bought her when she turned sixteen. I can't stress enough how incredibly hot she was. And Isabelle wasn't hot enough—for me. Not that Isabelle wasn't hot. She was. She was hot the way the lead girl in a teen movie is hot, you know, she's the girl that seems a little dorky at first but she has that spark in her eyes, the cute body and vivacious personality. And fifteen minutes into the first act she's the girl that everyone loves. The problem was I needed more than that. Or, I should say, I needed more than that standing next to me.

Not that Brooke was a model, or that I was after dating a model, but she was about as close to that type of girl as I had been exposed to in my life, and I wasn't ready to let go of what she did for me. She not only made me look good, but she worshipped me, and when she really tried or just forgot what she was doing she could be perfectly well behaved. Isabelle might need a little training—no, she needed taming. She was totally uncontrollable.

There was this one time when Isabelle attended a formal at a fancy hotel. The dance floor was right by the pool. It was kind of packed and this girl who Isabelle hated was dancing right next to her, acting real slutty (in fact pretending to go down on the guy she was dancing with) until all of a sudden, Isabelle jumped up, barefooted, and kicked the girl square in the back, launching her into the pool. Isabelle might've seemed like a total bitch, but she dove in after the girl and then her date followed and then everyone went swimming. That kind of shit intimidated me. I admired Isabelle for doing it, and from a distance I was entertained by it, but when I imagined myself as her date it scared me. Would I follow her into the pool, or just lurk back over to the bar, smirking and smiling as I ordered us another round of Sea Breezes?

The deal with Isabelle kind of caught me by surprise. I had met her a couple of times through Keating, but never really paid any attention to her or knew her name. Then one night a few weeks into the school year I was stumbling across the Delta Theta Chi lawn to puke in the bushes. I didn't realize that the entire lawn was a few feet higher than the hill that bordered it, so when I slipped and unleashed my vomit on a choice patch of roots and tried to step through the bushes to steady myself, I toppled, still puking, off the terraced lawn. I landed on my face on the opposite side of the hedgerow.

I was lying on my stomach when I noticed that Isabelle and her friend were standing downhill from me in the center of a brownish delta, bitching about their shoes. I tried to apologize, but the girls wouldn't hear any of it. All Isabelle did was throw a five-dollar bill at me and told me to get something to eat. Even though I didn't remember her name, and could barely recall anything else that happened that night, I tracked her down and repaid her the money she chucked at me.

I think this impressed her, and as Isabelle quickly became my best friend at school I slowly fell in love with her. I was in denial until one day when Brooke was visiting. I realized that I couldn't stop fantasizing about Isabelle while Brooke and I were having sex. After that I still tried to resist acknowledging it until one night when Isabelle was hanging out in my dorm suite. I was in the room with the bunks, lying in bed. Everyone left and she came into the room with me. I don't know what she said, but she was talking and I was looking at her, convinced that at any moment she was going to climb up and get into bed with me. She had done it before, but this time I knew it would be different. And I was scared, because I wasn't sure if I wanted to take the risk of hooking up with her, but as she spoke I forced myself to honestly and deeply assess if I was in love with Isabelle. I was.

She must have seen the change in me. I may have looked at her too hard. I don't know exactly what happened, but something suddenly changed. She looked terrified. She said she'd call me later and left.

She vanished for a while. Everyone was puzzled as hell and kept asking me about Isabelle and why she wasn't around anymore. All of my friends thought she was in love with me. And I did, too— to a degree. But what my friends didn't realize was that it was impossible not to love Isabelle.

Enough time passed and eventually we became friends again. Isabelle kindly pretended that she didn't know I was in love with her. I dealt with it by bragging about Brooke. As I've said several times, I wouldn't be with Isabelle anyway, because she wasn't hot enough, but I could still hang out with her, which was the best.

We had to spend time together alone, though, because in public I clammed up around her and got jealous when she'd pay attention to anyone else. And when I saw her at parties I got that good old sparklers-in-your-stomach feeling. Sometimes if I was stone-cold sober and hadn't seen her in a while I'd get so nervous and excited that I thought I might puke.

Thank God, Isabelle had yet to arrive.

Woodsy called game and started filling a rack. I stood by the bar, chugging beers. I wasn't the type to approach girls I didn't know and I didn't like watching pong so all there was left to do was drink. Plus, I was really worried Isabelle would show up, so I wanted to be as drunk as possible when she got there.

I began to loosen up. They served "Beast" at Delta Theta Chi. Milwaukee's Best. It was really hard to drink unless you were drunk. I was headed there fast. The Beast tasted sweet and cold. I slid over to Hellman. "I dare you to hit Laura Fleming."

"Laura's a senior."

"Don' care."

Hellman waited a sec. "Okay, you throw it." He handed me the beer. Fuck. This was a problem. Laura was the hottest girl at Dartmouth. She had huge cans.

I had a crush on her and I had never thrown a beer at anyone before, let alone a girl who was probably pretty nice. I looked at the beer. I swirled it. Suddenly it was sailing. The froth looked like the tail end of a comet. It hit Laura in the head and exploded in her face. The beer then magically shot out of the cup, rose in the air, fell down, and then—like the sand in an hourglass—disappeared, twirling, into her cleavage.

The chatter in the basement stopped abruptly. A Phish song played on the radio. Laura ran over. There was a beer slick in her hair. That part laid flat. The rest rose up behind her like a bent wing. Crack. Her hand hit my face. "Who the fuck do you think you are, you ugly brace-faced faggot?!"

She screamed *faggot* so loud that I jumped back. Her lower lip was wet and shaking. The beer running down her face was getting blown at me in misty plumes. It looked like she might cry.

No one made a sound. I was terrified, but I also wanted in the worst way to correct the situation. To this end, I said as timid and sincere as possible, "Sorry. I was trying to hit Stuey." I pointed to Stuart, who was in the general area of where Laura got hit. "Aim's off."

She didn't look at Stuart, but I did, for some sort of help. He was standing frozen in position, with his beer poised next to his mouth. I waited for him to nod or say something or throw his beer at me . . . And that's when I saw it. He had a piece of chewed-up blue bubble gum stuck to his finger on top of the boogerlike scar. He was saving it.

I locked my lips under the edge of my braces, stifling a laugh. I breathed through my nose and thought to myself, please, don't. She raised her hand. My lower lip popped loose, and titters came out of my mouth. They caught on. All-out laughs started bouncing off the walls. Her arm dropped and she ran out. When the door slammed there was applause.

I immediately knew I'd done something hilarious and legendary, but somehow I kept my cool. I just stood there for a while, sucking it all in, when Brice leaned over and handed me a beer. "Here you go. Looks like you lost yours." I thanked him and he asked, "You friends with Isabelle Sloane?"

"Yeah."

"She a ho?"

I thought about it. I didn't want him to get any ideas, but I wanted him to like me, and the truth was that although she wasn't necessarily a ho, it would have been extremely easy for Brice to hook up with her. It took me a while.

"No," I said.

He looked disappointed and said, "Good. My girlfriend's been hanging around her lately." The sly bitch was trying to cozy up to Brice through his girlfriend. But nonetheless this was good news. I had even more reason not to hate Brice.

Hellman was smiling weirdly at me from the bar. I felt a hand on my shoulder. "Hauser. Come upstairs." It was Defossy. Defossy was a linebacker and sort of a Hellman-in-the-making. He was cool and I suspect fairly good at football, although he didn't start. I looked at Hellman. He winked at me.

"Okay."

I started walking out and Woodsy yelled, "Hauser, we got next game!"

"Let Panolini play if I'm not back."

My dudes watched me as I followed Defossy up the stairs.

We didn't go to Defossy's room. We went to Cutch's. Cutch was in there with another kid, Pete San Francheesie. Cutch was from Chicago. Pete was from San Francisco. Cutch was a quarterback, the star of the football team and only a sophomore. He had long hair and smoked a lot of pot. One time Zeda told Cutch he didn't want him smoking pot during the season, and Cutch said, "Sorry, bro. I'm not stopping. You can kick me off the team if you want." I heard it. He actually said, "Sorry, bro." It was in the locker room, after practice and late. Cutch had to stay to ice his ankle. I was there because I had to make up with Bigs for a missed session, after practice. I was sitting on the floor, trying to take my shoes off, but my forearms were so sore I couldn't untie the laces. Zeda didn't know I was in there. The freshmen lockers were separated from the rest. I couldn't see them, so I can't tell you exactly how Zeda reacted. I could tell that he didn't flip, because there was only a short pause. I held my breath so I didn't laugh. Zeda said, "All right," and then his footsteps went out the door.

I didn't laugh right away, because I thought Zeda might come back, and then I heard Cutch say, "Ya hear that, Hauser?"

"Yeah." And the laugh I had bottled up in my face deflated. "That was awesome."

"You can tell your buddies about it." Then I heard an ice pack hit the floor and he walked to the showers.

Cutch was mixing drinks when I walked in, and he turned and handed me one in a plastic cup. He had flip-flops on and a faded silk robe with a flower print. A cocktails sign glowed behind him, il-luminating his long, grimy mane.

"Thanks."

Pete stood in the corner of the room looking freaked out and holding a bong with half a tube of smoke still swirling in it. He was actually halfway in the closet. I suppose he jumped in there when he heard the door open and didn't know who was on the other side of it.

"Hey, Pete."

Pete was also a linebacker. He looked like a cool guy but didn't say much. "Heyyyyy," said Pete, blowing out a lungful.

Cutch put his hand up for a high five. I slapped it. "Nice job fucking soaking Fleming's tits. That's balls-out. She's a fucking up-tight cunt too. Good job, man. I mean it."

I said "thanks" but I was seriously feeling bad about what I'd done.

Defossy said, "She's got great tits, though. Fuckin' awesome."

"I know," said Cutch. "I came on them all freshman spring. Fuckin' cum shot queen."

I started fiddling with a ukulele Cutch had hanging from his bedpost.

Pete spoke, "Oh . . . right, you dated her."

Cutch shrugged. "Sit down." He had a dingy corduroy couch. I sat on it and noticed a small foam mat sticking out from underneath it.

"Is that a *yoga* mat?" I guess it was the way I said it, sort of sincere, but sort of incredulous. Pete and Defossy started laughing their asses off.

Defossy looked at Pete. "I told you he was cool. He fucking threw a goddamn beer at Laura Fleming! Soaked her fucking tits!"

I sipped my drink and looked at Cutch. All of this attention was making me nervous.

"Yes it is a yoga mat." Cutch was trying not to smile. "You have a problem with the ancient art of yoga?"

"No. It's great . . ." I was struggling to come up with something funny to say when Defossy cut me off.

"It's the gayest thing I've ever heard of."

"Whatever. I pull more wool than you fuckers could ever dream of. I'm trying to learn about tantric sex. You know what that is?"

I answered, "It allows you to fuck forever and you don't come. Instead, you have a body spasm."

"Right. How quick are you, Hauser?"

"Shit. Real quick. Like two minutes at most. Can I borrow your mat?" They all laughed. "Fuckin' need that thing."

Cutch smiled. "You got a girlfriend? I see you running around with that short strawberry blond chick. What's her name?"

"Isabelle." I started to get nervous. I didn't like Cutch, with his yoga mats and affinity for cum shots, asking questions about Isabelle. But then again, Cutch wasn't Isabelle's type. And she had a crush on Brice, who I just found out fortunately had a girlfriend. So I knew that momentarily, Cutch also was safe. He'd probably have to cut his greasy hair before she'd sleep with him anyway.

Defossy said, "Yeah, Hauser's got a girlfriend. She's fucking smoking. You met her at Homecoming."

"I remember . . . You should probably be banging that Isabelle, though. She looks like she could be fun." Cutch drew in a deep breath. "Do you know why we called you up here?"

"No."

"Do you know what it means to be tapped?"

"Not really."

"Every fraternity is allowed to tap one person a year. It means that you automatically get in the fraternity. And you don't have to rush."

"It's an honor, Hauser." That was Defossy.

"Once you're tapped, you try to get your friends to join. We like you. We want you in, and we think that you can bring in some good guys."

Pete, "We don't want any meatheads. Only meat whistles."

I laughed. "Would I have to go through pledge period?"

Defossy got indignant. "Of course you have to! What'd you think, we'd just make you a brother?"

Cutch said, "Don't worry. I'll go easy on you."

Defossy, "I won't." He smiled. Pete grinned sadistically.

Delta Theta Chi had a very difficult pledge period. They shaved funny shapes into their pledges' heads and called them "shit birds." That's what they did out in the open. There were rumors about sheep and that sort of crap, but I didn't believe them. What I did believe was that they treated their "shit birds" like shit and basically tortured them. I didn't want to be tortured or to join a frat.

"I don't know. I wasn't really thinking about pledging anywhere."

Cutch, "What?"

Defossy, "Big mistake."

Pete, "Get out."

I stood up.

Cutch, "Sit down. Pete, shut the fuck up. Listen, I know where you're coming from. I didn't want to pledge either, I thought it was gay. But I'm telling you, it's not. It's fun. You want to be in a frat. If you don't want to be in this one, fine. But you want to be in one."

Defossy, "Hauser, you ever go to the cafeteria late at night?"

"Of course."

"You see the losers hanging out there, playing Dungeons and Dragons? That's the alternative. No shit. I ain't fucking with you. This is an honor we're offering you, a real honor. And it doesn't just stop here." Cutch coughed. Defossy looked at him. Cutch nodded. "The love continues . . ."

Cutch, "Listen to this."

"Did you ever meet a guy named William Musineki?"

"No."

"Willi Moosenutts? He was here for the pig roast."

"Don't recall."

"Anyway, this guy, he's a great guy, but he's just about the biggest dumbass to ever take a shit on campus . . . Where's he working now? Goldman Sachs. How? Fuckin' Dan Abrams, a '93 hired him. Both played football, both Delta Theta Chis, both earning a hundred K outta college in jobs they didn't deserve."

Cutch, "And that's not the best part."

Defossy smiled. "Basically, you go Theta. You get taken into the womb."

I was lost. "The womb?"

Defossy and Cutch in unison, "The womb is in the tomb. Dragon!"

"What are you talking about?"

"They're a secret society on campus. The Dragon. There's a couple, but only two that matter: Sphinx and Dragon. You've seen the Sphinx house. It's that pile of shit across from the football office with no windows and a door on the roof."

"Sure."

"They suck, but they're the oldest. The Dragon house is up the hill, you can see it from the computer science building. Anyway, dude, if you want to get in one of those, it all starts right here."

I handed Cutch my plastic cup. "Can I get another?"

Cutch took my cup and mixed a stiff one.

"Thanks. What about my dudes?"

Defossy had taken over. "Who we talkin' about?"

"Woodsy, Panolini, Keating, Parsi."

"All solid."

Cutch made a sound. "Aborwoods's gonna be tough."

Defossy, "You're right. He'll probably get dinged."

"Dinged?"

Pete answered. He put his leg up on the couch and leaned his forearms on his knee, the bong still in his hand. "All it takes is one brother to deny you. It's called a ding."

I asked, "Who's gonna ding 'm?"

Pete, "Probably about half the house. The guy is fucking annoying."

Cutch, "He's all right."

Pete, "Hell, I got no problem with him personally, but if he didn't get dinged, I'd ding 'm just on principle."

Cutch squinted and pointed his cup at me. "There's one other thing you can do as a tap." He sipped and flexed his neck. "You can argue for him during rush. If you can convince the brothers who hate him that he's cool, he could get in."

"Honestly, what do you guys think?"

Cutch, "Honestly, I wouldn't count on it, but dude, you can't always make decisions based on what your friends do. A lot of my bros went to Gamma Delt." GDX was all football players and somewhat dorkier, because of the meathead factor. "We're still bros. And it's even cooler, because I can go over there and have a nice time and they can come here and hang, so it's all good. Anyway, I'll ask around and see what Woodsy's chances are, but in the meantime, how's your drink? Need a refresher?"

"Sure."

The moon looked like a million yellow and silver snakes slithering down the Connecticut River. The rope swing hanging over it was a black stick. Hard. With a ball on the end of it. Panolini reached out for it with a tree branch. The silhouette broke as he pulled it over.

Panolini backed up the bank, stepped on the ball, and swung out. As the rope arched, he leaned back, flipped over, and disappeared softly into the water. He reappeared ten feet downriver and swam ashore. The rope swung back to me.

I hit the water squarely on my back. The needles shot into me, but I was drunk and it didn't hurt so much. Still, I floated, waiting for the burn to go away, and when it did I felt the current and the boils swell up and push me. The water came in bunches at different angles. The sky passed overhead.

I could hear my friends calling to me. I didn't want the river to stop. Bizarrely, I didn't want to disappoint it. It occurred to me that I could stay in the river. Drift all the way to the ocean. Then I remembered the dam and the water got cold and I didn't want my friends to think I was in trouble, so I swam to shore and walked up the bank to meet them.

I usually sleep late, but for some reason I woke up around ten. Keating and Steiner, my other roommate, were still asleep. I lowered myself down from my bunk. I almost fell over. I felt like my eyes were going to pop out and two spouts of beer would pour all over Keating. I stumbled into our common area.

Woodsy was passed out on our futon. We could never close the futon because he'd broken it a couple months earlier. His body was partially covered by a thin, greenish blanket. The futon was completely covered in Doritos shards. Woodsy loved Doritos, Cool Ranch in particular. The empty bag stuck to the sweat on his back, and he had a pillow between his legs.

"You can get into my bed if you want. I'm up."

"Huh?" Woodsy blinked. His face was white and pink and puffy like a baby lab rat. His eyes were blind too.

"I'm up. Get in my bed if you want."

Woodsy groaned.

I sat at my desk for a while, waking up. I stared at my computer screen. Woodsy smelled. I opened the window. The Doritos bag blew off his back. I smoked a cigarette and checked my "blitzmail." That's what we called e-mail at Dartmouth. I had a bunch of e-mails from friends and whatnot, but Isabelle's name immediately caught my attention. I opened it. It was from the night before. The first part of the e-mail was asking me where I was going that night; the second part was about Cutch. She wanted to know if I was friends with him and if he had a girlfriend. I replied, saying, "Yeah, sort of friends . . . And yeah, I think he's got one. They seem pretty serious." Fuck.

I lit another cigarette. Woodsy moaned again. "Put that out. I'm trying to sleep." I didn't say anything. Then in one quick movement he jerked out of bed, staggered, and smiled.

"C'mon! Let's go get breakfast."

I came to Dartmouth with an enormous amount of stuff but barely packed anything to take home. Most of it was going into storage. However, I didn't pack that either, nor did I plan on actually taking it to storage. I had an alternative method of dealing with this problem.

Keating was packing up his desk stuff. I saw him put a book called *Fun Christian Things to Do in College* in the box. The first day Keating got there, I noticed that book and others like it on his bookshelf and made a joke about them. I said something like, "Your mom and dad left, you can take that crap down." Keating seemed like a cool guy. I was genuinely surprised to see he had these books and just assumed someone forced him to put them up. Instead, he got upset with me and said, "They're my books. That's not a cool thing to make fun of at all." I felt bad about it, because Keating was the nicest person at Dartmouth. And I was impressed that he owned up to having those books, which I'm sure he knew were dorky. I wouldn't have.

Anyway, this is how I planned to pack—I zipped up my bag and said, "I'm done."

"Dude. You didn't even pack up your TV or your stereo or anything."

"I'm leaving them."

"What?"

"You can have them. I'm leaving them. I want to be more minimalist."

"You can't leave a TV, and that's a stereo. They probably cost a couple hundred bucks—at least. And what about your other shit? Your fuckin' bedsheets and your books and your CDs and your movies? And your . . ." Keating looked around. "You haven't packed anything!"

"I packed some clothes and my computer."

"It's a laptop."

"Whatever. It's all I need. I'm leaving the rest."

"But it's a lot of shit."

"I don't care. The janitors can have it."

"Dude, that's ridiculous."

"Then take it. It's yours."

"Okay."

I walked out.

I was almost all the way down the hall when Keating practically fell out of the door, laughing. "Dude! I figured it out. We're going to be roommates next fall!"

I knew that Keating would pack up all of the shit and put it into storage. He would probably get it out of storage and unload it in our apartment in the fall too, but I couldn't just sit there and watch him do it without helping, so I had to find something else to do until my dad got there. Everyone else was packing. I didn't feel like helping them, nor did I like to be in anyone else's dorm room. Most of the rooms weren't as nice as mine, largely because no one brought as much crap as I did.

It was hot and muggy. I'm not big on sitting in grass, and I didn't feel like walking very far, so I crossed the green and walked into the Hanover Inn. They had copies of all of the newspapers, attached to rods hanging on a rack. I picked up the *New York Times,* settled into one of the nice chairs they had, and fumbled around with my newspaper on a stick. It wasn't long before I dozed off.

3

My dad has a way of walking into a place. He's a big guy, six three, handsome, with a fair amount of dark hair left and no gray. A snappy dresser in a way that's never too snappy. He's smooth without being too smooth. He's nice to everybody and polite without being obsequious. He's smart. A member of Mensa, if that means anything. He was president of his class at Yale, where he was also an all-American swimmer, a graduate of Harvard Business School, and when he was drafted he worked in naval intelligence. After serving in the navy my father was offered a job with McKinsey & Company, but declined in order to return to Michigan and start his own consulting firm. He's honest in all matters, except marriage. He's an excellent judge of character and fair to a point that borders on annoying. Everybody likes my dad, except his ex-wives, who are obsessed with loving him and hating him at the same time.

At that very moment he was in the process of divorcing Sherianne, my stepmother. The day he dropped me off at school, Sherianne was with us. He gave me a kiss and a hug, and the two of them left my dorm room. I remember Sherianne was crying. Then he came back to my room in about five minutes, alone and a little out of breath.

"I forgot my hat."

"Oh, yeah, it's right there."

"Jay, would you walk with me down the hall? I have something to ask you."

"Sure."

I followed him out into the hallway, and he said, grinning, "I actually didn't forget my hat. I left it on purpose. What would you say to me if I told you I was thinking about leaving Sherianne?"

"Dad, I can't tell you how to live your life, but don't let Sherianne tell you how to live it either."

"Okay. But would it upset you?"

"Not really. I'll be fine."

"Okay. Thanks. Thanks a lot." He gave me another kiss and a hug and left. He waved, held his hat up so Sherianne could see it, smiled, and trotted over to the car.

He walked into the lobby with a bag slung over his shoulder, his briefcase in one hand and a piece of paper in the other. "The damnedest thing just happened to me."

"What's that?"

"A woman eating outside just gave me her telephone number."

"You going to call her?"

"No. She looked expensive. Let's check in."

I helped him take his bags up to his room. He looked it over. "Seems all right. I wanted a room with a view of the green, but they were all booked up. Bed's a little small." He set his stuff down on a chair. "And damnit! They gave me a smoking room." He looked at me. "Or is it just you, reeking of smoke?" I smiled. He opened the window. "I can also smell the alcohol you drank last night." He looked at his watch. "What time is dinner with Isabelle and her mother?"

"Seven."

"Okay. Where?"

"Simon Pearce."

"Oh, terrific. That'll be just wonderful. I love the river there."

I sat down. "Would you like to stroll around, or I was thinking that we could maybe take a swim?"

"I'd love to, but you know what? I'm supposed to get on a conference call in about five minutes. It'll probably eat up most of our time. You're welcome to stay if you'd like."

"No, that's all right. I could use a swim."

"You're damn right about that. Just don't drown the fish in all that booze you're sweating out. Meet me here at six-fifteen. We can have a drink before we go. Invite your buddies."

"Okay."

I was dying to get in the water. As I walked down to the river, it crossed my mind that my dad might've hustled me out to call that woman, and I laughed.

The swim did me good. I took my time getting back to the room, which was empty save for my roommates and the bags we were bringing home with us. Keating was sitting at his desk, sweating profusely. He shook his head when I walked in. Steiner laughed. "Nice, Hauser."

"Yeah. Real nice," said Keating. "My roommate's a dick. I dropped your TV and I think I broke it."

"Glad you didn't break your back."

"I broke that too. Thanks for the help." I could see Keating's lips curling up for a smile. He was pretending to be mad.

"Well, I can tell you one thing, the river's fucking nice. Keating, you should go for a swim."

"Yeah. I think I'll do that."

"Listen, my dad's in town. I'm going to meet him for a drink at six-fifteen over at the Inn, if you'd like to come I'm sure he'd greatly appreciate it." I was addressing both of them.

Steiner. "I'd love to, but my parents are on their way to pick me up for dinner."

"Keating?"

"Maybe."

"C'mon. Come after the swim."

"All right. But I want you to buy me the drink, not your dad. Okay?"

"No problemo."

As we drove over the Quechee Gorge I looked out. It was a dark silver cut. Black at the bottom. The car swayed a little bit. My dad had gotten to the bar early. "Would you look at that!"

"Watch the road, Dad."

"What? Are you worried I'm going to take us out?" He laughed. "Those friends of yours are just great. They'll be great connections for you all of your life." Panolini, Stuey, Woodsy, and Keating came for a drink. They all got kind of dressed up, too, for my dad. "And that Cutch! I hadn't met him before but he seems like a great guy. He said he was from Chicago, right? His parents are both lawyers."

"Yeah. I think so."

While we were there having a drink, I noticed Cutch hanging in the lobby, waiting for someone, so I asked him if he wanted to join us. He was real nice to everyone—Woodsy included—and after a while of us standing around the bar and chatting he got real close to my dad, and I overheard Cutch tell him that his parents were lawyers, but they weren't. His father was an unemployed machinist who was confined to a wheelchair and his mother was a school-teacher. Then he started bragging to my dad about me and my friends and what great guys we were. This really made me uncomfortable. Then some girl showed up. He offered to pay for his drink, but my dad picked up the tab, and shortly thereafter we left. For some reason, it kind of frosted me that my dad thought Cutch was such a prince, but I had to admit it, Cutch could turn the charm on when he wanted to. I'd also noticed he'd washed his hair.

My dad swerved again. "Easy . . ."

"Don't 'easy' me. Now, tell me again, what's Isabelle's mother's name?"

"Emma Denton."

"She doesn't go by Sloane?"

"No. She's divorced."

My dad glanced at me. "Holy smokes!"

"What?"

"You're trying to grow a mustache."

"No, I'm not."

"Well, you didn't shave it. I just saw the sun hit that thing. It glowed."

I pulled down the mirror. "Oh, shit." I was so distracted thinking about Isabelle that while I was shaving I forgot to shave above my lip. To say it was a mustache was an extreme exaggeration. I couldn't grow a beard. Just the tiniest amount of very thin, very blond facial hair. I started to get nervous, and the hair thickened with sweat. "Do you think it's noticeable?"

"Not very. But if the light hits it right it lights up like one of those Christmas tree bulbs. The thin spiny ones. That thing's pretty nasty."

"It is. Do you have a razor?"

"Left it in the hotel room. We'll probably pass a gas station, they may have one."

"What if they don't?"

"You could always burn it off. There's not much hair there."

"Damnit. It looks retarded."

"What do you care what it looks like?"

I didn't say anything.

"Are you interested in this Isabelle girl?"

"No." I looked out the window. "I'm interested in her mom."

"Leave her mother to me, boy."

I stared at Isabelle. The river twisted behind her like a big black boa. She wore a tight blue shirt, and it was cool in the room so her nipples perked up a bit. She wore small ruby earrings and a single pearl necklace, which rested on her collarbone and drew attention to her neck. Isabelle thought her neck was her best feature. It was nice, but the thing I loved best was her mouth. She was always kind of pouting. And if I looked close I could see the scar on her lower lip from being thrown from a horse when she was younger. She had those lips . . . I loved her beautiful, fucked-up lips.

She leaned over to me. I smelled her and went cold.

She whispered, "Stop looking at my lips. I'm not getting a cold sore." Isabelle knew I had a phobia about cold sores. It was my main phobia, by far the strongest. My seventh-grade science teacher, a total bitch, lectured us endlessly one day on the horror of herpes. She didn't tell us about genital herpes, just herpes. She showed us pictures of them, and drawings done by people who had them of what the pain and humiliation felt like. There was one of a guy getting his lip crushed by a giant hammer. Another one showed a girl, tiny, trying to cover up the gigantic, bulbous lump on her lip, but it was bigger than her hand, and the people around her stared and laughed. It was crazy. My grandmother had cold sores and I asked the teacher what to do when my grandmother kissed me "hello," and she said, "I'd turn my cheek and wash my face off as soon as I could." I really hate this woman for giving me the phobia. I no longer have the phobia entirely, but I had it then and I'd spent many years of my life in complete terror that someone would give me a fucking cold sore. I can't imagine a bigger waste of time.

Anyway, as terrified as I was about cold sores, I wasn't thinking about that, and in fact, I would have gladly kissed Isabelle's cold sore if she had one. I would have eaten it. She could have rubbed it on my dick or shoved it up my ass.

"I wasn't," I said. Isabelle smiled nastily and leaned back. Something was getting to her. I felt my upper lip tingle. I shaved it dry in the car. I checked it earlier in the mirror of the bathroom and it was bright red. It was probably blinking at her with every breath I took. I was sweating. I had my hands in my lap. I wanted to touch hers.

Suddenly, my dad asked her, "Isabelle, do you have a boyfriend?"

Isabelle took a while thinking about the question. I almost shit my pants. I'm sure my face matched my upper lip in color. "No, I don't." The steam went out of me. "I like boys with charm, and most of the boys I know don't have much, and the ones I do know are taken."

"Jay's charming and taken."

"He's a friend. And he's not always charming when he's around me." She nailed it, the bitch. Months earlier, when I told Isabelle that I was thinking about selling knives, she laughed in my face and said I wouldn't be any good at it. She said you have to be "charming" to sell knives. I didn't respond. I just stared out the window seething and decided that by August I was going to prove to her what a goddamn, slick-Rick, shit-eating, snake charmer I could be.

Isabelle continued. "So I don't really get to see that side. Plus, he's got something else." I was waiting to hear what that something else was when she said to my dad, "You've got charm. Mom, don't you think Mr. Hauser is charming?"

"Oh, yes. Very much so."

My dad added, "And recently single."

I left my dad at the Inn and headed across the green, thinking about the evening. After Isabelle's little flare-up and her sweet comments about my lack of charm, her mood improved nicely. Mine was slow on the rebound, but it did improve eventually. In the parking lot of the restaurant she took me aside. She had heard about the beer-throwing incident. She obviously got a huge kick out of it, and then she told me, while hanging on to my arm and staring out onto the river that looked like a cold wet black stone, "It's good to know you can be a dick sometimes. You're always so nice to everyone."

"Just you." Isabelle nodded. I could tell she liked hearing this but it also made her uncomfortable. Sweat dripped down my back. I tried to think of something to say that would impress her, so I told her, "Cutch tapped me for Delta Theta Chi."

Isabelle almost jumped out of her underwear. "He did not!" She sank her nails into my skin.

"He did."

"Oh. Jay. I hope you go there. I hope you do it. You'll be in with all the cool boys. You'll be . . ." She paused, like something bothered her or upset her, but slowly she smiled. She looked up at me with a face so pretty and perfectly evil and said, "Well, now, I guess you'll know everything about all the people who I hook up with."

Isabelle was like an endless swamp that I got stuck in. And it was slowly eating me alive. I lived on her happiness, and being around her was always something of a thrill that was terrifying in the moment, but as soon as she was gone, I was left with only the empty feeling of profound need, sickness, and longing.

I stood on the green. I knew my dudes were probably at GDX— the football frat. I thought about going there, but I needed to be someplace dark. The moon was out and bright and I wanted to find a giant tree to crawl under. There were trees around the green, but there were also streetlamps, so it is never quite dark.

I thought about going into the library and hiding in the stacks, but it would be hot in there whereas the night air was cooling off. I could have walked into some of the forests around campus, but I was suddenly tired and couldn't muster the strength.

I closed my eyes and walked. I thought about being under a giant shade, with empty desert on all sides and then miles away a huge wall built up hundreds of feet high so no one could see and animals couldn't get in.

When I got back to my dorm room, I called Cutch. Pete answered. It took a while for him to come to the phone.

"Sorry, dude. I was in the basement. What's up?"

"Did you find out about Woodsy?"

"Yeah. Sorry, dude. There's no way he's getting in."

"Okay . . . I'll do it. I'll go with you guys, I guess."

"Fuckin' great! You want to come over, play a game?"

"No. I have to get up early. Headed back to Michigan."

"Come on. You should come. That friend of yours, that chick with the red hair, she just showed up. We're getting fucking wasted right now. I never knew how cool she was!" This comment made me want to die.

"I really can't."

"All right. I'll be in touch with you this summer. Maybe we can hang."

"Cool." I hung up.

It was still early in the morning when we crossed from the spiked green mountains of Vermont into the rolling green hills of New York. I'd just woken up. My dad had coffee for me, which amazingly was still warm. I sipped it.

"Dad, you know what? I don't think you're going to have to support me this summer. I think I'm going to be making the big bucks."

"I like the sound of that, but you should hold on to my credit card just in case. Do you have a job lined up?"

"Yes."

"Really? Doing what?"

"Selling knives."

My dad laughed. "You're kidding me, right?"

"Nope."

"And you can make enough money doing that to support yourself this summer?"

"Sure. I can make a lot of money."

"But you've got to sell a lot of knives to do it. The problem is that whenever you sell something there has to be a *need*. Everybody has knives. Hell, your mother has about a thousand of them." My mother cooked a lot.

He drove on a little more. "Who are you going to sell them to?"

"I've been thinking about that. Do you think you could give me the names of some of your friends?"

"Oh. I see. Hit up the old man's buddies."

"I'll just start there. Then I'll go after *their* friends."

"Okay. I'll help you out. You should really talk to your aunt, though. She knows a lot of mothers." My aunt was ten years younger than my dad and had one son in high school and another in middle school. We drove around in silence for a while. "I'll tell you what . . . If you're going to sell knives you're going to have to be a lot more talkative than you've been lately."

"I'm sorry. I've been out of sorts."

"Because of Sherianne?"

"Oh, god, no." I thought for a second. "Shit, you kind of reminded me. I should probably go see her."

"She'd appreciate it."

"Dad. I'm not kidding. I really think I'm going to sell a lot of knives."

"Listen, I don't mean to discourage you. I think it's great that you got a job. Really it is. But I want to tell you, if you sell one knife this entire summer, I'll be goddamn amazed."

It didn't take long for me to fall back asleep. If I could float out of the car and fly west, like a satellite in a dream blasting its way around the earth, over New York State, Lake Erie, and then drop down past Detroit, gray, empty, and smoking, the suburbs increasingly green and lazy, sweeping through the tops of elms and eventually stopping at 1152 Pheasant Drive, I would find my mother sitting in her kitchen staring dully at the TV. Her coffee cooling in its cup, amaretto cream on the counter. Feeling her stomach aching as if it'd been punched the night before, the same way she felt every morning for the last decade, as it did that first morning after she got *the call*. It was my father calling from his car phone. Her four children were somewhere in the house generating a constant stream of noise that in a small house would have driven me crazy but in a large one was muted, faint, and comforting. I've heard the details of the conversation, thousands of times. My mother repeated it to us verbatim only moments after receiving it—trying to process what she'd just heard.

"Hello."

"Caroline. It's Hal."

"Hello. Where are you?"

"I'm not coming home."

"Okay. When are you coming home?"

"I'm not coming home."

"What, Hal? I don't understand you."

"Caroline. I'm never coming back."

"What? What are you trying to say?"

"I'm not coming home. Ever."

And then she heard Sherianne tell my father to hang up.

The call. The punch. There would be many years of pain to follow. But that day was the worst. That call was the surprise. That's what my mother remembers when she wakes up every morning, trying to figure out why her stomach hurts.

Had I been able to transport myself to her and crawl back inside of her, I would have discovered another source of pain—or rather an empty uncertainty. I was coming home that evening. My mother felt I deserted her when I moved in with my father and Sherianne when I was fifteen. Although she admitted that she lost her mind and kicked me out, she would later argue that I was at fault because I signed a form requesting that primary custody be transferred to my father. She fought it in court. It took nearly two years and according to her hundreds of thousands of dollars in legal fees, but my father won. I hadn't spent a night in her house since then. Now the plan was to spend the entire summer with her. She wasn't sure if she wanted me to. She said I reminded her of my father. The same swagger. The same attitude. She thought I just did whatever suited me and didn't care about anybody else.

She got mad and sad thinking about how my father and his

whore had stolen me, and I agreed to it. Went along with it. Apparently, I loved it. And Sherianne was all over me. At every football game and every lacrosse game. Hockey. Wrestling. The trips. Four years of hell. For my mother there was a constant humiliation in having to see Sherianne with me. Everywhere. She stopped going to the events. She cried for an hour before she could bring herself to attend my high school graduation.

There was one thing, though, that I'm sure made her feel good that morning. The bitch was gone. Even though he had spoken to me about it, my father never got around to telling Sherianne he wanted a divorce. Instead Sherianne got *her call* from the manager of The Four Seasons in Chicago. "Mrs. Hauser, we have your watch."

"What watch?"

"Our cleaning service found a woman's watch in your suite after you checked out this morning. We just wanted to call and tell you that we are sending it to you, but we wanted to confirm your address first."

"Wait. When was I at The Four Seasons in Chicago?"

"This weekend."

"Over the weekend? I was here this weekend. Are you sure?"

"Positive. You were with your husband. You left this morning. I checked you out myself."

"Oh . . . What do I look like?"

When Sherianne heard the answer to that question she wanted to kill my father. She actually told him she would have. Fortunately he wasn't around. She ended up attacking their bedroom with a golf club instead.

In a way, I was looking forward to living with my mother. We had had a particularly bad relationship for the past four years and I was hoping that might change.

My father stopped the car in front of my mother's house. It was still light out.

"You're going to need a car."

"Oh, yeah."

"I really didn't want to do this after you fucked up the car I bought you in high school so badly, but I'm getting a new car, so you can have mine for the summer."

"Sweet." My dad drove a BMW. It wasn't even two years old.

"You can walk over tomorrow and pick it up from the office. If I'm not there, I'll leave the keys with Kathy. Oh!" My dad reached into the backseat. "By the way, before I forget, I have something here I need you to sign."

"What's that?"

"It has to do with your trust and a recent tax issue due to an increase in its value."

"Yeah?" I said, kidding around. "What am I worth now?"

"Jay." My dad looked at me like I was an asshole. His face turned red and twitched a little. "Your grandparents were extremely generous with you, your brother, and your sisters. I think it was a huge mistake . . . As evidenced by your shitty attitude."

"I'm sorry. I was just joking . . ." I took the pen he was holding and quickly signed my name, feeling kind of guilty and undeserving that I was nineteen and already a millionaire.

"You know, maybe this job will teach you not to be such a brat. You might find out what it means to earn something for yourself."

"Dad, I really appreciate the ride and you letting me borrow the car and everything. I mean it."

"Okay. I love you, pal. Let's see each other soon."

"I love you too." I kissed him and got out of the car.

The door was open, but the screen was locked. I knocked. The cool air coming from the dark house felt good. Fancy beat my mother to the door and licked at the screen.

"I'm sorry to keep you waiting. You got here sooner than I expected. I was taking a nap."

"We drove through Canada. Dad hauled ass."

"I'm sure." She opened the door and we hugged. I bent down

and kissed Fancy on the lips. She was a black standard poodle, but her coat was graying in spots. Her chin was silver.

"It feels weird not to hear Bentley barking." Bentley was Fancy's son. He died that spring in my mother's bed.

"I miss him so much." She looked like she might cry. "I still have his ashes in my bedroom. I don't know if I'm going to stay here forever, and I don't want to bury him here if I'm going to move."

"Remember the last time I saw him he tried to bite my face off."

"You're here so infrequently. He probably didn't recognize you."

"I'd like some of those ashes. I don't care that he tried to bite me." I meant it, too. She didn't say anything about the ashes.

"It's good to have you home. Are you really going to stay here? That's not a very big bag."

"I left my stuff at school."

"What did you do with it?"

"Nothing. I left it up to Doug Keating."

"Your roommate?!"

"Yup."

"That's not very nice of you."

I noticed a framed photograph of my mother from when she was a model hanging on the wall just inside the door. A magazine cover. She is sitting on a horse standing on a bluff, a wide savannah spreading out behind them. My mother's got the riding crop in her hand, held loosely in her fingertips. Both she and the horse look very determined.

"I love that photo of you."

She smiled. "Are you going to stay in Courtney's room?" Courtney was the younger of my two older sisters. She lived in Portland. "Or Coulter's?" This was something that irritated me. After my mother kicked me out, she had to sell the house that we'd been living in before the divorce. It was a big and beautiful house. We had a vague plan that I would move back in with her after I came back from summer camp, and she always held it against me that I never did. However, while I was gone she sold the old house and bought a tiny one in the same neighborhood, a house without a room for me.

"Coulter's."

"Why don't you just stay in Courtney's room?"

"What do you mean? Because it's her room!"

"Well, she's not here."

"What happens when she comes back?"

"We can deal with that then."

"Mom. It's not my room. Besides, she's got some of her shit in there from high school, like her lollipop collection."

"Suit yourself."

"Okay."

I followed my mother into the kitchen. She was always cooking and the kitchen always smelled good.

"Mom. I haven't called Brooke yet. I'm kind of not looking forward to it, but if I do, she'll want to have dinner with us or at least I'll have to invite her."

"You can do whatever you want." My mother was being an icy bitch.

"What do you mean?"

"I mean, you don't have to have dinner with me if you don't want to. I cooked something, but Coulter can have it later or something. Maybe I'll give it to the neighbor. Mr. Bradly's teeth aren't good, but it's soft food, so he'll be able to chew it."

"What did you cook?"

"Well, I haven't *cooked* it yet, but I was going to grill salmon. I also made beet soup. Of course we'll have a salad, and I'm trying a tomato soufflé that I think could be good, but I don't know."

"Is that what's cooking?"

"Yes."

"It smells nice."

46

"Thank you."

"Where's Coulter?"

"He's at lacrosse practice, I think."

"When is he supposed to come home?"

"Not till later. He's going to study at the whatchamagigs, which really frosts me, because I bought enough salmon for four people and if he's not here and you go off with Brooke, then it'll just be me or, like I said, Mr. Bradly can take a crack at it with his gums for all I care."

I laughed. "No. I'll eat here. I'll tell Brooke I'll see her later. I'm not really looking forward to calling her."

"Why not?"

"I don't know. When she answers the phone, she's going to make some big noise and I just don't want to hear it."

"I know the sound. It's not pleasant. I spoke to her mother the other day and I'm not one hundred percent certain that she's not retarded."

I laughed again.

My mother was warming up. She loved going off on Meg Ambrose. "She's sweet and pretty, but boy, is she dumb. I couldn't believe I was actually hearing what was coming out of her mouth, it was so stupid."

"What was she saying?"

"I don't know, some drivel about Brooke getting a calling plan and she wanted to know if I'm going to get one for you."

"She was trying to be nice."

"I know, but what do I care if Brooke has a calling plan? And if she wants one for you, she should call you. Or your father. He's the one you talk to all the time. So she—"

"Were you nice?"

"Of course I was nice, but if I hadn't been, I doubt she would have known the difference." My mother drank from a silver cup that was white from condensation. "Would you like some sangria? I made some yesterday and it's excellent. I don't like to offer my children alcohol, but you're in college and it's too good not to."

"I'd love some in a minute. I want to take a shower and make some calls."

In the shower, I thought of Isabelle. I imagined her sitting in my lap and leaning in close to me, her breasts on my neck and her cold mouth kissing my forehead. The steam from the shower was choking me.

Using Courtney's room as an office, I called my aunt and my grandparents and arranged to meet them at ten and one respectively. I wanted to take my time with them and really grill them for a list of names to call.

I stared at the phone for a while and at the list that my dad and I made. Cold-calling is not an easy thing to do. It's humiliating. Apex, the marketing company for Bladeworks, teaches its salespeople scripted formulas for both cold-calling and the actual sales call in which the salesperson gives his "demonstration." They recommend that you call people closest to you to do your first appointments, because they'll be easier on you. However, I viewed this as being a little tricky, because I thought that these people would also be the ones who, if you did a good job, would be most inclined to buy more knives. A lot of the people my dad recommended were extremely wealthy. I knew some friends of my mother's that would be easy on me and didn't have much cash, so if I blew it, it wasn't a big deal. I wanted to save some of my better recommendations for when I got better at selling.

As I studied the list some more I realized I had a problem. Most of the people on the list were men. I wanted the wives. I'd have to get their names from my dad. I went back to the list and did some more figuring.

According to Apex, the best window for calling is between 6 and 9 P.M., when people are most likely to be home. Ideally, a salesperson would stagger the calls closer to six and nine to hopefully catch people right before or after dinner instead of during it. Another good time is in the morning, between 9 and 11 A.M., which was actually my favorite time to call housewives because the husbands weren't around. So I always liked to put in a few calls before heading off to my first demonstration of the day. Anyway, my mother eats dinner around nine, so I had to start making calls soon. There were some other female names on the list that I didn't know well if at all. I looked over my dad's notes next to those names, searching for people who might be professionals. I wanted to lower the risk of disturbing someone's family time.

There was one major thing that I didn't agree with Apex on about cold-calling. Apex recommends that when calling a client, the salesperson says, "Hi, is Joan there?" They recommend using the person's first name and not really identifying yourself, so that whoever answered the phone would think that the person you were calling knows you and wouldn't sniff out that you were trying to sell something. I found this method unbelievably rude.

The Bloomfield Hills/Birmingham area is a very conservative place. There was no way I wouldn't completely offend my father's friends by calling them by their first names. Plus, my mother was a maniac about phone manners and has always lectured us children on how to be polite. She grew up in South Carolina in one of these old families with a lot of money that was eventually lost over several generations. But they always kept their manners.

Once I got the person I wanted on the phone, I was supposed to act professional and say something like, "Hi, this is Jay Hauser, I'm Hal Hauser's son. I have a great opportunity to win a scholarship this summer selling Bladeworks knives, and my father thought you might be able to help me. All I have to do is come over and give you a demonstration and I get points toward the scholarship. I get paid to do it, so you aren't required to buy anything. It'll only take about an hour, and I can speed it up if you're in a rush. Would eleven o'clock tomorrow morning be good for you?"

You don't want to be on the phone too long. You don't want the customers to think about it. You just want them to hear the name of your contact, the word *scholarship,* that they <u>DON'T HAVE TO BUY ANYTHING,</u> and when you hit them with the time, they should just say yes. You get their address, thank them, and hang up. But it's not that easy. According to Stuart the rate of refusal is around 80 percent.

I found the scripted call a little pushy, phony, and unnatural. It might be okay for the average idiot, but I really didn't want to risk offending anybody or embarrassing myself by doing something that I didn't believe would work. At that time, I felt like the in-person demonstration as taught by Apex was pretty solid, because I understood it. It starts from the moment the salesperson steps out of his car onto the street in front of a customer's home.

You, a Bladeworks salesperson, stride up to the front door carrying a sales binder, a roll of knives, a cutting board, a handful of pennies, a length of rope, and some shoe leather. Your job is to give a demonstration that is geared toward selling the Deluxe Kitchen Set, which includes eight cooking knives, a carving fork, shears, a turning fork, eight table knives, a cutting board, and a block to store the knives. With a good lead and a little luck you can do it.

Once the customer opens the door, introduce yourself, thank the customer, enter the home, and ask where the customer would like to see the presentation. Suggest the kitchen table and remind the customer you will be paid and receive points toward your scholarship regardless of whether or not he or she buys anything. Stuart always warned me not to talk too much about the scholarship because if the customer starts asking questions you will be forced to either lie or tell the truth—that the first-place scholarship is less than five hundred dollars, and clearly not enough to pay for school. It seemed to me that the scholarship was a device created by Apex solely to get the salesperson in the house.

The first step in the sales process is to create the need for new knives. Bladeworks suggests using the fact that you are new at your job as an excuse to educate the customer about knives. Begin by saying something like "I'm sure you know a lot about knives, but I've got a routine that I've got to follow, so I'm just going to tell it to you. A sharp knife is a safe knife . . ."

Discuss the life of a knife, the general wear and tear, rust, the importance of a balanced knife for healthy wrists and forearms, etc. Then, hit them with the fistful of fungus. "Wood is a porous material that soaks bacteria up like a sponge." Add a bogus stat—"the average kitchen sponge has more bacteria in it than the average toilet bowl. Most knives have wooden handles." Hopefully the customer will connect the dots, but if not, there's an old knife-selling story that will shock the customer into listening to you if you don't already have their complete attention, the one about the salesperson who lopped off a client's handle and found it filled with maggots.

Explain Bladeworks's features: the high-grade carbolic steel, the rivets, the tang, the balanced weight, the expertly engineered thermal resin handle (nonporous), the handle's ergonomic design, and Bladeworks's patented serrated blade, the Tri-part Recessed Edge. Most people ask if the knives ever get dull, and they do, but it takes a long time. "Sometimes twenty or thirty years, but you can always send them back and the factory will replace the entire edge for free." Show them Bladeworks's lifetime warranty and money-back guarantee. The warranty is rock solid: the life of the knife—not the person. Emphasize there is zero risk.

Stop the demonstration here and ask them to bring you their favorite knife. Here is where the actual "need" portion of the pitch pays off. Most people will feel embarrassed about the piece of crap they think of as their favorite knife because it's almost certain to have a wooden handle, so it's important to compliment the knife no matter what the condition. Then ask the customer to cut your rope with their knife, counting the number of strokes as they go. If the knife has a straight edge the customer may not be able to cut all the way through the rope. On average it takes at least thirty hard strokes, but it can take up to one hundred or more.

Next give the customer the Petite Carver. Let them feel the high-quality knife in their hand before placing the blade on the rope and instructing them to pull back. Ninety-nine out of a hundred times it takes one stroke to completely sever the rope. I never saw the number exceed one and a half. The customer will be impressed and ready to buy, so you want to move quickly through the rest of the demonstration.

By now you've created a problem and provided a high-quality risk-free solution, but remember your goal is to get the customer to buy a multitude of knives instead of just one, so you need to justify this by listing each knife's specific use. "See how nicely the paring knife fits in your hand, it's ideal for . . ." A common mistake that most salesmen make early on is to bore the hell out of the customer with too many uses for each particular knife. One or two will do. Move, move, move your way through the knives!

Hand them one of the forks. Point out the other products in your sales binder that you don't have with you. Whip out the cooking shears—your magic wand. The shears have tiny serrated edges that pull objects into the crux of the blades as you squeeze the handles together. They cut a penny. "Some salesmen can cut a penny into one long corkscrew-shaped piece." "Really?" Leave the cooking shears in their hand so they can feel the product.

"Okay, so now that I've shown you the knives, wouldn't you say they're pretty great?" They agree—they are great. "Let me show you some other great knives." Turn the page to the photo of Henckels' Five Star line of cutlery. "Many people say Bladeworks knives are ten times better than any knife they've ever used. This is a stretch. But, in all fairness, wouldn't you say that Bladeworks knives are at least *twice* as good as Henckels?" Typically, they agree. You then tell them what a complete set of Henckels would cost in a department store. I would say $1,400. "So, according to what you just said, it would be fair to say that a comparable set of Bladeworks knives should cost twice that much?" Let the customer process this very large figure and close.

"Fortunately they don't." Smile. "Our Deluxe Kitchen Set costs only eight hundred and five dollars." Feel the customer's relief. "The reason Bladeworks's knives are so much less expensive is because we don't advertise and we don't sell our knives in stores. Instead, young college students like myself make them affordable by selling them directly from the manufacturer to people like you. We have several different payment options. If you don't want to pay the whole fee now, I can bill your credit card, interest free, over five months for only a hundred sixty-one dollars per month."

Regardless of whether the customer buys the knives or not it is essential that before you leave you ask them to write down a list of their friends who might be interested in helping you with your scholarship. You must have new leads if you want to keep selling. After they write down the names go over the list with them and ask some general questions about the people on it to help you evaluate the quality of the lead. "Are they married? Do they have children?" etc. After you get the information thank the customer and ask just one last favor. "Would you mind calling these people and telling them I might be in contact?" They always say yes because they want to warn their friends that the knifeboy will be calling.

No matter how good a knife salesman is at giving a demonstration, however, his best pitch isn't worth shit if he can't set up an appointment. Back to cold calls . . . They suck but you have to make them. And I had yet to make my first. I was still sitting there, watching the phone in its cradle, wasting time thinking about how little I believe in Apex's scripted call, when I got an idea. My little brother is the phone master. Every time he calls a friend and a parent answers he's so obsequious and indirect on the phone it's almost painful to listen to him giggle, suck ass, and beat around the bush. But he's the ultimate mother-charmer. I picked a name. A former office manager that my dad had recently run into.

I dialed. A woman's voice answered.

"Hello?"

I tried to make my voice seem as high and young as possible. "Hi . . . This is Jay." I gulped. "Hauser. May I please speak to Mrs. Jenkins?"

"Speaking. May I ask what this is about?"

"Yes. Mrs. Jenkins. I'm Hal Hauser's son."

"Oh. Hi. How are you?"

"Fine."

"How is your father?"

"Very well, thank you." I paused, then forced my voice to crack as I said, "This is a little weird and I'm pretty nervous, but my dad gave me your number and he thought that maybe I could call you."

"About what?"

"Well. I've got a pretty bad job this summer selling knives, but it's mostly about winning a college scholarship."

"A scholarship?"

"Yes. I've got to do these demonstrations. They're pretty embarrassing. You're the first person I've called."

"Oh . . ."

"It won't take very long and I get paid ten dollars an hour, so it's not about buying anything. I've just got to show up and do the demonstration. It's kind of funny too. You might like it."

"How long will it take?"

"Twenty-five to thirty minutes." A total lie. "But I can try to speed it up."

"Hmmmm. Knives, right? Well, I can promise you I won't buy any. I never cook. But I'd love to help you with your scholarship, especially if it won't take that long. When can you do it?"

"Anytime. You tell me what is convenient for you and I'll be there."

"How about six o'clock tomorrow?"

"That'd be great. Thank you so much. This is so nice of you." I got her address and thanked her about fifteen more times.

My whiny, half-retarded call took longer than I would have liked, but it worked. Apex recommends that you call around twenty or more people each night, hoping that you would get three or four appointments a day. That would be ideal. And in order to do that you had to keep the calls short so you can fit them all into the six-to-nine window. Mine took longer, but it was better. I had three appointments for the following day. For my first day of selling this was good, but I wanted to start selling hard, so I made one more call using the same technique I used on Mrs. Jenkins. It worked again. This woman wanted me to come at 8 P.M., when her husband would be home from work.

My mother and I had a nice dinner. We ate outside on the patio. I drank a fair amount of sangria and told my mother about knife selling. She thought the idea was humorous. We laughed a lot. Fancy sat on the ground, leaning against my leg, panting.

Brooke lived in a gated community, and I found it incredibly insulting to have to get permission from a guard to go to my girlfriend's house. The guard didn't know me. He was an old guy. He actually had an oxygen tank next to his chair and tubes in his nose. It was late when I pulled up, and he looked at me like I caught him doing something wrong, like he shouldn't have been getting his oxygen.

I asked him to please look in the permanent guest book and not call because I didn't want Brooke's parents to wake up when the phone rang. He called anyway. The tubes jammed up in his face were getting tangled with the spiral cord. It was so sad to watch. I almost told him to forget it but Brooke answered lightning-quick. The guard apologized and raised the gate. I felt like hell driving away from the guardhouse. My grandmother takes oxygen when she sleeps. She hides her tank in her closet.

Brooke came running out of her house as I rounded the corner, and I don't know why but I felt a brief yen to hit her with my mother's car. Not kill her. Just tap her. And send her body sailing into the marble fountain at the end of her drive. She opened the car door giggling and said, "Don't you love the new guard? Isn't he so cute?"

Brooke and I took a walk. There was a fake lake with swans in it in the middle of her community. Huge houses graced the perimeter. There was a small park on the shore with a gazebo built under some giant elm trees. We went down to the gazebo. I pressed Brooke up against the rail and pulled her pants down. I came pretty quickly, despite jerking off in the shower earlier. The cum glimmered on the small of her back, just like the surface of the lake behind her. She looked at me, deliriously in love and beautiful in the moonlight.

As I was leaving I said, "Listen, Brooke. I'm going to be working really hard this summer."

"I know. That's great."

"So, my days . . . I'm probably not going to be able to come over during the day."

"What about lunch?"

"I'm not going to have lunch."

"A few . . . Pweeese . . ." She was putting on her baby voice.

"We'll see."

"Okay. But I really want us to go on a trip. A couple of days or maybe a week or two alone. Just us."

"Sure. That sounds cool. Where?"

"Mackinac Island."

"Why?"

"I love it there. They have the best food. And you've never been."

"Okay. We'll do it. I promise."

"I love you."

"I love you."

I wanted to talk to Coulter to say hello when I woke up, but he was impossibly tired and babbling nonsense as I shook him in his bed. So I drank a bunch of coffee and walked over to my father's office. My father wasn't there, and it was nice and easy getting the keys to his BMW from his secretary. I said hello to a few consultants at the firm and left.

Coulter was gone by the time I got back. My mother offered to cook me breakfast but I wasn't hungry. I was nervous. I thought about wearing a blazer but opted for a shirt and tie instead. I combed my hair and took a long time brushing my teeth. I had braces, gold ones. They were hypoallergenic. They sucked. However, there's a certain ease in wearing braces in that you look stupid and there's nothing you can do about it, so it takes a lot of pressure off trying to look good. I was getting them off in a week anyway. The appointment would take a couple of hours, and I made a mental note to schedule knife sales around it.

I had two days to get good at selling before the first "push week" of the summer. The push week is a ten-day period wherein Apex sets up a competition to see who can sell the most knives. At the end of it, there was to be a conference in Atlanta for all of the knife salesmen in the Southeastern division. I didn't really know what was going to happen there, but I wanted to win, so I didn't have much time to fuck around. (You may find it confusing that I lived in Michigan and I was part of the Southeastern division, but you have to remember that I was working out of Stuart's office in Covington, Kentucky, right across the Ohio River from Cincinnati, which was the northern-most city in the Southeastern division.)

I grabbed my roll of knives and headed over to my aunt's house a couple of blocks away.

My Aunt Tina was still in her bathrobe when I arrived. The kitchen smelled like a family. A smell I missed. Burnt toast. Coffee. Dirty lacrosse gear molding in the corner. The bottle of Grand-dad that fueled last night's fight sat next to an overfilled recycling bin. A divorce was imminent. But not yet, because the maid would come at noon and clean the slate. Then there would be Pine-Sol and stillness until around five when swim practice got out and the chlorine and video game tournament invaded the basement. And then Tina could be upstairs, without Uncle Steve, listening to the racket in the basement and fantasizing about what wonderful children she had and how her marriage would work. They'd make it work.

I listened to the rhythm of the house. The toilet flushes. The faucet running. A slow creak from the bathroom to the staircase. Brothers shouting at each other. Four feet pound a steady beat on the wood stairs followed by more shouts and a tremendous clang as one brother slips on the Oriental rug at the foot of the stairs and crashes into the coffee table.

The hooligans came screaming into the room and tried to wrestle me. One of them, Cole, looked like me. The other, Porter, looked like his father, Steve, who was leaving for work. It was ten in the morning. He supposedly had a job as an "architectural consultant," except he could never point out any buildings he's worked on and he was a bit of a running joke in our family. He was also abusive to Tina and the kids, so he wasn't well liked. And he was always getting drunk and loved telling racist jokes. But he saved me from drowning once. It was 1981. I was four. I'd just learned to swim. We were at my old house, which had a pool and a separate pool house. It was summer and my parents were having a midafternoon cocktail party by the pool with my aunt, uncle, and some of their friends. They were all drinking and chatting and my mom was showing Coulter off and I was the only one swimming. I tried to get everyone to watch me take my first dive. I was typically a quiet kid, but I made a lot of noise before I dove, so I thought they were watching. But they weren't.

I went straight to the bottom of the pool. I remember how the party looked from down below: just a bunch of pants and skirts and bare legs shifting around. My father wore pink pants. I could see them standing beside the pool facing other pants, but I couldn't get to the surface of the water. I kept watching the pink pants and the roof of the pool house and then everything went white. The next thing I remember I was puking water on the tile next to Steve, who was soaking wet. Legend has it he noticed me below the surface when his drink spilled into the pool. But he saved me, and I always loved him for it.

Steve and I chatted for a moment.

"How you doin', Bub?"

"Good. You?"

"Great. Listen. I've got to run off to work." He turned to Tina and said, "Don't be such a goddamn cheapskate. Buy some knives off this kid, will you?"

"I already told this joker, I'm not buying anything. We don't need new knives."

"You're just cheap. Bye. Cole, if you break the couch I'm going to kill you."

Tina smiled and Steve left. Tina was immensely wealthy and notoriously cheap. Her wealth had nothing to do with her husband. It had to do with my grandfather and Tina's stinginess.

Tina and I sat in her kitchen. She slapped the table. "Okay, Buster Brown, let's have it."

Tina had absolutely no control over her children whatsoever. They kept running in and out of the kitchen during the demonstration until finally Porter sat down to watch it, and later so did Cole. As much of a pain in the ass as the kids were, Tina had them beat. I was doing my best to recite the pitch verbatim, and she interrupted me about every five minutes to remind me that what I was doing was pointless because she wasn't going to buy. I had to keep telling her that what I really wanted was advice on my pitch and someone to listen. I would have gotten frustrated with her, but she's my aunt and I'm used to dealing with her. Also, the knives she owned were complete crap and in reality, she could have used a new set.

"Okay. I know you are not going to buy, so I won't hit you with the closing line."

"What is it?"

"The closing line?"

"Yeah . . . Give it to me."

"Well, no. I mean. If you're not buying I don't need to—"

"Give me the line! I want to hear it."

"Mrs. Pierce, would you like me to order the Deluxe Kitchen Set for you?"

"Absolutely not! I told you I wasn't going to buy anything and I'm not going to do it. I love you, Mister Man, but I am not made out of money." It chapped my ass that she made me say the line so she could jump all over it.

"I know. It's okay. Really. I just want to get some advice. What did you think about the whole spiel?"

"I thought it was fabulous. You could maybe be a little faster in places. I don't think people need to hear so much detail about the knives."

Porter piped up, "Mom. You got to buy those, they're great."

Cole added, "Yeah. Our knives suck. They wouldn't even cut one of Spanky's turds."

"Watch your mouth! They were a wedding gift and I agree that they're getting a little old, but I am simply not buying. I'm sorry Jay, I—"

I cut her off. "Tina, it's okay. I think you're right. I've got to speed it up a lot. They're good knives, though, aren't they?"

"They're great. You're going to see Gammy and Pappa next, aren't you?"

"Yes."

"You might remind them that I have a birthday coming up. Or, you know what? I'll call them myself."

I started putting together my stuff and cleaning up the mess that I'd made.

"Is there really a scholarship?"

"Yeah. It's for the top three salespeople in the country and around four hundred dollars."

"That's better than a sharp stick in the eye."

"Yeah, but get this . . . In order to win the scholarship, you have to sell around sixty thousand dollars' worth of knives, and if you sell that much, according to the pay scale, you'll have already made twenty-five thousand dollars in commission."

"Holy moly!"

I finished cleaning up and mined her for names. Tina gave me a ton, then a piece of advice. "Before you go see your grandparents, you might want to put on a sport coat."

My grandmother terrified most people, including her grandchildren. She was Scottish, but had gone to boarding school in England, and she spoke with an affected English accent. She weighed less than ninety pounds and stood ramrod straight and was extremely elegant and somewhat famous for her style.

My grandfather had enormous hands. He had a habit of aligning and realigning items that were placed in front of him. He was a big man with soft features and the kind of face that you trusted. He had authority without ever asking for it. He was quiet, humble, generous, and always made a tremendous impression on people.

He didn't give a damn about what he wore or how he looked, but he always looked sharp. My grandmother had all of his clothes made for him and told him what to wear, so even in the nicest suit he looked a little bit like a boy who had been dressed and couldn't wait to take it off, which on an old man bore a great charm and sweetness, although he was not sweet. He was brutally honest and extremely demanding. But those who didn't know him thought he was sweet, and people loved him anyway.

Neither of my grandparents ever explicitly demanded respect but they commanded it nonetheless. Most people, even if they said they loved my grandparents, secretly feared them. I did at least. And I'm fairly certain my father did also. Because what they did demand (quite verbally) was accomplishment. When they were disappointed, their wrath could be terrific.

When I was eight years old my grandfather asked what I wanted for Christmas. I had just learned what the stock market was and I wanted to show off, so I asked for stocks. I had no idea that I had been receiving stocks all my life, but my grandfather took offense to what I said, and after that comment he and my grandmother stopped giving me and my brother and sisters stock.

That year for Christmas I got a dictionary instead. I remember, after I unwrapped it, my grandmother said to me, "Don't pretend that you're happy about this gift. I know you're not, but someday you will appreciate it." She was right, and many years later I wrote her a thank-you note telling her so.

My mother claims that my grandparents never really loved us. She says that they loved my father too much and that they hated anything that took his love away from them and so they weren't capable of loving us, or my mother. There may be some truth to this but I doubt it.

I was sitting at my grandparents' kitchen table, asking my grandfather for advice on the sales pitch I'd just given. He sat thinking silently for a long time and finally said, "It seemed all right to me. I never was a salesman, but I know that whenever one would come to me with a new product I would listen to what he said, and the good ones always said very little. I didn't need to know everything about the product, but I needed to feel comfortable that the person selling it did. You should also be an expert on your customer. Hell, some of these guys knew more about my company than I did. What a good salesman should know is the essential difference in what, why, and how. If they could tell me what they had, why I should buy it, and how it would help me I would probably buy it. That's about all I know." He straightened his pocketknife out on the table. "Betty, what do you think?"

My grandmother turned her glazed eyes toward me and said with complete insincerity, "I didn't know knives could be so interesting. Perhaps you could trim it down a bit." I smiled but was hurt. "Jay, tell me, why should I care about you selling knives, when there are so many other better and more important things you could be doing with your time?"

I couldn't really tell them about impressing Isabelle so I said, "I want to be able to support myself."

She grinned. "Well, then I suggest you try selling them to people other than your grandparents. And perhaps turn up the charm a little bit." She stood up. "I'll get my checkbook."

5

My father laughed on the speakerphone, "Don't worry! They can afford it. And trust me, Mother wouldn't have bought anything if she didn't want to." This made me feel a little better, but not really. I hadn't intended on shaking down my grandparents, but I did.

I noticed when I was explaining the particular functions of the knives that the description I gave of the spatula spreader got a very strong reaction from both Tina and my grandparents. I said to them, "The spatula spreader is like a three-in-one tool. It slices, it spreads, and it serves." Stuart told me this line, but neither Tina nor my grandmother knew what a three-in-one tool was. I'm not all that handy myself. I guessed that it's the tool used in painting as a paint-can opener, a scraper, and a paint knife, but I didn't really know exactly what the hell it was, so I said, "It's the kind of thing that Bob Vila uses." Both Tina and my grandmother laughed at this and later referred to it as the "Bob Vila Knife." They even seemed to get a bizarre thrill out of saying it, like they learned a new word. I decided to call the spatula spreader the Bob Vila Knife in my next demonstration.

I would later name most of the knives. I wouldn't drop the Bladeworks name, I would just say, "This is the spatula spreader. I call it the 'Bob Vila Knife' because it's like a three-in-one tool . . ." This kept me from having to go too far into too much detail. The use of the knife was often implicit in the name. For instance, I called the trimmer, the tomato knife, and the carver the Saturday Night Special.

I parked on the street outside of the two-story Colonial job in Troy. Close to Bloomfield Hills but low-end by comparison. The yard was bare. There were no decorations on the exterior of the house, except an empty clay planter next to the door. I could hear the Toyota sedan's engine clicking as it cooled in the driveway. The garage door was open, revealing a neat and spare room with a few grimy JCPenney boxes stacked along the back wall. This was not a promising lead. There was no indication of children, of extravagance, or that this woman took any pleasure in homemaking whatsoever.

Naturally, I was nervous. This was the first customer that wasn't family. This was not even a family friend—it was a former employee of my father's. There's a possibility that I'd met Mrs. Jenkins in passing at some point in my life, but I would have been nine or ten years old and had no recollection of her. I racked my brain thinking of the various secretaries that worked for my father in the '80s.

I pressed the buzzer. Mrs. Jenkins swung the door open. She was taller than most women, pretty, brunette with her hair in a bun and a short summer dress. "Come in." She had a phone in her hand and immediately turned away from me, twirling her skirt back to her kitchen.

Mrs. Jenkins's perfume was strong and smelled more expensive than the kind that most secretaries wear, but still verged on cheap. I followed her to the kitchen, glancing into the living room as we passed. An empty mahogany picture frame on a small table beside a mirror. An Ansel Adams print hung on the wall above the television and a large bowl of potpourri sat on a stand that stood awkwardly at the foot of the staircase.

"How do you do? I'm Jay."

"Hi. Jennifer Jenkins. How's your father?"

"Great."

"He's the best. He was always so nice to all of us."

"Yeah. He's a nice guy."

She studied me. "You seemed a lot younger on the phone last night."

"Oh, did I?" It looked like my stammering call might have backfired. "Maybe you thought I was my younger brother."

"Maybe. So, where would you like to do this?"

I motioned to the kitchen table. "This is perfect."

We sat. She checked the clock on the wall. "Listen. I don't mean to be rude but could we try to make this as fast as possible? I'm happy to help you with your scholarship, but I have to tell you that I never, ever cook. You can see this kitchen is not a cook's kitchen." I looked around. It wasn't. In fact, there wasn't a single indication that the kitchen had ever been cooked in.

"Really, it's okay. You don't have to buy anything. I get paid anyway. And honestly, right now, I am just starting off and so if you could tell me what I'm doing wrong or give me pointers . . . That would be great."

"Okay. But I have to tell you, Jay, my husband is coming home in thirty-five minutes and we're going to dinner. I'm leaving town tomorrow morning and I really want to spend time with him before I go. We both work long hours. I'm a paralegal now and it's just . . ."

"I'll be superquick. I promise." I started fiddling with my bag to get out my roll. The zipper was stuck. She was staring at me, impatient as hell. I bent farther over the bag and as I did this, the handful of pennies that I had in my shirt pocket fell out and scattered all over her kitchen floor. She let out a big laugh. "Oh, God. You're a mess!"

"Sorry." I crawled off the chair and onto the floor and went after the pennies.

She jumped out of her chair, laughing again, and said, "Let me help you."

"God. I'm so sorry. Normally I wouldn't worry about these pennies, but I've got to cut them."

"You're going to cut pennies?"

"Shoot. I think I just ruined the surprise."

She helped me collect the pennies off of her floor. When I get nervous I ask a lot of questions so I asked, "Do you remember a woman named Saundra who used to work at my dad's office?"

"Saundra Place? Of course. God, she was a trip. You know how she got fired, don't you?"

"Sure." She was fired for stealing. "I kind of had a crush on her as a kid. I always wondered what happened to her. Do you know where she is now?"

"She's living in Tempe and married to a contractor. She's doing really well."

"I always liked her. She babysat for us a couple of times."

She stood up. "There, do you have them all?"

"I hope so. I'm real sorry about that. I'm pretty nervous."

"Oh. It's okay. Just relax. You'll do fine."

"Okay. Should I start now?"

"Why not?"

I launched into my pitch.

Conscious of her husband coming home and remembering my grandfather's advice, I cut the superfluous crap and observed Mrs. Jenkins carefully.

There was something extremely attractive and stylish about the lady. Although her home was clearly neglected with a minuscule amount of attention paid to the decor, her dress, on closer inspection, was actually quite nice—it was well fitting with a tie around her waist, and a neckline that plunged exactly as low as a professional office might allow. Her jewelry, though not excessive, was all high quality and her diamond earrings were small enough to be real but large enough to catch your attention. Even the way she sat and listened, shoulders straight, head tossed back, legs delicately crossed, her hands smoothing out the skirt of her dress as she peered at the satin tip of her high-heeled shoe, made me think, this woman cares about how people see her and she'll spend money on it.

When I asked her to bring me her favorite knife she got up and smiled. She had a pretty smile. "See, I really don't cook." She pulled a set of knives out of a cupboard.

The block was still wrapped in plastic. I had to cut it open. The knives were the cheap serrated kind seen on infomercials with black plastic handles and thin, flimsy blades. Her brand-new chef's knife took seven strokes to cut the rope. The Bladeworks took one. I used the "Bob Vila" line. She laughed. "That's funny. I usually have toast in the morning. I could maybe use *that* knife."

"No way. Cooking is not allowed in this kitchen." This line got her too.

But then she shrugged. "You have a point."

I blasted through the rest of the demonstration as quickly as possible. I was sitting down, as Apex teaches its salespeople to do, so that you're at the same level as the customer and not threatening. This rule irritated the hell out of me. I felt awkward and slow, immobilized in my seat, and found myself having to either get up or rudely reach across the table to turn a page in the catalog or hand a customer a knife. Every time I did this, my tie dragged through the pile of chopped rope, leather, and bread.

When I got around to the close, I looked down at the table with genuine embarrassment and tried to make it clear that this next line was not my own. "Would you like me to order you the Deluxe Kitchen Set?"

"Yes."

I was shocked. "No. You can't. You have a set here that you haven't even opened."

"That's because they're so nasty. I don't even remember who bought them for us. I guess they're not that important, right?"

"Sure. But c'mon. You're not going to use this whole set."

"I know. But I like the look of the block. And Rob's family is coming for Thanksgiving this year. I'm supposed to cook, but I know his mother's going to be in here. She'll be going crazy if I don't have good knives." She motioned to her set, half unwrapped. "She sure as hell can't use those."

"Okay. If you say so."

I was shaking slightly as I filled out the sales form, and out of nervousness and with nothing to say I gave her a vegetable peeler for free. Salesmen are allowed to give up to twenty dollars of product free for every hundred dollars spent. Apex recommends that you use this as a bartering tool to get the sale. I never did. I thought that bartering was bad business and corny (plus your commission was determined from the net sale), but later on I would often throw in a vegetable peeler after a customer had paid for the order as a thank-you. It was a twenty-dollar item.

Although Mrs. Jenkins did not necessarily have the money to squander on the set of knives, nor any practical need for them (they would be about as useful to her as a bronzed turd), Mrs. Jenkins got a thrill out of the purchase. Her cheeks were pink and flushed. Her motions were exaggerated and her breathing was heavy. Instead of looking at me while she talked, she sort of gazed back over her shoulder through the doorway, panting and posing, thinking about herself and what she'd just done. Mrs. Jenkins was proud and excited that she'd just bought something that would arrive in three weeks by mail, be placed on her counter, where the block of knives would collect dust and possibly a compliment or two from her mother-in-law in November. It took me a moment to figure out why she was so pleased with herself, and it finally struck me. The knives were actually a smart buy. For a mere eight hundred dollars, Mrs. Jenkins justified owning a kitchen.

We thanked each other as she walked me to the door. She looked down the street at a car approaching the house. The driver wore a mustache and a greasy hairdo. "That's Rob . . . He'll think I've gone crazy."

I was sure of this and wanted to get out of there as soon as possible. "Well, I better get going then. Thanks again, and have a wonderful summer."

"You too."

As I was walking away Mrs. Jenkins asked, "Is that your car?"

My father's BMW was fairly glowing at the curb.

"Oh. Yeah. I mean. It's my father's."

She smiled. "Well. I'm glad I bought the knives, but you're going to have a hard time convincing people you're in need of a scholarship when you're driving around in a car like that."

I tore through Mrs. Jenkins's development, cutting late turns and chirping the tires as I rounded the corners. "We Are the Champions" blared from the speakers. I'd found a Queen CD in the glove box.

I reflected on my demonstration and realized that although I had done a decent job of selling, the stroke of luck that changed the momentum of the appointment was when the pennies fell out of my pocket. That and our chat about Saundra.

My next customer wanted to wait until eight when her husband got home, so I wouldn't have time to make calls afterward. I realized because I had no appointments set up for the following day I would have to make calls on the move. I didn't like this for many reasons. It would be hard to take down directions and drive at the same time. It would also be hard to do my mamsy-pamsy act. But most important, I didn't want to make the calls from a mobile phone. This was before everyone in the world had cell phones, and much like a college kid driving around in a BMW, in my hometown, cell phones were viewed as an extravagance. Still, I had no choice.

Even though I wanted to save my sure things for later when I was kicking ass, I figured that I'd better call people that I knew well enough that I wouldn't have to worry about where they lived or laying my act on too thick. Plus, my aunt Tina had coughed up a veritable gold mine of names. I fumbled around with my list, the phone, and the directions to my next gig.

For my last appointment I was selling to a very wealthy guy with a mildly hysterical, and I suspect agoraphobic, wife who was wound so goddamn tightly that I was scared she might work herself into an epileptic fit during the presentation. That is—until she got ME so goddamn nervous that, as I bent down to pick up my sales bag, I again launched the pennies out of my front pocket and across the floor. I have no idea why, but both the rich guy and his bugged-out wife found this so hilarious, and it relaxed them so much, that they were practically drooling on each other for the rest of the sales pitch. In this more comfortable state I was able to drive the rest home nice and easy and close by creating an entirely new set of knives. I called the new set the Jay Special. It was a slightly smaller set of knives (the Studio Set) but in the big block with a specialty knife (the Handy Slicer) and a pair of kitchen shears. The

Jay Special was "I'm not sure but I think a little over five hundred dollars" (actually $595), and the Deluxe Kitchen Set cost "eight hundred and five dollars." A much easier sell, but still a big one. Anyway, I guess I did all right, because as the guy—who I noticed looked like a country club version of Jack Palance—walked me to the door he asked me to quit my knife-selling job and work for him that summer.

"Selling to your grandparents doesn't count. If you're going to win the push week you're going to have to step it up. You've got one day to get ready." I had Stuart on speakerphone.

"Dude. I got offered a job."

"It happens all the time."

"Sure. But the first day? I sold over two thousand dollars' worth of knives."

"Yeah. And I told you, good job. But you can do better."

"All right." I ashed my smoke out the window.

"How many appointments do you have set up for tomorrow?"

"Four."

Stuart moaned so loudly I thought he might've been faking it. "You've got to do better than that."

"Yeah. I know. I've been driving all day. I had to call from the road."

"When's your last appointment tomorrow?"

"Four-thirty."

"After you finish, get your ass home and hit the phone. Try to schedule as many appointments as possible. It's great to get a nice sale late in the day, but if it prevents you from scheduling your following day it's not worth it. Try to schedule a day or two in advance and then call in the morning to confirm."

"All right. Talk to you later, douche."

I hit the end button on the steering wheel. The music automatically turned back on. "Fat Bottomed Girls." Isabelle had a nice ass. In my life before Isabelle I didn't like big butts, but I loved Isabelle's. Not fat, just round. Kind of like the perfect Brazilian ass you see in the Ja Rule video for "Holla'." It's right underneath the template "Rio de Janeiro" . . . Just a couple of sandy butt cheeks on the beach swinging in the breeze. I wondered if Isabelle had left for Colorado yet. She was working on a ranch for the summer. I wondered if she was thinking of me, about how I was doing.

I considered calling her. Not yet. I did an extra lap around the hood and wondered if Isabelle knew why I was selling knives.

I walked through the door and immediately my mother was griping at me from the kitchen. Her footsteps quickly clipped across the glazed brick floor and into the hall. "Jay. It's almost ten o'clock. I told you we were having dinner at nine."

"I know. I was at an appointment or I would have called."

"What good does calling do if you're already late?" She cornered me in front of Coulter's room.

"I don't know."

"Jay. I don't want you living here if you're going to behave like this."

I snapped. It was the threat of throwing me out again. I slammed the wall with the palm of my hand. "No! Goddamn it! You're not going to pull that bullshit on me! If you don't want me here, tell me, but I'm not going to have that shit hanging over my fucking head!"

"If you want to leave, fine."

"Mom!" That was Coulter calling from his room. He came running out. "Don't say that." I didn't pay any attention to him.

"No. Come on . . . Just tell me if you want me to leave. Come on . . . Tell it to me. Tell me you want me to leave right now."

My mother started to cry. "You're such a bully." She turned back to the kitchen.

I called after her. "Yeah? Who's the one trying to throw me out for being late to a goddamn dinner when I'm just trying to work?"

I went into my sister's room. I threw my stuff down onto the bed. Courtney had a phone and desk in there and I was using the room as my office. I didn't really understand why she had a room in that house when, as I've said, I didn't and she lived in god-damned Portland. "Coulter. Get in here!"

Coulter came in. "She's crying. You've got to say something to her."

"Wait. Coulter. Do you understand what she's trying to do? What she's fucking doing? It's unacceptable."

"I know . . . But c'mon. It's Mom. You have to understand her."

"Maybe." I cooled down a bit. "All right. I'll talk to her in a minute, but I want you to do something for me."

"What?"

"I want you to get out your Cranbrook directory, go through it carefully, and write down the name and number of anyone you think I could call to sell knives to. No. Wait. Just write down the names and numbers of people who like you. The parents. We'll go through the list and I'll have to ask you questions about them to see if they're good or not."

"Okay. But what if they're not in the book?"

"Well, if you know some parents that don't have kids at Cranbrook, great. Write those down too."

"Are you going to talk to Mom?"

"Yeah."

"When?"

"As soon as you start with the names."

"I've got finals."

"Oh. Come on. You need a study break. I'll give you a cut if they sell."

"You will? How much?"

"A lot. Listen. I got a big week coming up so I need good names now. Okay?"

"Okay."

"Good. I'll go talk to Mom." I walked out of the room. "Mom!"

I thought of a solution to the BMW problem, in the form of a car my older sister had bought, never used, and left to rot in the parking lot of one of my father's companies. I would use that car for business and my father's for pleasure. Coulter took me to pick it up.

It was blue and boxy. The streak of early morning yellow sun glowing across the hood like a puddle of urine. The parking lot was wet from the previous night's rain, but the sky was blue and empty, and it was going to be a hot day. I hoped the Escort's air-conditioning worked.

"Thanks, dude." I shook Coulter's hand.

"Is everything okay with Mom?"

"Yeah. It's fine."

"Okay. Good luck today."

"Thanks. Wait. Don't pull out until the car starts."

"Okay."

I lugged my crap over to the Escort, tossed it in, and fired it up. It actually wasn't too bad. It was clean—frankly, almost brand-new—and a stick. I laid an excellent patch of rubber as I did a squealing three-sixty in the parking lot and whipped out onto Maple, rolling on westward to my next victim.

Margi Tammerstein. Tina's best friend. Her kids were wearing bathing suits. They were waiting for me to finish my presentation so their mother could drive them to swim practice at their country club. They were beautiful and calm and had large dark eyes that looked at me like I had a bonsai tree sticking out of my ass.

My ten o'clock was some old guy who used to work as a driver at my father's office. He lived by himself in a dark and cramped condo. He only bought two knives and a potato peeler. About $150 worth in sales. My dad was convinced he'd be a great lead because he loved to cook and always talked about me. Obviously he wasn't. Still, he was a nice guy. His apartment reeked of garlic and loneliness. I was probably the only person he'd see that day.

Stuart used to tell me that these were the best sales. The unlikely buyers. The sales you had to fight for. I didn't agree with him. I left the man's condo in deep gloom and didn't feel good until speeding north on Telegraph with the driver-side window rolled down and my head hanging out of it with a cigarette pinned in my teeth. I had to be very careful about smoking—so I didn't smell like it. If I was ever asked if I smoked, my line was: "No. But the last person I met with did. It was awful."

I unloaded a Studio Set on Rose Greenway, the wife of my father's lawyer. Her husband was going to speak at my brother's graduation. She was a very close and longtime family friend. Selling to her depressed me, because instead of doing my shtick, she just wanted to listen to me talk about my mother. They hadn't seen each other in a while. The sale was payment for catching up.

Out of earshot from Rose's house, I gunned the motor, threw the car in neutral, cut the wheel, and yanked the parking brake up, putting the Escort into a long power slide down the dirt road. The car ground to a halt, facing in the opposite direction. It worked. I felt better.

Dust and rocks flew from my back tires and I carried on.

My next sale was painless and profitable: a Jay Special to a mother of two. I tried something out with the customer, Mrs. Arkin. When I walked in she seemed nervous. I purposely made the pennies fall out of my pocket and immediately she relaxed. This trick would permanently become part of my act.

I got some excellent referrals out of Mrs. Arkin, went home, and hit the phones. Cold-calling really sucks, but I didn't stop to reflect on this or anything else, I just kept plowing ahead, planning my push week. Ten days. I stopped calling at nine. My last call was to Stuart to tell him I had a fifteen-hundred-dollar day. He seemed unimpressed.

I went out to the patio, sat down, and closed my eyes. I sat there, like that, until my mother came out of the kitchen with a tray of hors d'oeuvres.

"I thought you were having dinner with Brooke."

"I am."

"Aren't you late?"

"I am."

"Did you call?"

"No." She didn't say anything. I spread caviar and cream cheese onto a piece of melba toast.

9

I found the newsletter on Courtney's bed, where my mother had put my mail. Apex sent it to me. It was a listing of their top five hundred salespeople. Worldwide, Apex employed over fifty thousand salespeople. At the very top of the list was the name JORGE ACUÑA.

Acuña was a knife-selling legend. He was the number one salesperson in the country for the past three years. In his dorm

room at Dartmouth Stuart had a photo on his wall of Acuña stepping out of a limousine with a glass of champagne in his hand. He
was a slick-looking fucker. Handsome, with greased-back hair and a
charming smile. He wore a tux well. He wore that charming goddamn smile even better.

Acuña sold around three hundred thousand dollars' worth of
knives each year. Since he was selling at the 50 percent commission
rate, he was making over $150,000 a year. The most amazing thing
about Acuña was that he sold in Puerto Rico, where the GDP per
capita (purchasing power parity) in the year I was selling was $8,600.

Acuña's trick was that he didn't put up huge numbers. He just
put up constant numbers. He didn't cold-call anymore. He only sold
to people who'd previously bought Bladeworks knives. If you've
sold enough you can get a list of leads of all the people in your
area who've bought before, what they bought, and when. He would
scan that list for likely names, then call up and say that he was a
Bladeworks representative and that he'd like to come by to clean
and sharpen their knives. It takes about fifteen minutes. So Acuña
would show up, sharpen and clean the knives, and then sell them
more knives or other Bladeworks products, like cookware. He was
very fast and would just sweep through neighborhoods peddling
the crap. He drove a Mercedes but did his sales rounds on foot.

Acuña was in his late twenties and technically still a college
student. (Many salespeople would remain enrolled in community col-
leges or universities so they could continue to say they were trying to
win a scholarship to complete their studies.) He had already sold over
twenty thousand dollars' worth of knives that summer. Fuck him.

Stuart kept telling me that my numbers were good, but not high
enough. He said that there were other people in his office who
were selling as much as I was. If I had a day where I sold less than

one thousand dollars it was a disaster—someone in the office would always beat me that day. I had no way of knowing what other people were selling. Nor did I have time to find out. All I knew was what was in the newsletter.

All I did was sleep, eat, sell knives, set up appointments, fight with my mother, and dodge Brooke, who was starting to get mad at me. I kept promising her time. "I've just got to get through this first ten days. I'll be better afterward." I did occasionally find time to fuck her. Late at night I'd drop by. We'd go to the lake or to her basement. Sometimes I'd fall asleep for a couple hours afterward, slumped over on the couch or in her bed, with my dick hanging out sticky and wet. She'd wake me after a while. I'd jerk upright, like my father, drooling on myself and angry at her for letting me fall asleep. Later I'd apologize.

I had a mental list of people who I decided I didn't want to sell to, people who weren't family but who would feel socially uncomfortable if they didn't buy knives from me, like my godmother and Sherianne. My dad's new girlfriend, who I had yet to meet, was on there, too. I ended up selling to those people and everyone else on that list (except one) during the first push. Sherianne bought because she wanted to see me. My dad's new girlfriend had another more obvious reason. I introduced myself; she talked about how much she loved my father and bought a Studio Set. My godmother, "Aunt" Blake, didn't buy because she had ulterior motives or out of guilt. She bought because I sold the hell out of the knives.

The only person or family that remained on the list that I didn't sell to was Brooke's mother. Brooke, like Sherianne, wanted her mother to set up an appointment so she could see me, but out of some clinging duty to dignity I refused to use my girlfriend to make a sale. At that point, so early in the summer, no sale, no matter what it would have done to my ranking—and it probably would have done a lot, since the Ambroses were quite generous—could have persuaded me to attempt to sell to Brooke's family.

When I first told Mr. Ambrose that I wouldn't sell to his wife, he had quietly taken me aside. The guy looked like Clark Gable, super handsome with the same thin mustache and haircut. He dressed like him too and even acted like him, except maybe Mr. Ambrose was smoother. Definitely more gentle. His parents died when he was very young and so he had that sort of light touch when dealing with people, like everything was fragile. And when he took me aside—into a corner, really—he laid one hand on my back, smiled, and turned his huge yellowish eyes on me as he swore that there was absolutely nothing wrong with "practicing" my routine on Mrs. Ambrose. Wink-wink. *Every good businessman was a salesman. And after all, she didn't have to buy if she didn't want to.* But there was something faint in the offer—not a trap, but something like it, like joining a secret society that scared me. *All you've got to do is sell to my wife to be one of us.* I couldn't do it. The Ambroses already had two complete sets of Bladeworks knives and they didn't need any more from me.

Now, just because I didn't jump at the first opportunity to sell to the Ambroses don't think I was a saint, because when I looked at my greater list of potential buyers—the people who I planned on calling—there wasn't really anyone on it that I originally intended to sell to either. I liked them all and didn't want to use them, but I did. All they had to do was answer the phone. Deborah Callahan. I called her "Aunt" Debbie. I called Antoinette Fraser "Aunt" Toni, too. Mrs. Ruby. "Aunt" Sharon Showalter. Karsi Graber. Betty Mills. Duffy Wizenstein, whose husband, Marty, had recently passed away. Carol Hankoff. Rebecca Pitts. Martha Newberry, my godmother, and my godmother's sister, Jody, my best friend's mother. Christine Leonard, wife of novelist Elmore Leonard. Robert "Bobby" Beaufort. Joanne Herman, my football coach's wife. Joanne Waldon. Cathy Pollux. Eldon Manfrey. All of my female elementary school teachers. Teresa James. Lucy Brody. Janet Gross . . . You get the idea. I sold like crazy.

I honed my pitch to well under thirty minutes. On the seventh day of the push, I set up ten appointments. I made them all and sold knives to them all. I wasn't keeping track of my numbers. I didn't know the total of what I sold. I only knew the figures for each particular day and if they were more or less than the previous day. I didn't want to know the total. I just wanted to keep pushing, selling.

Only three notable things happened that week unrelated to my knife activities.

One. I attended Coulter's graduation. I saw some people who I'd sold to. It was embarrassing. Jack Greenway, Rose's husband, spoke.

Two. I got my braces off. I couldn't believe how white my teeth were. I kept staring at them in my rearview mirror as I drove around, constantly running my tongue over the glossy crowns. Brooke practically creamed her jeans when she saw the grin.

Three. Right after I got my first paycheck, I went to a local market and bought a bottle of expensive champagne, a bottle of even more expensive wine, and a pack of English cigarettes. I had them sent to Isabelle's ranch in Colorado with a note attached that read, "Hope you're well. I'm sure the dude ranch is turning you into a hard-ass. Please don't let it get too hard. Maybe these will help. Yours, Jay."

The BMW bombed down I-75. Black on black in the night. I luxuriated behind the wheel, loving the lack of late-night traffic and the cigarette burning between my fingers. I had the windows down. The air sitting on the Ohio plain was hot and muggy. It felt soft and then got cold and wet on my skin. I sped into the big flat empty darkness that lay spread out before me. Cincinnati came up like a neon backhand, slapping the night away.

I cruised through downtown, ghettos on my left, the financial district on my right. I dropped down to the Ohio River, hit the bridge, crossed into Kentucky, turned left, and pulled into the second strip mall on the right.

Stuart's office was a plain storefront, recently vacated by a shoe store and rented for the summer months. An APEX MARKETING sign hung in the window. The interior was bare, except for rows of folding tables with chairs and phones.

I tried the door. It was locked. I looked inside. The lights were on, but I couldn't see anybody. I went back to my car and called the office. It rang a few times and then Tammy, Stuart's secretary and girlfriend, came out of the back room, wiping her mouth and pulling the sleeve of her blouse up.

"Hello. Apex Marketing."

"Hi, Tammy, it's Jay. Would you put Stuart on the phone?" She did. "Stuey, I've been sitting out here for *ten* minutes while you've been in the back with your goddamn girlfriend."

"Secretary!" Stuart squinted out the window. "Is that you in that fuckin' Bimmer?" I brighted him.

He unlocked the door. Tammy was embarrassed as hell. Stu gave me a hug. "How you doin', man?"

"Good. You?"

"Great. Just sorting out some stuff in the back." Stuart was grinning big and wide. It was good to see him. Tammy stepped forward, and I noticed what looked like a thin streak of glue shining on her forearm. I gingerly shook her hand. "Hi, Tammy."

"By the way, this . . ." Stuart pointed at Tammy and himself. "Keep it private. No one in the office knows that Tammy and I are dating. I'm trying to be professional."

I laughed. "Professional!"

"Another thing. And, this is really important, don't tell anybody in the office or at the conference what you've sold. I know. Tammy knows. So does Bobby, my assistant manager. But no one else."

"Why?"

"You'll see. Dude. Just trust me. Don't tell anyone."

"Okay. But I don't even really know what my total is."

Tammy told me my total and picked up her purse. "I'll see you boys back at the house."

"Wait, why don't we all go together?"

"Bobby's coming here. Stu didn't know how late you'd be."

"He'll be here in a minute. He wants to meet you, anyway. We'll take off soon. Plus, like I said, I'm trying to keep this thing with Tammy a secret, okay?"

"A'right. Do you have a beer in here or something?"

"Yeah. I got some in the back."

Stuart and I sat drinking for a while. Bobby seemed excited to meet me. He was a nice guy, polite, a couple years older than Stuart, good-looking, neatly dressed, and seemingly smart enough. At first glance you'd think he'd be the manager and Stuart would be his assistant. But he looked at Stuart like a god. He kept his left hand balled up in a fist.

Stuart was telling some old war stories from his selling past when he said, "Bobby was a great knife salesman. Could've been one of the best."

Bobby blushed. "Nahhh. I wasn't that good."

"No? What did you sell last summer?"

"Thirteen thousand. Okay, I guess I was pretty good. Never thought I'd be a manager, though. I only do it because I can't sell no more."

I asked, "Why? What happened?"

He took a deep breath. Stu winked at me. "Well. Last year, I was doing a presentation for this really rich woman. She'd already told me that she wanted to buy a Studio Plus Four in a block. She said she was in a rush, but I wanted to sell her the kitchen shears and maybe get her to upgrade to a Studio Plus Six. I was rushing. She was putting her things together to get out of the house. It was a huge house. Filled with new stuff, like she'd just won the lotto or something, and she had this little dog, a shih tzu that kept running around and yapping. You know those little yapping ratlike dogs?

"This one was nasty and kept barking like crazy and nipping at me on occasion. Anyway, I was nervous and sweating and I told the lady to just forget the presentation and went right to the cooking shears. I said to her, 'Mrs. Anthony, you gotta see these shears. They cut a penny.' So she stops packing her bag and watches me. I didn't have any new pennies on me, but I had an old hard one, so I had to make do. But this penny was a tough son of a bitch, pardon my French, and I couldn't get through it, so I just wrapped both hands around the blades and squeezed as hard as I could." He looked up at us.

"I didn't feel anything, I just heard a pop. Suddenly the woman screams. I looked down, and my finger was spraying blood all over the place. I pretty much knew what had happened. I accidentally slipped my finger between the blades and cut it off. Suddenly the little shih tzu goes tearing after my finger, which was lying about four feet from me on the floor. I tried to grab it, but the dog got it first and took off out of the doggy door." Bobby laughed. "It's funny now, but I was scared as heck back then and right when the dog grabbed my finger, the woman looked like she was going to vomit, but instead, she turned white and passed out."

"Oh. My god."

"Yeah. It was pretty crazy. But the worst part of it was that I had to wake the woman up and ask her to drive me to the hospital."

I couldn't stop laughing. "That's hilarious. Did you get the sale?"

"Hell no. But when I went back to her house to get my car, she'd left a Ziploc bag under my windshield wiper with some melted ice and my finger in it all chewed up and dirty. There was a note that said, 'I don't know if they can reattach this, but here's your finger.' I was hopped up on painkillers and it all seemed . . . I don't even know the word."

"Surreal?"

"Yeah. It was pretty darn surreal."

"Could they attach it?"

"Heck no. Look." Bobby held up his left hand, and his ring finger was cut off just above the first knuckle. "You can't really sell knives with a hand like this . . . So that's why I'm working for Stuart, here. Hopefully next summer I can have my own office."

Stuart crumpled his beer and hucked it into the trash can. "That's one hell of a story, Bobby, but you never told me what you did with the finger."

"It's in a drawer at home."

Stuart lived in a dumpy house that he rented on the ghetto side of the expressway. I left my father's car in the lot outside of the office. It would be safer there. In the morning, I was pretty hung over and asleep when we met up with the rest of the caravan that was following us to Atlanta. Tammy drove in a separate car.

I woke in the car, drooling on myself with some dirty-looking kid with a thin mustache asleep in the back, balled up around a backpack.

I turned to Stu. "Where are we?"

"Tennessee?"

"Huh . . . Dude. Your oil light is blinking."

"Oh, shit! This is my dad's car. He told me a couple of weeks ago that the car needed an oil change. Is that bad?"

"Could be."

"Why?"

"You could throw a rod if the engine seizes. If the light's on, it's bad."

"Fuck. We have to pull over."

I could smell the alcohol evaporating from my skin. I was sitting in the shade, under the awning of the gas station. Stuart was pacing back and forth, talking on his cell phone. "Chuck. We're on our way . . . I don't know. We got off to a late start . . . Ask 'em to wait if you can . . . Okay."

The rest of the cars in our caravan were parked in a small lot beside the station. There were seventeen other office members just hanging out. Apart from basic introductions, no one except Bobby and Tammy were speaking.

I lit a cigarette and watched the others. Greasy limbs hanging on car doors. The heat swirled up from the blacktop, obscuring features. Boozy salt water dripped into my eyes. I could hear squealing laughter. Which one of these jackals kept outselling me during the week? Probably the girl with the blue eyes, sucking on a soda that Stuart bought her. She sat on the curb, her legs spread out, slick with sweat.

"You got a light?" The little guy with the 'stash was standing over me. He had a gritty Kentucky accent.

"Yeah. Right here." The matchbook was soggy from the humidity, and I had trouble getting the pad to strike. Once I did, the sulfur burned my index finger.

"Thanks. Name's Skeeter."

"Jay." We shook.

"I know who you are. You're selling up in Michigan, aren't you?"

"Yeah."

"Mind if I sit?"

"No. Please do."

He sat. "You've never been to one of these conferences, have you?"

"No. You?"

"No. I hear it's a pretty big deal, though." He paused. "How about the hotel, you ever heard of it?"

"Nope."

"I hear it's a big one. Real fancy." Skeeter spat. "You got a roommate yet?"

"Nope."

"Wanna share one with me?"

"Sure."

"Cool, man. You seem like a cool guy."

Skeeter stubbed out his half-smoked cigarette, knocked off the ashen end, and stuck it in his pocket. "I'm gonna buy a motorcycle with the money I make selling these knives. I had a Ninja but I wrecked it."

"So you're going to buy another one."

"Yip. Faster one too. You know what a Hayabusa is?"

"Yip."

As we drew closer to our destination Stuart explained what the conference would be like. The Southeastern region was divided into geographic divisions based around a central office. The divisions were comprised of the branch offices. Stuart's Covington office was part of the Ohio River Valley division. In addition to the salespeople competing with one another to win the push, the branch mangers were competing for the highest office totals, and the division managers were competing for the highest division totals. Everyone would be excited. Everyone wanted to win.

We didn't have time to check in. Those of us who had coats and ties put them on in the parking lot, and we entered the hotel en masse.

A big dumb-looking ex-athlete type in his midthirties was waiting for us in the lobby. "Oh, boy! You guys just made it. Quick! Let's go down to the ballroom. We're about to get started." He stuck his hand out at me. "Chuck Schick. I don't think we've met."

"Jay. Hi."

"Jay Hauser?"

"Yeah."

"Wow. Nice to meet you." Chuck motioned for us to follow him. "Like I said, I'm Chuck Schick. I run the Ohio River Valley division. Stuart sold for me last summer. Hell of a kid. Made him a branch manager." He grabbed me by the arm. "Listen, whatever you do, don't tell anyone what you've sold." He pulled Stuart over. "I think we're going to have a little coup. That dick Chokewater thinks he's got it locked up with Susanne Beatle."

"Chokewater runs the Nashville office, right?"

"Yeah. The guy with the lisp. I overheard him saying that she sold around seven thousand." Chuck made a very high-pitched giggle and then, elbowing us in the ribs, he said, "I let it slip that we didn't have anyone who sold half that much. Oh, man. This is gonna be fun."

The hotel was huge—fifteen stories with a gigantic three-story lobby and a glass elevator. An escalator took us down to the level with the grand ballroom. Outside of the ballroom there were around two hundred salespeople in nervous clusters waiting for the festivities to begin. Everyone was checking each other out, but no one seemed to notice me as we cut through the crowd.

Stuart pulled me aside. "You nervous?"

"No."

"Bullshit." He was right. I was nervous.

"Put on your game face."

We entered the ballroom. It was enormous and filled with more than fifteen hundred people. Salesmen. Secretaries. Branch managers. Division managers. All milling around. Coordinators held up signs, conducting people to their seats. The branches and divisions had sectioned-off areas. All of the chairs faced the stage. An audio/light booth was set up in the back.

Skeeter and I walked over to the Ohio River Valley, aka the "Cinci-Slicers" area, took our seats in the Covington rows, and waited. Skeeter kept rubbing his hands together. "Jay, I'll tell you what I sold if you tell me."

"I'm sure you sold more than me."

"I doubt it."

"I'm serious. I didn't sell that much."

"I know you sold a lot. I heard Stuart and Bobby talking about it."

"Nah. Not that much. Someone in the office has me beat."

"I don't know, man."

"I guess we'll find out soon enough."

"This is pretty nerve-racking, ain't it?"

"It is. I'm not sure how much I like these other people."

"Me either. That girl over there with the soda pop's pretty hot though, ain't she?"

"Yeah. You know what she sold?"

"Nope."

"Damnit."

Chuck Schick came running over. "Okay. It's about to begin." He sat with us.

The lights dimmed, almost to black.

A single spotlight illuminated a woman standing at the podium. "Welcome to Apex Marketing's first push week for summer '97!" The crowd cheered. "My name is Kathy Jacobs. I am the assistant director of the Southeastern region. And I just want to say that I'm proud of all of you and of the work you've been doing. It's just great to be a part of such a wonderful organization that gives you guys a chance to work hard during the summer, succeed, and for those of you still in school, the opportunity to win a scholarship." Cheers.

"So, without further ado, I want to introduce a man who's been my inspiration for many years. My boss and mentor, the director of the southeastern sales region and senior vice president of Apex Marketing, please welcome my distinguished colleague Mr. Bud French!"

Huge applause accompanied by music drew Bud French out from behind a curtain at stage left. He was chubby, probably in his midsixties but looked a little older and a lot like Seymour Cassel. He sounded like him, too. He wore a tuxedo with a red flower pinned to the lapel and several rings on his fingers. He had a full head of glowing blond hair and a shiny well-trimmed blond mustache to match. He jogged across the stage floor, carrying a dozen roses. He kissed Kathy and gave her the flowers.

"Would you put your hands together for this fine woman? Kathy Jacobs, everybody! She should be an example to all of you!" Kathy bowed and walked offstage smelling her flowers. The cheers died down with the music. Bud slowly approached the podium. He looked out over the crowd, like he was admiring the sight.

"Man! Am I happy to be here today! It's a real honor for me to be in a room with you people. You excellent salespeople. Come on! Give yourselves a round of applause! Let's hear it! Let's hear it!!! How about that! You guys and gals are just great. I'd also like to point out that we all have a special honor tonight. Normally, she can't come to these things, but since my youngest son, Buddy, Jr., is away at basketball camp this week . . ." He leaned toward the crowd, as if sharing something private. "Don't worry, as soon as he's old enough to sell, he'll be here. Ha! Ha! But seriously, would you please give a rousing welcome to my lovely wife, Judith!" He motioned to the back of the ballroom, where another spotlight beamed down on an extremely fat woman wearing what looked like a white tablecloth. There were more cheers. Judith waved. "I love you, honey." Some people hooted.

Bud had a deep, raspy, showman's voice. He played it like a saxophone. "I want to tell you a story before we begin. I ummmm know a lot of you are in schools all across the country. I really applaud that. But when I was a kid, I came from a very poor family and I was what a lot of people would've called a bad seed. I just couldn't get it together in school. I wasn't dumb. I just found it boring and I didn't understand why people worked so hard for nothin'."

"I graduated from high school at the bottom of my class. The next couple of years I went from job to job without understanding why I had to put in eight hours and why if I worked harder than the other guys I wasn't rewarded for that. So I never worked hard. And as you might guess, I got fired from a lot of jobs. My parents threw me out. I had no home. No money. It was fun at first, but it wore off real fast. Like, as soon as I got cold and hungry." Lots of people laughed.

"Now, I'd come from a pretty small town in Pennsylvania, and most of the businessmen in the area knew me and knew I didn't like to work real hard for the peanuts they shelled out. So, I figured that my only chance to find work, which I really didn't want to do, was to go to the next town over and see if I could fool those people for a little while, bum around until I'd been fired from all of the bad jobs they had, and then move on. At some point, I'm sure I would have moved on to a life of crime. I'm certain of that.

"So I hitched to the town over, and as I was walking down Main Street, I saw a sign in a window that read, APEX MARKETING. EARN AS MUCH AS YOU WANT TO MAKE. What was this? This couldn't be true. There isn't a job where you can earn as much as you want. I didn't believe it and I would've passed by it, but there was a pretty girl sittin' in there. Judy!" He called out. "You saved me!

"So I went in there after a pretty girl, but I came out with the opportunity of a lifetime. I had an interview with the local branch manager, a great man by the name of Joseph Papandello, and he told me that what the sign said was true—if I worked hard at selling knives I could earn whatever I wanted. The sky was the limit. I was so excited that, like a fool, I told him about all of the jobs I'd lost and how lazy I'd been, and you know what he said? He said that he'd done the same darn thing! He told me that he was also one of those guys that just didn't get how bustin' your butt for nothin' made sense until he'd come across a storefront just like I'd done.

"To make a long story short, I started selling. It was tough at first, but I learned how to do it and I learned that you *can* have a fresh start and that if you show purpose and determination you *can* succeed. Hard work *can* get you up that ladder. But you've got to have an incentive. There's got to be a ladder to climb. Apex gives you that ladder.

"I sold a lot of knives and I made a lot of money. I probably would still be selling knives today if good ol' Joe Papandello didn't retire and offer me his job. Well, I took the same principles that I learned from selling knives and applied them to the job of helping other people sell knives. Years later, a lot of those people are in this room right now as division managers and some corporate executives like myself and the lovely Miss Jacobs you met earlier.

"Let me tell you what happens at Apex. If you want to succeed, you can. Everybody can sell knives, and every knife you sell is something special. I wish I could get back out there, and thanks to you, in a way, I do. And I'll tell you something else. I continue to work harder every year, and like I was promised that very first day when I walked into Joe Papandello's office, I MAKE MORE MONEY EVERY YEAR!" Lots of applause.

"I'm not going to lie to you. I make a lot of money. We all know what kind of money a good salesman can make. And let me tell you, if you stick to it, it only gets better. That is my promise to you. The sky is the limit, ladies and gentlemen.

"Enough about me! We know why we are here and I know you can't wait to get to it. So what I want you to do is this: everybody who's sold anything in the past ten days, I want you to come up here to the front of the room, by the stage. Come on. Come on up here." A little over half of the room got up and moved to the front of the ballroom. I was surprised that there were people there who were not managers who had not sold any knives.

"Okay. I want everyone in this ballroom who's not standing to take a look at these people. Look at them. What a great bunch. If you haven't sold your first knife yet, just look at this group of people and let them inspire you. You can sell knives. Now, I want all of you to give yourselves a round of applause. Selling is not easy, and you've all done it. You make me proud." Bud reached into the podium and pulled out a silver trophy about the size of an Oscar, of a man midstride, carrying a bag in his hand. He held it up.

"Someone is going to walk out of here with this trophy. And we all want to find out who. So we are going to start with a number. One hundred and fifty dollars. If you've sold one hundred and fifty dollars or less I want you to come forward to the microphone, tell us your name, what you've sold, and what division you sell out of. Okay. Let's begin. Who here has sold one hundred and fifty dollars or less? Come on."

A guy standing close to Bud stepped up. "Bob Manning. I sold fifty-six dollars for HOTLANTA!"

All of the people in the Atlanta division cheered in chorus "Hot! Hot! Hot!"

Most people had sold less than $500 worth of knives. It took a long time to get through all of the cheers and rattling off of stats. Skeeter bowed out at $650. By the time Bud got to the $2,000 mark there were twenty of us left. By the $4,000 mark there were three of us left: me, the girl from Nashville, and an older guy who looked like a human sock monkey, peaked and flaccid. "Take a look at these three salespeople. What a bunch of winners!" The girl from Nashville had the snottiest, most pompous expression I'd ever seen, and smiling out at the crowd, she dropped her head in a deep bow. She knew she'd won.

"So, who of you have sold four thousand one hundred dollars' worth of knives or less?" No one moved. The crowd cheered, "Higher! Higher!" "Four thousand two hundred? Four thousand three hundred? Four thousand four hundred?" The older guy stepped forward. He looked like he was on the verge of passing out.

He was panting. "My name is Donald Merryweather. I sold four thousand three hundred and sixty-five dollars worth of knives for Chattanooga."

The Chattanooga division cheered, "Choo! Choo!"

"And I just want to say that Mr. French, the words you shared with us earlier really touched me. For years I'd been working as an elementary school teacher and I just didn't find it satisfying. This summer break I decided I'd try something new, something that I always wanted to do but was afraid to try. One month ago I started working for Apex, and last week, with my wife's blessing, I tendered my resignation to the Chattanooga school system."

Bud didn't miss a beat. "Thank you, Donald! What a tremendous thing to say! What a great story. Your students are going to miss out, I'm sure, but I'm glad you're with us doing something you love. We have just two salespeople left." Bud looked at us. "Which one of you thinks you've won?"

"Me," snapped the bitch.

"Oh?" Bud looked at me. "And what do you have to say about that?"

I shrugged. Bud laughed and then yelled at the ballroom. "Do you want to find out?!"

"Yeah!"

"You want to find out who's going to win this push week?!"

"Yeah!"

"You want it? You got it! Which of you two has sold four thousand five hundred dollars' worth of knives or less?" The girl from Nashville had her hands clutched behind her back, her shoulders square to the audience and her chin up high. She stared ahead, smiling. I was slouching, sweating profusely under the spotlights. My clothes were crumpled and smelly, and I'm sure I looked like a giant, teetering drip castle of alabaster guano. Nobody there could have thought I had any chance of beating this girl.

"Higher! Higher!"

"Four thousand five hundred? . . . Four thousand six hundred?" Bud kept going up. When he got to seven thousand he stopped to wipe his brow. "Now, I can't take much more of this. One of you has got to break sometime soon. I just can't take it. Okay. Seven thousand one hundred." The bitch looked at me, desperate. Her eyes begged me to move. I stared at her. Fuck you. "Seven thousand two hundred dollars." The bitch broke. She stepped forward, her head still turned back at me, waiting, hoping. She practically stumbled to the microphone.

"Susanne Beatle. Seven thousand one hundred and thirty-seven dollars." She started crying. "Nashville." Shocked at the fact that she was crying, no one cheered. She quickly walked off the stage.

Bud's voice changed to a soothing tone. "You did a great job, honey. Let's give the lovely Miss Susanne Beatle a big round of applause!" Bud switched back to the old gruff style. "Okay, big guy. I want to find out what you sold . . . Seven thousand four hundred?" Bud looked at the crowd and then back at me. "We've been up here for a long time and I just want to know. Do I have a long way to go?"

"Yeah."

"Yeah? How about ten thousand?!" I shook my head. He looked out at the crowd in disbelief. "Twelve? Thirteen? Fourteen? Fifteen? You sold more than fifteen thousand dollars' worth of knives in ten days?!" I nodded.

The crowd started cheering, "Higher! Higher!"

The guitar intro from the song "Eye of the Tiger" began to play, low at first, slowly building—looped.

"SIXTEEN THOUSAND! SEVENTEEN THOUSAND! EIGHTEEN THOUSAND! NINETEEN THOUSAND!" I stepped forward.

"Jay Hauser. Eighteen thousand six hundred and forty-four. I work out of the Ohio River Valley division."

"Cinci-Slicers!"

Bud raised my hand up in the air. "The Eye of the Tiger" blared from the speakers. Beams of light swirled around. The crowd leapt up, applauding wildly. Bud kept pumping my hand again and again, singing along with the lyrics.

After the first verse of the song, the fervor died down. A woman came running up to Bud onstage. Bud spoke to the woman and came back to the mic. "Kill the music. Kill the music!"

"I've just gotten some news . . . that's going to be pretty shocking to a lot of people." I began to worry. Maybe all of my orders had been canceled. He held up the sheet of paper and waved it around. "Jay. I've just received word that you have beaten the all-time Apex first sales push record, by three thousand two hundred and eleven dollars." I looked out at Stuart in the audience. I swear to God he had tears in his eyes.

I was mobbed exiting the ballroom. Autographs. Photographs. Handshakes. Hugs. I was told that I'd sold more, individually, than most branch offices. A contingent of fifty people followed me out to Stuart's car, where I collected my bags. Chuck checked me in. Skeeter hung close.

I stuck my head under the showerhead. I began to get scared. How am I going to keep building the legend?

The following night we drove back to Cincinnati. Tammy beat us to Stuart's house. Stuart went inside to have "five—no, four" minutes alone with Tammy while I sat on his front steps and smoked a cigarette. I thought about Isabelle and how she must have gotten my package by now. She might have even been smoking one of the cigarettes I bought her or drinking the wine. It was Sunday. She probably had the day off. I hoped she did. I could not wait to get home to see what she wrote back.

After a while Stuart came back out and sat next to me.

"So, you think you're going to play football this fall?"

"Yeah. I think so."

"Great. That's great fucking news."

Some people say knife selling is addictive. And there is some truth to this. You get a rush out of the sale. It's something that you don't want to do. You know it's wrong. But you sell and sell and eventually you destroy yourself. I was a long way from rock bottom but I had taken my first step in that direction—off the gangplank and into the sea, where I would become the shark.

When I got back to Michigan I developed the first and primary facet to what I would later call my Seven Steps to Selling. My "six degrees of selling" theory.

I started running out of people I knew personally or were referred to by Coulter or my aunt. I had to do my homework. At night, after I'd made my calls, I'd study my list of names and try to figure out who to call next. I began to see a certain pattern in my references. The same names would be referred to me by different people. I saw how people grouped themselves into respective cliques, and I created associations that could be used duplicitously to my advantage.

When I first walked into a customer's house, on my way from

the front door to the kitchen, I would take the time to ask a ton of questions, often directly related to the person who had referred me to them. In doing so, I would create the illusion of strong connections between myself and the person who referred me, thereby connecting myself to the customer; all the while I would also be learning details about future customers. The more distant the referral the greater the lies would be in order to bridge the gap.

In addition to lying verbally, I began to lie more and more with my body language. Every twitch of my skin had a purpose. Every movement was premeditated. Everything was fake. After two more weeks I would move up to number three on Apex's list of top salespeople worldwide.

Chuck called. He wanted me to come to a knife-selling retreat in the Cumberland lakes area for the Ohio River Valley division offices and give a lecture on my selling method.

"Sure. I'll do it. I have some thoughts on it anyway."

"Okay, great. I'll let everyone know."

"Hey, Chuck. Listen, I want to start selling cookware. Is that possible?"

"Why do you want to do that?"

"Increase my sales. I've been seeing a lot of people who already have Bladeworks, so I know I'm not going to be selling them a set, but I think it'd be easy to sell 'em some pots and pans."

"You got a point there. But Jay, Apex policy is that a salesperson has to have sold knives for at least a year before they can sell the cookware too. It's a tricky pitch. I don't have anyone in my office who sells it."

"Well, let me try. I think I can make it work."

"Let me think about it."

"Chuck, don't take too long. The next push is coming up, and I'd like to have the cookware by then."

"Okay. I'll see what I can do. I'm gonna have to call Bud French on this one."

"Call 'm."

The lowest sale I made all summer was to a science teacher from Coulter's school. The school itself was near my mother's house—a big private job with boarding students, a graduate art program, and housing for teachers, so I figured it would be an easy in-and-out-type sale. Unfortunately, though, this Dr. Arnken guy lived off campus in the country and about an hour and thirty minutes away. I didn't learn this until he'd already agreed to meet with me. His lawn was like a giant, thick green sponge, dank and oozing with summer rain. After squishing my way up the short walk, I got hit with the usual scent of a low sale—garlic.

The guy was about fifty and had longish white hair and a drooping, thin pale face. He looked like white asparagus. Right away I could tell he was a vegetarian. I could also tell he was smart. Real smart. His house was warm, cluttered, and dirty. A Harvard alumni magazine sat in the wastebasket. He had a library of six thousand books stacked up around the house. He offered me a cup of tea. I accepted, and when the pot hit a high note, I broke into my routine.

Dr. Arnken knew more about composite steel and the resin handles than I suspected the knife designers knew. He immediately recognized why they cut through the rope so easily, dismissed the notion that a sharp knife is a safe knife, thought it unlikely that maggots would breed inside a wooden handle, was humored by the seriousness with which I stated my bogus statistics, and didn't agree at all that Bladeworks knives should cost twice as much as Henckels. By the end of my presentation both Dr. Arnken and I were laughing at the entire construction of my sales pitch.

Nevertheless the guy fell prey to some of my charms, agreed that the product was quality, and decided that he needed a new paring knife and could always use a new vegetable peeler. A sixty-dollar sale. I would have made just about ten dollars an hour for driving out to see him, but as I was filling out the form I decided to give him the vegetable peeler. I liked Dr. Arnken. Plus, he was Coulter's teacher, and I knew Coulter thought he was the greatest. Although the cost of the paring knife wasn't high enough to just throw in the peeler for free. I had to actually give him the one I used in my demo—the one that I had bought as a sales tool. Apex sent me a spare as part of winning the first sales push. It was in a box in my car and I didn't really know what I was going to do with it. So I handed over the old peeler as a thank-you. It cost me seven dollars to buy and $7.50 in commission.

On the way back to town I called Stuart and told him about the sale and the net loss. I told him it made me feel good. He replied, "When there's not a competition a lot of salesmen get complacent and that's when they slip up. That's where they lose. Jay, you have to remember, the entire summer is a competition." Thanks, Stuey.

It was one of those hot-as-hell muggy late afternoons. The pine trees on the street smelled heavily. "Oh, Jay. Come in. How's your mother? I haven't seen her since the Martins' cocktail party two weeks ago . . ." All of the lights in Mrs. Tammersol's house were off as I followed her in.

"She's fine. Thank you so much for having me."

"My pleasure. Since Doctor Tammersol and I divorced I've been just about plumb out of entertainment." Her face and chest were damp with sweat, and her blouse was unbuttoned just above her bra strap. She stopped at a closet on the way to her kitchen and removed a towel. She patted her face and her neck with the towel. She nodded to a weedy patch of slate rock beyond her screened-in patio. "I was just sunning on the terrace." There was an empty highball glass next to her reclining beach chair. She was holding her shirt out and patting the tops of her breasts, which I knew from her constant drunken bragging to my mother were fake. Maybe I looked a second too long. She flashed an embarrassed smile. "I've heard from Cathy Pollux your little show is quite impressive." She led me toward the screened-in porch. "It's so hot, is it okay if we just leave the lights off? There's a little sun coming in through the screens."

I didn't like the idea of doing the demonstration in a dimly lit area, but I said okay. On the way, I glanced into Mrs. Tammersol's kitchen. It was obliterated, shit everywhere, like she'd gone to have a midnight snack and had a food fight with herself.

"You sit down. I'm going to fix myself something cool to drink. Would you like something?"

"I'd love a glass of water."

She put her hands on her hips and looked at me. "Jay. It's after six in the afternoon. You know it's okay to have a drink with me. Maybe I'll put something in it."

She smiled at me like we were playing a game. I smiled back.

Mrs. Tammersol returned from the kitchen with two drinks and a platter of cheese and crackers. "I'm not a cook like your mother, so I won't even try, but here's something that you can nibble on if you'd like." She set the platter down in front of me, deeply leaning over. I noticed she'd taken off her bra. Her breasts nearly flopped out of her blouse. I looked away but felt her watching me. She sat down on the squishy cushion next to me, handed me one of the drinks, and tapped it with her glass. "Cheers."

"Cheers. Now, before we begin I'd like to tell you a little bit about Bladeworks . . ." I set my glass down on the small table in front of me. "The company was founded by two brothers in Orion, New York—" She set her hand on my leg. I stopped. I was so shocked that I actually just went on with my demonstration, very distracted by the hand now moving slowly up and down my leg. After a while I desperately wanted to tell this woman to stop, but at the same time, I wanted the sale, and to avoid any kind of embarrassing exchange that might get back to my mother. So I just kind of pretended not to notice and hoped she'd forget about what she was doing, which seemed unlikely, because the force of her hand on my leg became increasingly strenuous. Remembering my sales pitch also became increasingly strenuous, but I pressed on.

I had a brief respite from my rubdown when in the middle of showing Mrs. Tammersol the specific uses of each knife she excused herself to fix another drink. Now, it wasn't that I necessarily found Mrs. Tammersol attractive, because I didn't. But the woman certainly knew how to use her hands, and even though she had not touched my penis, I was definitely suffering from an extremely painful erection. As soon as she was gone I stood up and paced around the patio to walk it off. What Mrs. Tammersol was doing was weird, for sure, but it didn't really bother me that much, and I kept saying to myself over and over, you've come this far, you might as well get the sale. Again, "fixing" her drink took a goddamn long while.

When she came back she made up for lost time by winding her left arm along my shoulders so she could reach around and touch my chest—rubbing and then pausing to hug me. She began to murmur, "I miss touching someone, Jay. I do. You understand it. Don't you?"

"Yes. I do. Here is your Bob Vila Knife. It's a three-in-one tool." She slid her right hand down between my legs. Her fake tits pressed up against the back of my elbow. She was sweating through my shirt, her lips about an inch from my ear. I continued with the sales pitch as if this woman were not hanging on my back. I felt a little bit like a marionette controlling the puppeteer's hand. I could smell her boozy breath and felt her lips brush against my ear.

At some point I realized that the situation had gotten completely out of hand, and for the first time that summer I really had no idea what I could do to steer the sale my way. As I neared the price comparison, Mrs. Tammersol actually bit down on my ear, ran her hands up between my legs, and grabbed the end of my penis.

"Please, stop." I said it quietly—like a girl.

Her right hand jerked back, slightly, but stayed between my legs. Her left hand kept rubbing my chest.

"Why?"

The question made sense. Why shouldn't I—it'd be kind of gross, but why the hell not? The answer came very clearly to me. I said, "I have a girlfriend who I really love and I don't want to cheat on her. I'm sorry, Mrs. Tammersol, we can't do this."

Mrs. Tammersol pulled back a little and looked me over. Her features softened and her hands stopped moving. "Jay. I'm going to buy your knives, but I want you to do something for me."

"I can't do what you want."

"Just stay where you are."

"Okay."

"Keep talking."

"What do you want me to say?"

"Say anything." She took her right hand off my leg and put it between her own legs.

"So, now that I've shown you the knives, wouldn't you say they're pretty great?"

She closed her eyes. "Yeah. I can't believe I'm doing this." She parted her sarong, revealing a very pink, clean-shaven vagina.

I continued with my demonstration. "Let me show you some other great knives . . ." She nearly had me in a headlock as I moved into the close, choking me with her left arm and fingering herself with her right hand. Her lips were very wet, she was drooling a little, her eyes were closed, and she looked like she might go into a fit at any moment.

Fortunately, she came quickly, emitting five or six short hard breaths and curling spastically on the couch next to me. I never stopped speaking. Slowly she folded her sarong back into place on her lap and sat back up.

Then she interrupted me. "Jay." She was breathing very hard. "I want to spend four hundred dollars on knives. You pick them. I'm going to fix another drink. You want one?"

"No, thank you."

She left. I filled out the form.

15

I made my way through the house toward the pool, which was packed with people I knew growing up. I was still fairly amped from the last sale I'd had and all of the caffeine I'd consumed, so I probably wasn't as friendly as I might have been otherwise. My head was still in it, you know, and I was twitching, so it was hard to be chitchaty. I saw one of Coulter's best friends smoking weed in front of the kitchen. "Hey, David."

"Yo. Jay, what's up?" He gave me a hug.

"Have you seen Coulter?"

"Yeah. Earlier tonight at Katie Fortenblau's. Her parents are in Greece. He'll be here in a bit. Want some?" He held up the joint.

"No, thanks."

"Is Brooke with you? I haven't seen either of you this summer."

"She's at home. I've been working my fucking ass off."

"So Coulter tells me."

Someone tapped me on the shoulder. I turned. It was Doug, one of my closest friends from high school. I smiled just seeing him and went to slap his hand. "Doug! Yo, man!" He caught my hand and didn't say anything, just stared at me with this serious look, like he was going to tell me someone died. "What's up? You okay?"

"Dude. You should go talk to Hanagan."

"Why, what's going on?"

"Just talk to him."

"Where is he?"

"The theater in the basement. He heard you were here."

I nodded. David patted me on the shoulder. "Tell Brooke I want to marry her, will ya?"

I laughed. "Sure, and if Coulter gets here tell him I'm in the basement."

Doug followed me downstairs, close and somber, practically stepping on the backs of my shoes.

Hanagan was another really close friend of mine, one of my very best. You wouldn't think it, because he acted like a tough guy and could be sort of a bully, but he was quite sensitive. When we were arrested together (I was fourteen and he was seventeen) the police split us up into different cells to scare us. I remember thinking it was pretty funny and so I was smiling and laughing when they took the mug shots, which pissed off the cops, but they knew me through my mother and I knew everything was going to be fine. The last I'd seen of Hanagan he seemed fine too, right before they separated us. But as the officer led me back to my cell, I was wiping off the ink they used to fingerprint me when I heard this strange gurgling-choking-crumpling-sound. I looked up to see Hanagan sitting outside of his cell, blowing into a brown bag, hyperventilating and crying hysterically. I walked over to him, touched his shoulder, and told him not to worry, that as soon as our parents got there everything would be all right. He just erupted, snotting and shouting, "I told you I didn't want to do it! I told you it was a bad idea! I told you to leave me alone!" The officer took me back to my cell. We didn't speak for a while but eventually made up and probably became closer for it. Anyway, that was the last time we had a "problem" and that was five years earlier, so I figured whatever was wrong might be bad but couldn't be that bad.

I found Hanagan in the theater with a bunch of his new friends from Northwestern University. I didn't know any of them. They looked small and irritating, like the kind of guys that would watch their friend play a video game at a party, which is exactly what Hanagan was doing. I dropped my hand for a shake. He kept staring at the screen, but all his friends were staring at me. "Ah . . . Listen, if you don't want to talk it's okay, but if you do, there's such a thing as pause."

"There's such a thing as friendship," Doug said. "You should have called when you got back."

"I know, I'm sorry. Let's just get wasted tonight and get over it." I looked at Hanagan's friends. "Anybody got a couple beers?" Again they just stared back at me. "Anyone want to go grab a couple beers?" I laughed. No one else did. "Hanagan, I apologize for whatever. I told Doug I was going to be super busy this—"

"You called my mom, Jay."

"What?"

"You called my mom. You sold her some shit."

"Dude, I asked her to listen to me. She didn't have to buy anything."

"You told her you were trying to win a scholarship." The fucking asshole was still playing his video game. "I know you're not trying to win a scholarship. And even if you were, you don't need it."

"So what?"

"You called my mom!"

"Hanagan, calm down. You're being a baby."

"You sold knives to my mom!" Hanagan really belted it out this time.

Doug nodded toward the door. He said, "Let's go, Jay."

"Fuck off. Hanagan, I can't believe you called me down here in front of all these douche bags who don't even know—"

This tiny fucker stood up out of his seat, "No, *you* don't know—"

Without thinking I shoved the kid back into his seat, except I pushed him more back than down, and he flipped over the couch behind him. "Sit the fuck down!" Hanagan's lips started puckering. I couldn't take it anymore. "Oh, FUCKIN' A! Stop crying, for god's sake!" I noticed that a crowd of people I knew from the party had come into the theater to see about the yelling. Hanagan stopped playing his video game but didn't pause it.

"J-j-j-jayyyy." He was slobbering all over himself just like the night outside of the jail cell.

I started feeling bad for him and embarrassed. "I'm sorry. I'll buy the knives back. I have a check right here. I'll make it payable to you. It's for a thousand bucks. Cash it, give it to your mom. Just stop crying."

Hanagan looked at me, blinking. His hazel eyes were clogged with tears and turning bloodshot. He sniffed and wrung the sockets out with his knuckles. "That's not the point, Jay. My mom is dying of cancer, and you sold her knives." There was a gasp in the room.

"I had no idea . . ."

"I know. You never asked."

"I'm so sorry. Please accept my apology."

Hanagan restarted his game. "Get away from me." I did.

* * *

When I wasn't working, or scheming, I would hole up with Brooke. I was sad, and sometimes I'd tell Brooke about it. She loved listening to me and trying to make me feel better. She never thought I did wrong and believed that I deserved to be happy more than anyone else in my life. Hearing these reassurances from her when I was beginning to slowly question the things I was doing was a wonderful relief. She became an expert at picking me up when I took myself low enough to tell her about it.

Most of the time, though, I wouldn't say anything—just that I was tired, and I would sit, sullen and waiting for something—what, I didn't know. Often I'd go to a lake near my mother's house late at night when the water would be black and steaming to smoke a few cigarettes and think about Isabelle and how she was not only not hot enough for me, but also maybe she wasn't good enough or a nice enough person either. She had yet to thank me for the stuff I'd sent her, but I wasn't too worried about it because I figured it must have taken a few days to get to her and she'd probably wait a week or so before sending a response. It'd been a few weeks since I'd mailed her the stuff—no big deal. I'm the worst person at sending thank-you notes, but Isabelle was usually pretty good at it. When I really thought about it I was confused and I'd get myself so worked up that the only thing that could take my mind away from the pain and irritation I felt toward Isabelle and toward myself was to sell, sell, sell, and let Brooke coddle me.

When I drove down to Cincinnati for the retreat, I was fairly irritated by an unpleasant phone conversation I'd had with Mrs. Murray, an old family friend. I'd called her to see if she'd help me out with my scholarship, and she told me to stop bothering her and hung up on me. I was astounded. I told Brooke about it. I also told Brooke's parents and several other people who knew Mrs. Murray, including my father. It was the first time in my selling career that anyone of that age and social status had been so rude to me, and what made it worse was that she and her husband were really good friends with my father and my grandfather. I didn't understand it and I let a lot of people know that I'd been treated unfairly.

I met Stuart at his office again, and we drove to his house. It wasn't as late at night as the last time we drove down, so we decided that we'd visit Keating at the club where he worked right over the bridge in Kentucky. The club was a series of bars and restaurants that had been built inside a derelict riverboat. Keating told us a hilarious story about a time when he took the trash out to the back of the restaurant and saw a rat that had an ass as big as a small dog's.

There were no more beers when we got back to Stuart's place, so he took his car and went to go buy some. He didn't come back for several hours. I fell asleep. Eventually Tammy woke me up and told me that Stuart had been arrested for drunk driving and that she had to go bail him out. The police confiscated Stuart's license, so I drove his car (after Tammy dropped us off where he got popped) to Chuck's office to meet up with his caravan. We left Stuart's car in the parking lot and climbed aboard Chuck's RV—his personal RV. The entire way down, a guy from Chuck's office, Judd, kept bragging about how much he was selling and bitching about how cheap some people could be. He had lots of theories on selling, and I more or less dozed off as he rambled on. The hot girl, who I remember looking so sexy drinking her soda pop my first trip down, came over and sat next to me. She fell asleep on my shoulder.

Chuck repeatedly got lost when we arrived at the state park. It was about to rain and he'd pull down a road and we'd see a silver strip of one of the lakes, we'd be dying to stop and swim, and then without saying anything, he'd pull over and begin the long process of turning his damn RV around while all the other cars behind us did the same. He did this about ten times, and each time a new cloud added itself to the thickening sky. Eventually he wheeled into an extremely nasty trailer park and proudly found his spot. The instant he opened the door of the RV the sky broke open and turned the world around us into a stinking bog.

The lakes were all gray with a rainy gray ceiling overhead. The water was warm, sickly warm like a mud bath. I swam anyway with the soda-pop girl, whose name, I found out, was Julie. We swam out to a raft and just laid on it in the rain and then spent the rest of the day hanging out in Chuck's camper, warming up and bullshitting with good old Skeeter and the gang. Judd began to get on my nerves.

Around six o'clock Chuck had everybody gather under a large tent built off the side of his trailer. He provided me with a dry erase board and battery-powered microphone. I laid out my Seven Steps to Selling.

1. The sale is made from the door to the kitchen. Six degrees of separation. Establish connection. Do your homework. Cross-reference names.
2. The pennies. Have them fall out of your pocket. Relax the customer. Make them feel as if they are in charge.
3. Stand and deliver. Standing on your feet helps to make a quick and dynamic pitch. Do not sit.
4. Name your knives. Associate with use. The funnier the better. Don't worry about being corny.
5. Build up the price comparison to Henckels knifes. Convince the customer that there's *no way* she's going to be able to afford Bladeworks knives. Then explain that because of you, a college-age salesperson, they are easily affordable.
6. In the close, direct and personalize the sale. Bladeworks wants you to buy this set, but it's not right. This set is better for you—the Jay Special.

7. Never barter. Only offer to give something to the
   client when you fill out the form as an act of kindness
   so that they feel gratitude and they don't change their
   minds before you walk out the door.

The rain seeped off the edges of the blue tarp hanging over our campfire. The light was blue, orange, and sad. I played to the faces watching me. They smiled and laughed and I began to get bored and depressed and wanted to leave desperately.

When I finished the demonstration we ate hot dogs that were burnt and charred on the outside and cold and mushy on the inside and hamburgers that were like solid pellets forged in hell. A lot of people came over to me to ask questions. I tried to listen to what people were saying, but I couldn't concentrate. I couldn't think about anything but Isabelle, and the fact that I'd never been to a trailer park before.

Fortunately, Skeeter and some of the other salespeople had beer in their luggage. Chuck also brought beer, but since most of us were underage, he couldn't actually give it to us. He just said, "I have a couple cases in the back of the RV. They are on ice." And he left.

Getting drunk made me feel a little better, but not good enough. It had stopped raining. Julie and I found a relatively dry patch of ground and lay down. She had pale white skin, large blue eyes, and big red lips. I thought about kissing her and I wanted to kiss her, but I didn't. I had never cheated on Brooke. For a long time I'd been waiting for an opportunity to cheat, but for some reason that night I couldn't. I watched Julie's eyes flutter shut, and I lay awake for several more hours, feeling miserable.

Everyone was hung over and soaked the next day. We could not have gotten the hell out of that trailer park soon enough. Of course, it took Chuck ages to get his shit together and figure out how not to get lost on the way out. We finally left, but it was raining like hell, and it took us twice as long to get back. I stared at the clock, waiting, waiting, waiting, and wanting that fucker behind the wheel to just please speed the fuck up.

The sun broke through when we arrived at Chuck's office. I asked him for the cookware kit, which consisted of a pan and a videotape. He gave it to me and then, like a sword slamming into my spine, he said, "Hey, you mind if I ask you one more tiny favor?"

"What?"

"One of the guys from my office, Tim, he's a big fan of yours, and he really wanted to come down to the lakes to hear your presentation but he couldn't make it because his wife was in the hospital."

"Okay."

"Well, he has an appointment tonight and he thought that you could just take that appointment and he'll come along to watch you sell."

"Chuck, I'm really tired and am looking forward to getting back to Detroit."

"Okay . . . but . . ."

"What?"

"Some of the guys in the office think that the only reason you've sold so much is because of the area you're selling in. A lot of them think you're selling just to your parents' friends. I think this would be a good way to dismiss those rumors."

Tim was enormously fat and had a gruff voice, but was nice enough. He drove me out to a middle-class house in a rural area. It was not a promising lead, but things like that didn't bother me anymore. I was kind of mad at Chuck for putting me on the spot like he had, because as soon as I got in Tim's car I could tell that he didn't doubt me. I guess Chuck did. Anyway, it was sort of funny when we arrived and Tim said he was my "colleague and just there to observe." I unloaded a Jay Special on the couple plus a set of steak knives. Tim bought me dinner—a Cincinnati specialty, spaghetti served with fast-food chili. Tim talked about Apex and wanting children.

I sat there the entire time, condescendingly watching him move his beans around in the plastic bowl, thinking about how unattractive his zits were and basking in his admiration for my knife-selling skill. He was a nice guy. I was just an asshole. He thanked me for taking the time to show him my technique and drove me back to get my car at Stuart's office.

I didn't stop in to see Stuart before I left. I just got on the expressway and smoked my way back to my mother's house. I started thinking about how I could sell knives in Hanover remotely and I came up with the idea of a personalized catalog. A lot of Bladeworks representatives will send out a Bladeworks catalog around Christmas with a note attached. I felt that the personal connection the salesperson makes with the customer is a large part of why the customer buys or not. When they buy knives, they are not only buying a product that they want, but they also believe they are helping out a college student they like. I think most people are happy to do this. In my case the customers didn't see the complete con job I laid on them. The attached note was supposed to remind the customer of the personal connection, but I believed the fact that the catalog was manufactured by a large corporation diminished the note's effectiveness. I thought an excellent way around this would be to create a catalog that would appear as if it were created by the salesperson. I figured that it would be easy enough to whip together a decent-looking stock catalog (a template), with a written statement that would basically remind the customer of who the salesperson was, thank them for helping with the salesperson's scholarship, and finally say that in addition to going to school over the winter, that the salesperson has put together a catalog of Bladeworks products. Perhaps Mrs. Whomever might like to take a look at some gift ideas . . .

Once the template was created, if the catalog producer was so inclined, he could swap in the name of other salespeople and their customers in the blank spots and also insert a photo of the salesperson on the cover of the catalog. I figured that if I could get enough people at the next sales conference to let me take their pictures and to give me their customer lists, I could produce the catalog, swap in the names and photos, and mail them out for a small portion of the salesperson's commission. The salespeople wouldn't have to do any work but they would still make money. In fact, I was betting they would make more money because, even less my commission, their customers would be more likely to buy from this type of catalog than from the standard Bladeworks catalog. Anyway, that was my idea. All I had to do was figure out how to make it a reality.

Back in D-town a number of curious things happened.

One: I got a call from Lilly Abbot. Lilly's father, Trip Abbot, was my father's best friend, a hilarious guy and a former Indy race car driver. For a while, he drove for a team my grandfather owned a part of. I grew up going to these races. So did Lilly. We both found them incredibly boring and we'd sit around in the boxes and talk most of the time. We became very close and when her dad retired as a driver, I retired as a race fan. Lilly's family lived in a small town in East Texas, on this huge ranch that her dad bought because it was as close as he could be to New Orleans without leaving Texas. Since Trip stopped racing cars his main goal in life had been insinuating himself into New Orleans society so that when Lilly turned nineteen, she could have her debut there. Lilly was calling to ask me to be her escort to the first round of balls, during the summer season. It would require me to be in New Orleans and East Texas for ten days. I said I would do it but only if her father could arrange for me to meet with potential customers during the down time. The next push began toward the end of the period when I would have to be in New Orleans and on the ranch. He said he would.

Two: through a friend of my aunt's, I was referred to the wife of a former CEO of Kmart who then referred me to one of her husband's friends and business partners, a gentleman by the name of Ty Nakamori, a reported billionaire. His children went to my high school and during my senior year he visited and lectured us on how technology would affect our future. He said that we were living in dog years. Seven years in the days before computers now equals one year. He also said that he liked to sleep in and that his company started at eleven in the morning. It was a strange speech.

I popped a flat on the way to Ty's house and didn't have time to change the tire, so I drove on the deflated rubber. The tire ripped off a block away from the Nakamori home and I pulled up his driveway with a smoking hubcap. Ty answered the door wearing a karate outfit. It was kind of funny that he came to the door like that. He looked over my shoulder at the Escort.

"You don't know how to change a flat?"

"I do. I didn't want to be late, so I thought I'd brazen it out."

"I like that kind of spirit. Come in."

Mrs. Nakamori and their children were waiting in the kitchen. They all wore karate outfits.

"Am I interrupting something?"

"I was giving Candi and the kids tai chi lessons. It's okay."

It was rumored that Candi, Ty's wife, had been a Vegas show-girl. She was big and blond and looked a little banged up. Their daughter recognized me from high school and blushed when I walked in.

"Do you mind if the kids and I watch? Candi told me you were going to give some sort of demonstration."

"I am."

When I finished my routine, Ty said he was impressed by what he saw and how I acted. He bought a set. Ty asked what I planned on doing after the summer. I felt a little embarrassed about my cat-alog idea, because I found it totally deceptive, but I explained it to Ty and he loved it. And, as luck would have it, he told me that he owned a printing company and that his son, a little shit named Toby, was some sort of computer genius. He proposed on the spot to give me the best possible deal printing the catalogs if I would employ his son to help produce them.

"Do you think Toby would want to do it?"

"Toby doesn't have any choice in the matter. He's unmotivated. I think someone like you would be a good influence."

I laughed. "Okay. Yeah. That'd be great. The first thing that we'd need to do is come up with the template and create a few cat-alogs so I could show them to Apex and see if they'll let me do it."

"Sounds good. Let me know when you want Toby to start work-ing on it."

Ty walked me to the door. He went back inside and I suspect that he watched me change my tire through the drapes.

Three: Thanks to Brooke's mother, it'd gotten around the Bloomfield Hills Country Club that Mrs. Murray was rude to me on the phone and the rumor found its way back to Mrs. Murray. One night as I was poring through the BHCC phone book looking for new leads Mrs. Murray called, apologized, and asked if she could set up an appointment with me.

Vengeance was mine! Mrs. Murray bought two Deluxe Kitchen Sets, and a full set of cookware. It was one of my easiest and best sales the entire summer—almost. I had forgotten it, but Mrs. Murray was slightly cross-eyed. I didn't make this discovery until midway through the presentation, when it caught me off guard. Fortunately, I was able to fight through the distraction and focus. I made around $1,500 in commission.

Four: Brooke tried to break up with me (sort of). She laid it down for me as calm and cool as she'd never been before. "I've kept track over the past week and every time you've told me that you're going to meet me you've been three hours late on average. Don't try to deny it. You can ask my mom."

"You told your mother?"

"Yes."

"Why in god's name did you do that?"

"You've got to respect me. You can't tell me you're going to show up and then come three hours late and expect me to wait."

"It just slips my mind."

"I know. And that makes me think that you're not thinking about me and that's okay, if that's what you want. But I can't be with someone who's not thinking about me. I'm just . . ." She took a deep breath and looked really scared for a second, which made me think she was serious. I stared at her and really tried to think about what breaking up with her would mean. I was attracted to her and I would miss that. She was a good person who was loyal to me and loved me and I didn't know if I could find someone who would love me as much as she did. Certainly not Isabelle . . . Most important, though, she was one of my closest friends. I didn't want to lose that. Maybe things would get better. "Brooke, I don't want to break up. I've just been working."

"But you have got to make it up to me sometimes."

She was so direct about this I almost found it sexy. "I know what you're thinking."

"What?"

"Mackinac."

She got so excited she started shaking in her seat. It was pretty cute.

"I promise that as soon as I get back from the next push week, we'll go."

"What about right before the push week? Can we?"

"We could, of course, but I have to go to New Orleans and be Lilly Abbot's escort at her debutante party thing . . ."

"Lilly who?"

"Lilly Abbot. I'm sure I told you about this. She's a very old friend." Brooke's face began to shrink up into a wrinkly dot. I touched Brooke's hand. "Don't worry, baby, I'll only be gone ten days and I'll be selling down there too."

I watched as tears popped out of her eyes in rapid succession. Huge drops arched off her eyelashes. I could hear them gently thudding on the dashboard of the Escort.

Five: My father came to my mother's house for dinner.

This was the first time my father, mother, and I had had dinner in years. Coulter was somewhere else. I was late and my father was well on his way to being drunk when I stepped out onto the porch where they were having cocktails and hors d'oeuvres.

My dad said, "Nice of you to join us. Working late? When do I get my cut for all the names I gave you?" My mother was swooning all around him like he was the king of the world. We sat there for about twenty minutes before I told my dad that I felt bad about selling to my grandparents.

He exploded. "Then why did you goddamn do it?!"

"I didn't think they would buy them."

"Of course they were going to buy them, for Christ's sake! And if you feel bad about it, you can go buy them back. You've got plenty of goddamn money now. You need to have guts if you want to sell! Guts! Goddamnit! If you don't have the guts, then you shouldn't do it. You can't keep whining about selling to your god-damn . . ."

He was shouting and he kept shouting and I don't really know why or what exactly he was trying to say. My mother didn't stop him, but I could tell she was scared and embarrassed so I said, "Dad. Never mind what I said. Don't worry about it."

"You don't get it! You don't get anything!"

"Dad. Please stop yelling."

"No. You don't goddamn understand anything about guts!"

I shot up out of my seat. I tore off the bird feeder hanging from the tree near me, hoisted it over my head, and smashed it on the bricks at my feet. "This is not your house! You have no right to come here and start yelling! You have no goddamn right! Keep your voice down or get the hell out of here." My father's eyes were like drunken dead fish eyes. I was crying. The skin on my face felt like it was dancing. My dad started to say something but I cut him off. "I want you to apologize to her right now."

"To—"

"Right now!"

"I'm sorry for raising my voice."

"Say it to Mom."

"Caroline, I'm sorry. But, Jay, you've got . . ."

I didn't listen to the rest of what he was saying. I left.

I went to see Brooke. I tried to explain to her what had hap-pened but she didn't understand anything about it. When I got home my mother was waiting for me and started lecturing me on the subject of my father's alcoholism and womanizing. I broke something else, screamed at her, and went to sleep.

The voice of a stewardess woke me up. "For those of you seated in rows A and B, if you look out the window to your left you can see the French Quarter . . ." This was almost ten years before Katrina, but from high above New Orleans it still looked like it was constructed of rotted brown and grey boards. Everything looked wet and grimy. Then oily gray clouds blotted out my view and the plane descended.

I took a cab to my hotel, which was on the financial district side of the Canal. I dropped my stuff in my room and called Trip, whose voice was nasally southern and affected. "Mister Hauser! How's your hotel? I hope it's to your satisfaction."

"It's great. Thank you so much. By the way, I can pay for it. It's really no problem."

"Now, stop right there. If Lilly were feeling better you'd be staying with us in the Garden District, so consider the hotel my treat. And listen"—Trip muffled the phone—"you might have some fun down there on your own that you might not have with myself and Mrs. Abbot, so why don't you just take it easy, maybe find your way to Bourbon Street and we'll pick you up at four-thirty on the dot tomorrow afternoon. Now, don't be too hung over," he kidded. "And make sure you're wearing a sharp light-colored suit. You might end up in the papers." And he hung up.

Lilly had some sort of colon disease. I didn't know much about it, but that it occasionally flared up and she'd been taking steroids to keep it down. All her life, Lilly had studied to be a ballerina and was extremely proud of her slender and taut physique. The steroids she'd been taking made her gain a little weight, which I'm sure frustrated the hell out of her. Poor Lilly, she was a beautiful girl. I didn't reflect on this for too long (maybe thirty-five seconds) and set off for the Quarter.

There was a slight Disneyland feel to the French Quarter, but also the feeling that I could get mugged at any moment, which I liked. I found a dumpy bar that smelled like a Dartmouth frat basement, bought a drink, and sat enjoying watching the drunken crowds stagger by.

When I got tired of this I walked around until I got tired of that and finally found my way back to the hotel, where I tried to write a letter to Isabelle. I wanted to tell her that I was mad she hadn't thanked me and for about one hundred other things, but it seemed so uncool, so I tried to think of something cooler to write, but got tired of that so I fell asleep. In the morning it wasn't a matter of cool or uncool it was just the realization that she had obviously chosen not to write me. It wasn't that she was being rude, because I can understand that and could have gotten mad at her for that. It is fucking rude not to write your friend back if he sends you a gift. It was now becoming clearer that Isabelle just didn't want to write to me. Or maybe there was an issue with the mail? I mulled this over for a while, feeling like it was totally possible and highly probable, and this depressed feeling settled down on me like a cold giant fist around my head crushing my brains out my ears.

I tried to go back to sleep but couldn't. I decided the only way I'd feel better was if I put my mind to something else, so I started thinking of knife selling and my catalog and I snapped that chilly fist off my head like a tennis sweatband. My brain clicked into gear. I called Toby, who had just woken up and was as retarded and rude as ever. I tried to describe to him how I wanted the layout until I discovered it was useless. I'd have to show him in person when I got back.

At four-thirty Trip's car pulled up to the curb. "Hi, Jay." Lilly smiled through the open window. Her dimples were deep. She looked better than I thought she would. She didn't look fat, just a little swollen. "Sorry, I'd get out of the car and hug you, but I'm a little tired."

"That's okay. How are you?"

"I'm fine. You?"

"I'm very happy to be here."

Trip had a folder full of information (including the itinerary and dress requirements that he'd already sent me) on the various "clubs" that sponsored the debutantes and the floats for Mardi Gras. There were articles—clippings on a wide variety of topics, and a brief history of Lilly's life, which Trip'd written. I laughed at all the stuff while Trip lectured me on how important and serious it was while Lilly looked sick and green as the car plodded along some route I didn't pay attention to until we arrived at a country club.

Trip said, "As a debutante, Lilly is required to throw several parties for her fellow debutantes, and this is one of them. Of course, I'm the one planning and paying for this whole operation, but Lilly selected the band, so don't blame me if it's not to your liking."

His wife, Channing, chimed in, "I'm sure you'll love it. It's a young person's band."

Trip continued, "Nevertheless, I just want to point out that there is an unwritten code that one girl, or one girl's father, should not outdo the rest of the fathers too much, as far as these parties are concerned, so even though I'm sure you will find this a fine party, please understand that if I'd had it my way, there would be a goddamn troupe of circus elephants inside this country club, serving mint juleps."

As we stepped out, Lilly took my arm. "Don't worry, Jay, I'll feel better as soon as I have a drink." She smiled, painfully.

The party was not particularly impressive, nor were the other debutantes. There were some people from the newspapers taking pictures. When we'd finished our round of hellos and had our pictures taken, Lilly asked me to bring her a gin and tonic. It took a while and when I came back she was talking to some other guy. I held up her drink.

"Thanks. Spencer brought me one."

"Hey. I'm Spencer. I went to Deerfield with Lilly. I had no idea this was her party." Spencer then stepped between Lilly and me and continued with what appeared to be a private conversation.

I held up Lilly's drink again. "Excuse me. I'm going to put this down." I went outside to see if anyone was smoking. No one was, so I went back inside and thought about asking people who looked like smokers if they wanted to smoke, but I couldn't work up the courage to do this so I got a drink and went to the back of the room and watched people.

Spencer looked kind of familiar. He had one of those roundish faces with a thin nose and long eyelashes that he batted around like a girl. He hung his head back and smiled when he listened and sort of sashayed as he walked, but he wasn't a fruit. I fucking placed it. Isabelle had pointed out a photo of that douche in one of her photo albums. I wondered if he'd fucked Isabelle. She told some story about him that I couldn't quite remember, except how funny and crazy the kid was. A total loon. He didn't look too crazy now, bobbing his head as he listened to Lilly's mother talking about who knows what—her hand cream?

Damn Spencer and his fucking sockless loafers. He took off his coat and slung it over his shoulder. Whew! A menace. This guy was a real party animal. Then he said something and Lilly and her mother started laughing. Laughing hysterically with genuine mirth. Lilly put her arm around Spencer and gave him a little one-armed hug. Then the little fucker whistled at a waiter. Literally whistled. The waiter came over. Spencer practically flung his glass at the guy, snatched another one off the tray, and said something funny to the waiter, who walked away laughing! I started staring at Lilly, imagining Isabelle's head on her shoulders, giggling and squeezing that bastard when she glanced over at me. The joy disappeared from her face like it'd been blown off with a shotgun.

I turned awkwardly to my left, bumped into a banana plant, got embarrassed, quickly hailed a drink, downed it, got another, went to one of the service bathrooms, locked the door, lit a cigarette, and looked in the mirror.

My face was pale and greasy with stale sweat. My lank hair clung to my forehead, absurdly parted to one side. I had dark rings under my eyes, which might have made me look older, but I had a young face so it just looked odd. My face was puffy too—still fat from football. My suit didn't fit right. It was beige and I wore a pink shirt and a white tie.

Why in God's name had Brooke been telling me how goddamn handsome I was? Why had I believed her?

I didn't like the way I felt. I finished my drink and thought about smashing the glass in the sink, but didn't. What if Isabelle was here? What if she was watching me? I probably would have bummed her out too, especially since seeing me would make her feel guilty for not calling to thank me for the gifts. I hate making people feel guilty. The thought of Isabelle nearly made me cry. I was hiding in a bathroom at a debutante party.

I set my smoke on the edge of the sink and rinsed my face off with water. I slicked my hair back. My face was still dripping. I felt water rolling down the back of my neck like marbles. I stuck my smoke back in my mouth and stared into the mirror. No one can sell knives like you can.

Spencer was gone when I got back. The party was really lame. If it were my party, it'd be a fucking riot. I'd have Isabelle whipping waiters with banana plant leaves as she rode around on their backs in a golden saddle. I guzzled a few more drinks and suddenly became obsessed with the idea that it was my job to show all of the geezers mingling with the young people what a prince I was. Bring'm to my party. I strolled around, schmoozing away, cracking jokes and laying the good old Bladeworks charm on the fifty-and-over crowd.

Then, feeling quite incorrectly that I'd gotten my mojo back, I decided that as much as I was annoyed at Lilly's bitch act, which in retrospect makes perfect sense, since I hadn't seen her in years and her father probably forced her to invite me and she was constantly on the verge of shitting her pants, it was my job to show Lilly a good time—particularly since the legendarily wild and wacky Spence had hit the road.

I jerked Lilly away from a girl teetering on a pair of crutches. "Let's dance."

"Jay. I'm not feeling well."

As if on cue, the band switched songs and I boogied out onto the dance floor, lugging Lilly behind me. It was a country song and most people (not that there were many) were doing the typical college swing dance, of which I considered myself the master. Lilly was laughing and politely trying to pull away from me. She made a very poor effort at dancing. I started slapping my hands together and lurching around to get her moving. When that didn't work I snatched her by the wrist and slipped my hand behind her waist, and that's when I felt it. She was wearing a diaper.

She looked at me, horrified. I didn't stop. "C'mon. Move." Fuck the diaper. Who cares, right? I tried to slip my hand behind her again, to show her how little it bothered me, but she deflected my arm. She executed a few steps. I tried to follow her and then backed away to do a spin and by the time I came back around she was gone.

I stood there, shifting my weight from side to side for a few seconds. I didn't see any other girls without partners. I looked out at the party to see if anyone noticed me get dissed and I saw Lilly's mother watching me. Maybe she was embarrassed at Lilly's behavior. Maybe she was embarrassed at mine. I stopped swaying—my eyes still on Lilly's mother's. She began bobbing up and down, like she was imitating a baboon. I shook my head at her, as if to say, I don't understand you. But she didn't stop those grotesque motions. Was she making fun of me? I was confused and upset. And then I got it. *Keep dancing.*

After the party, there were more parties we were invited to, but Lilly, of course, wanted to go home, so I escorted her. The house Trip rented was beautiful and large and on a quiet street. "You can come in if you want."

"That's all right. I'm pretty tired."

"It's all that dancing." Lilly smiled. I was forgiven.

I started walking down the steps and then stopped. "Lilly, did you want any of this? The debutante stuff."

"No."

"Sleep well. I'll see you tomorrow."

I walked a couple blocks down the street, breathing in the strong smell of roses growing in the gardens along the sidewalk. I took my coat off and hung it over my shoulder. My body felt cool and slender in the night air.

I thought about Lilly. The last time I'd seen her was at a farmhouse near the Michigan International Speedway. She and her family were staying there for the race weekend. Lilly and I had a little fling. I was a real shithead back then—a freshman in high school—and I convinced her to skip the race and stay with me at the farmhouse. We made out a lot and I fingered her in a barn toward the back of the property. We fell asleep and didn't even know when the race had ended, until we heard the helicopter bringing her father back. We looked out the window to see all of the cars and the people waiting and when the helicopter landed, Lilly's father stepped off carrying a wreath. That's how we knew he'd won.

Over the next two days in New Orleans, Lilly and I finally got along. It was a tenuous sort of friendship, though. One based on absolutely zero assumptions. I made zero assumptions that she would understand my jokes or my behavior. She seemed stronger. On the last night, she even came with me into the Quarter, which she considered unsafe and had never been to without her parents or a large group of friends. We had a nervous drink at a jazz club.

The following morning we flew on the Abbots' plane to Orange, Texas, where Trip's mother and brother lived. Orange was very close to the Abbots' ranch, which was much more like a plantation than what you'd think of as a "ranch." I'm pretty sure it was, in fact, an old plantation house. It sure as hell looked that way. As soon as we got there we had an enormous lunch and I updated Trip on everything I could. How I'd almost gotten my older sister, Molly, enlisted in the marines when I sent away for the free socks. Lilly laughed and seemed charmed and happy, and for the first time I felt as if she was genuinely glad I'd come.

19

I couldn't get my mind off the white dress on Mae's black skin. It looked so perfectly ironed. Starched stiff. Her skin was surprisingly smooth for her age, but dry. Her wig was blacker than her skin. Her skin was dark brown, like her eyes, which stared at me completely uncomprehending why I should be in Trip's mother's kitchen talking to her about knives and why she, Mrs.

Abbot's cook, should have to listen. But she was instructed by Trip to be there and so she listened.

Trip's brother watched over her shoulder, leaning against the hospital-green counter next to the glowing metal sink. It was filled with the sunlight slanting through the windows. Monroe was almost completely deaf and mildly retarded. He grinned at me continually, like a doll painted with an expression of curiosity on its face. He wore loafers, pink socks, khakis, a leather belt with whales on it, a blue shirt, an ascot, and two giant hearing aids. The outfit had been chosen for him. His hair had been brushed for him. A perfect red coiffure. He also was there on instructions.

Mae's swollen arthritic hand held a Petite Carver. Her arm rested on the kitchen table, bent at the elbow, and the hand holding the knife lay curled—palm up. I swear I could hear the vein in her wrist pulsing when I finished my pitch. It was the only sound in the room other than bewildered silence. Slowly, Mae turned to Monroe, still grinning in my direction. "Mr. Monroe, wha'my supposed to do?"

"Say again?"

"Wha'my supposed to do?"

"Oh." Monroe blinked for thirty seconds—trying to remember what he had been told. "We'll take two."

I stopped in one of the rooms on the way out of the giant house to say good-bye to Trip's mother. She sat in a soft leather chair, a blanket around her legs, staring at nothing and thinking about the same. "Thank you very much, Mrs. Abbot. I'm sure you will enjoy the knives. They are very special knives." She was incapable of responding. Per my request and Trip's instructions, I'd just sold knives to a near vegetable. "And thank you, Mae. I hope it was fun for you."

"Oh . . . Yes. It was fun all right."

Monroe walked me to the door. "You come back and we'll have a nice cocktail with Mother." He put his hand on my shoulder. "I want you to meet my daughter. She's coming home for Lilly's party."

I was surprised to hear that Monroe had a daughter and wondered who the hell would have a child with him, but didn't ask. I just said, "I can't wait to meet her."

"You'll like her very much. She's soooo pretty and sooo nice."

Trip sat at his kitchen counter, writing in a thin paper notebook he always kept in his front pocket along with a finely sharpened pencil and his reading glasses. "So, how was Mother's?"

"It was nice."

"Mae's something else, isn't she?"

"Yes, she reminded me of Weesy." Weesy was my grandparents' maid.

"I remember Weesy. An amazing woman . . ." Trip shook his head and scribbled.

"I didn't know that Lilly had a cousin."

Trip paused and took off his glasses. "Beth. Of course. She's Monroe's daughter." Trip looked at me. I could tell this was a painful topic and I suddenly wished I hadn't brought it up. "I've arranged it so that all of Lilly's family will be in town for her debutante ball. You'll meet her on Thursday here in Orange before we drive down to New Orleans."

"Yeah, Monroe mentioned it—"

"She's ummm, not like Monroe, who you may have noticed, is not altogether there . . ." Trip put his glasses on the table and shifted them around like my grandfather. "Monroe is really a sweet person, but he's never been completely—I don't know. He never completely formed. I think you'll find that in life there are some people who will take advantage of people like Monroe. Beth's mother was one of those people. Now, don't get me wrong. Monroe loves Beth, but the fact is Beth's mother is not a good person."

"Were they married?"

"Yes. For about five minutes. She had Beth and left them."

"Does Beth talk to her?"

"Not to my knowledge. They don't know where she is. She got her settlement and left."

"That's awful."

"Her mother calls me, every now and then, asking for money."

"And you give it to her?"

"Yes. So she doesn't call Monroe." Trip smiled.

"What's Beth like?"

"You'll see."

Lilly and I met Beth, Monroe's daughter, for a glass of wine at Beth's house on our last night in Orange. Although Beth clearly considered herself to be quite a vixen, she was not attractive at all. She was overweight, wore too much makeup and too much perfume, and she talked too loudly. Her thin lips were dry, and the lipstick that she caked on them flaked outward and waved at you like okonomiyaki, the Japanese fish pancake. And her physical qualities were her best qualities. Beth was also bitter, argumentative, smart enough to irritate you but no more, chaffing, pompous, insecure, vulgar, and worst of all, mean.

Beth did have amazingly beautiful hair. It was nearly silver in color and apparently had been that way since she was very young. Lilly told me it was a familial trait and that her mother had the same color hair. Both women were sort of legendary for it. I hate to admit it, but I could see why. If I let my eyes lose focus and I muted the words coming out of Beth's mouth, she could, solely because of her hair, and very briefly, transform into some kind of striking creature. What kind, I wasn't sure, but through a blurry haze, the talking hairdo could capture your attention.

The three of us were sitting on her porch. "I don't know what Lilly's doing here this summer. Well—she's got that problem." She smiled at Lilly. "And her debut. My daddy wanted me to have a debut, but they're so stupid and such a waste of money. I'd rather have him save it so I can inherit it, frankly. God. I say, 'Don't even think of burying me here.' I'd rather be tossed on the side of the highway. This place is so full of idiots. What do you think, Lilly?"

"About Orange?" Lilly thought. "It's okay. It's peaceful. I like being with my parents."

"Well, at least you have cool parents. My daddy . . ." She rolled her eyes. "Is the biggest fool of them all."

I said, "I like your father. I like Orange. I may move here."

"So you can sell my grandmother more knives?" We stared at each other. I seriously considered slapping her. "Just kidding. I'm sure you'd love it here. Lilly, do you remember the time I brought my boyfriend, Alex, home?"

"I guess."

"He hated it here, but he said the funniest thing. He said, 'If there's one good thing about this town, it's that it's so boring and slow that all you want to do all day is fuck.'" Her laugh sounded like a pig being electrocuted. Lilly reeled back in her seat. "This wine is shit. I keep telling my daddy that if he's got all this money, he should at least spend it on something decent." She grabbed her glass with her meaty hand and shot its remnants over the rail of the porch. "Lilly, what do you have at your house?"

I sold about $4,500 worth of knives in Orange, Texas, in five days. The Abbot family bought $1,500 of them. Most of the other sales were fairly standard. They weren't all setups. Some of them were young couples—not necessarily looking for cutlery, but happy to have a high-quality product and entertainment. Orange is a long way from anything and a new anything rolling through is generally appreciated—including me. I was aware that my routine was talked about by my customers like summer theater in a small town.

Lilly and I got back to New Orleans around two and Lilly's phone started ringing at four. Her friends from UT and Deerfield were arriving. I had never seen Lilly so happy. She began describing to me who was coming, how she knew them, how great they were, and how much I was going to like them. A caravan of four cars was making its way across Texas from UT. My excitement grew with Lilly's. At around five she ran over to me and hugged me. "Jay. I haven't told you yet and I feel badly for not saying it, but I'm so glad you made it down. I promise. I won't be in a bad mood anymore and I won't be tired. I swear. I'm going to make you so happy you came." She didn't need to. I already was.

This would change, quickly. Lilly's friends were there for Lilly, and although I didn't necessarily care about their attention, I had recently grown accustomed to enjoying Lilly's and I started to lose that as soon as the first friend rang the doorbell. It would only get worse over the course of the night.

We occupied the top floor of a fancy restaurant. I sat across from Lilly. The anecdotes she and her friends were swapping melted together with the music that was playing. I don't remember what it was. I wasn't listening. My mind was somewhere else; with Isabelle and the U.S. postal service and thinking about how Isabelle'd probably get along well with Lilly's friends. Isabelle was so good at making friends. She'd blend right into the music and the chitchat and I'd feel even more like a black hole of charm.

"Jay . . . Jay! Why are you staring at me like that? You did it at the last party."

"What? Oh. I was spaced out. I wasn't looking . . ."

"Dude," the guy to Lilly's right said, "you look weird. That was creepy."

"I was just . . . Never mind. One of you was telling a story or something." I motioned with my hand. "I'm sorry I interrupted." I looked around at Lilly's friends. They were all staring at me. I lowered my eyes and fiddled with my glass of wine.

I heard a girl a few people away from me say, "Is he freaking out?"

Someone else said, "Yeah. I think he's stoned or something."

After dinner we went to a bar near Tulane. Trip paid for several rounds of drinks and left. I immediately went upstairs to the second floor balcony, sat down in a white wicker chair, smoked a cigarette, and decided I would leave. I went to find Lilly to say good-bye. She was halfway down the stairs and surrounded by her friends, laughing. I was standing there, waiting for an opportunity to interrupt, when one of Lilly's friends whispered something into her ear. Lilly stopped laughing and looked up at me. This time I was staring right at her. I just wanted to say good-bye, but it didn't matter. Three strikes and you're out. She made a disgusted face and shouted at her friends, "I don't know why he keeps staring at me! I fucking hate it!" Since the girls were blocking the stairs, I turned around, got a drink from the bar upstairs, and sat back down in my wicker chair.

Someone sat next to me. It was Beth. I didn't even notice that she was at the dinner.

"You have another cigarette?"

"Sure." I handed her one.

"Will you light it for me?"

She smoked her cigarette and said, "You want to get another one somewhere else?"

We took a cab to Charles Street. I paid the driver and got out. I had about five hundred dollars in cash on me. I guess I got confused when I paid the driver, because as I was walking down the street and went to put my money back in my clip, I noticed that I had a twenty-dollar bill in my hand. Shit. I'd kept the twenty I was going to pay the driver and given him four hundred and eighty dollars. The cab was gone. I saw a traffic jam a block down the street and started running.

As I came up behind the cab, the driver was counting the money I'd given him, firing the bills from his right to left hand. The window was open. I reached in and snatched the money out of his hands. "Sorry. I gave you the wrong amount." I tossed a twenty in the window. "Keep the change." I went running back.

"What happened? I thought you ditched me."

"I'll tell you inside. I need a drink."

She followed me into a restaurant with a huge courtyard. This was supposedly the place where the Hurricane was invented. I can't remember the name, it was something Irish. There were large groups of people around us who were all drinking out of one giant Hurricane. Their faces, the white bloated faces of drunken tourists, were lit by the flaming liquor, and their backs, hunched over the bowls, glowed red in the light coming from the many heat lamps set up around the patio. It all looked very pagan and midwestern, like a group of Satanists had just gotten off a bus from Minnesota. I'm sure Beth and I blended in nicely.

I sucked down three Hurricanes, split a hamburger with Beth (she hogged the fries), and then ordered a Jack Daniel's for a nightcap. Then I ordered another. Beth had stopped drinking after her first Hurricane. It sat on the table half empty. I drank it. It was warm and disgustingly sweet. I paid and we left.

In the cab I felt so relieved to be done with Lilly and her college cronies. They reminded me too much of Isabelle and how I felt around her and her friends. Somehow I was just happy to have Beth next to me talking about some shit that I really didn't have to pay attention to. I also didn't have to give a damn what Isabelle would think about me in a car with such a spiteful, boring slob like Beth. Fuck her. Fuck Isabelle. Fuck everyone. I wanted another drink.

When we arrived at Beth's hotel the bar was closed. Beth offered me some of the booze in her room. I accepted and told her I thought she had very pretty hair. She said she was planning on dyeing it brown, that she couldn't wait to get home to do it. That's when I knew she was a truly hateful person. Before I'd finished my second airplane bottle of whiskey, Beth grabbed my face and kissed me, hard.

It was revolting. I pushed her on the bed. She lay there for a moment, looking surprised. I stared down at her, wanting to walk out but was somehow immobile. She pulled off her dress and I saw that she was wearing some sort of an elastic diaper that held her gut in. When she pulled that off it made a loud snap, and her blubber went rushing away from her body in a wave. She pulled off her underwear, rolled onto her stomach, and slithered over to me.

I was still standing there, looking down at her, my hands in tight fists. I'm sure my eyes were bugging out of my head. My nostrils flared. I could smell her. I felt vomit inching its way up my throat. Then I noticed the arch of her back, and the slow, white round curve of her buttocks began. The vomit slid back into my stomach and I thought—very objectively—that there was something about the position of her body, the grimy paleness of her skin, that could be attractive. I remembered a glimpse of Isabelle's bare back when she pulled off a sweater and her T-shirt underneath stuck to the fabric. The memory flashed into my mind and I swatted it out. No. There was no comparison. And this was not something I wanted to drag Isabelle into.

Beth unzipped my fly and took my penis out. She sucked me until I got fully hard. She pulled me onto the bed and sat on me without taking off all of my clothes. Her vagina made its way down my penis. It was dry at first, like fucking a plastic bag, and then it was wet and hot. It occurred to me that this was the second girl I'd ever had sex with. Her weight was on my belt, which she was grinding into my pelvis. It hurt and it was distracting. This, along with my extreme drunken state, empowered me with the ability to not come quickly. Brooke had never gotten off from having sex with me, so it was sort of a shock to see Beth writhing around on my pants, pinching her nipples, biting her fingers, and making gurgling noises. She did this for some time, leaned back, let out a giant moan, and flopped forward onto my chest. She tried to kiss me, but I moved my face out of the way.

"How about I kiss you somewhere else? Come in my mouth." I did.

I lay there as depressed as I ever thought possible. I'd betrayed myself, Trip, his retarded brother, Monroe (whom I liked), and Brooke. All of the anger and rejection I'd felt because of Lilly and

Isabelle only intensified the depression. I hated myself passionately and not only for what I did, but also for who I was: the loser, the weirdo, the pathetic, cheating miserable drunk who could neither make new friends nor pleasant dinner conversation and wound up getting fucked by the girl who everybody, myself included, despised. Worst of all, I kind of liked it.

Beth clung to my waist. "Oh. You're good. I didn't think you'd be so good . . ." Normally I relish compliments, but this was completely preposterous. All I did was lay on my back, paralyzed and frightened. Beth started wriggling her way up my torso. I slipped away and put myself back inside my pants. I felt foam at the base of my penis and gagged. "I'm going to have a cigarette. Would you please brush your teeth?"

I got up from the bed and walked out onto the porch, which looked down into a narrow alley seven stories below. I shut the sliding glass and gripped the railing with both hands. I thought about what I'd just done. I gagged a few more times. I heard the door behind me slide open. I didn't move a millimeter. Beth crept out and looped her arms around me from behind. Slowly, she ducked her head under my arms and her face appeared below mine. I could only see the top of her head. I couldn't look at her. She hugged me. I looked down into the alley, and in an instant, I had visualized exactly what would be required to heave Beth up over the rail and send her hurtling down into the alley below. I saw it. I felt it. My muscles were twitching, ready to do it.

It scared the hell out of me.

I pushed myself away from Beth. I was shaking and breathing hard.

"What's wrong, baby? Don't worry, I don't want Lilly to find out either."

"Tomorrow at the ball, do not say anything to me. You got it?"

"Yeah. Relax. It's fine. I'm not going to say anything."

"No. Don't even think it."

"Okay."

Beth went back inside. I began to feel bad. There was no reason to be cruel. I smoked two more cigarettes and stepped into the suite.

Beth was in bed, pretending to be watching TV and pretending not to notice me. Her hair was wet, which made it look dark and gray like it was smeared with soot. She'd taken a shower while I was outside. I walked over and sat at the foot of the bed. "I'm sorry if I seemed angry. It's just that Lilly and I are old friends."

"Let me walk you to the door." She got up out of her bed with her robe open, and walked with me. She gave me a hug before opening the door, pressing her naked body up against mine. When I hugged her back, I felt her ass, which was still warm and damp from the shower. She kissed me and lowered herself down onto her knees. I would not say that she "blew me." A more accurate description would be that I fucked her face.

I woke up late the next morning. It was obvious everyone at the Abbots' house knew what I'd done. I felt like hell and spoke very little. My father had arrived early that morning and was off somewhere with Trip. I ate, showered, and went back to sleep. After I woke up I sat in my room very quietly, as if I were still asleep, until my father came back.

My father, Trip, and I went to a very late lunch at the Plimsoll Club. A heavy and oppressive cloud of shame hung over the table. And then my father and I walked home. He told me that when Coulter was born, he was gripped with a terrifying fear that Coulter would turn out crazy because of the history of mental illness that runs in my mother's family. I asked him why he didn't feel that with me. He said he didn't know. "There was just something about you that didn't make me worry. Plus, you looked like me and Coulter looked like your mother." I asked him if he was still scared about Coulter. "He seems to be coming along just all right." He took a few steps and added, "But it may be too early to tell. Same goes for you, Bub."

My duties were simple. First, the fathers came forward and stood next to the girls. Lilly looked extremely unhappy and uncomfortable in her gown. Some shit was said in Latin, French, and English. A group of men formally referred to as "Pages"—old guys wearing purple Dutch-boy outfits, highly embarrassing to watch—ran out and gave the leader of the ceremony, "The King," as they called him (another old fart in what looked like a purple Klan outfit), a staff. The King waved it around, said some more shit, and the music began.

I had to stand there while the fathers danced with their daughters. I led Lilly back to her seat, and then the remainder of my duty was to bring her whatever she wanted when she wanted it and to escort her wherever she walked, if she wanted me to. Lilly didn't want to dance. She didn't want to drink. She didn't want anything. Something was bugging her and that something was sitting two seats away and staring at me. I did not look at Beth at all, until, very abruptly, she started crying, threw her napkin into her plate, and stormed out. No one at the table said anything—at least not to me. I did nothing. After the ball, most of the young people went off to a party in the Quarter. Lilly went home.

On the plane the next day my father said to me, "I hear you hit it off with Lilly's cousin."

I said as passionately as I could, "Dad, I know that's what everyone thinks, but it's absolutely untrue."

21

It's a voodoo doll. Here are the pins. It's supposed to be Sherianne. I had the guy in the store cast a spell on her for you."

Coulter held the bag in one hand and the doll in the other. He really tried to act grateful. "Thanks, man. Thanks so much. I really appreciate it."

"Don't mention it. Where's Mom?"

"Did you get her anything?"

I belched. "Some Creole rice and shit like that. A cookbook too." I checked the clock on Coulter's bookshelf.

"Gotta get to work."

"You're working today? You just got back."

"Yeah. I fucked up. I sold $4,500 down in Orange, but only my last day of selling was technically part of the push week. I only sold around $700 that day and I've got five days left in the push, including today."

"Oh." Coulter didn't understand what I was saying.

I went on. "If I wanted to be a douche bag, I could change the sales forms so the Orange sales would have occurred during the push. I sold the knives, so I wouldn't be lying about that and I'm sure lots of people do that kind of thing, but I'm not going to. How does that make you feel?"

"What do you mean? Why would you cheat?"

"To win. Aren't you impressed that I'm not going to?"

Coulter had no idea what I was talking about.

"Okay. I gotta take a shower. Think about names we might have missed, will you?"

I walked out of his room, leaving Coulter holding the bag and doll like they were a hand grenade and pin.

I went straight to work—blitzed through a flurry of appointments (all lucrative) and then drove VERY late to have dinner with Brooke. When I arrived at Brooke's house and first saw her standing in the doorway with the door flung wide open, a blast of guilt from my escapade in New Orleans nearly broadsided me into the pachysandra beside their drive. Then her beautiful features became more clear in the light shining down on her—the top of her head illuminated in a sort of insect crown—the guilt evaporated from my body and was replaced with a cooling vascular pulse of relief. I tried to yell out a hello to her parents, but she pinned me to the wall outside of the door, rammed her tongue down my throat, and grabbed my penis. The brick hurt the back of my head, but Brooke's fake tits felt good and warm pressed up against my body and so did her hand. Never in my life had I been so happy to come home to Brooke.

It was kind of like playing house and I didn't want to let go of it. I knew, even as my arms wrapped around her, that there was something cruel in what I was doing. When my mother kicked me out and I was living with my father, Brooke and her family had taken me in and taken care of me. But that wasn't it entirely. My instincts told me that I probably should let her go, but as my arms eased around her back, she pulled me in closer and tighter, and as we whispered to each other, "I love you so much," I even felt it.

For once I even enjoyed the steamy plastic smell of I Can't Believe It's Not Butter wafting up from my sizzling filet mignon as Mrs. Ambrose slid my plate in front of me, and didn't mind the scent of Mr. Ambrose's whitefish, cooked in the same substance but seasoned with McCormick's allspice, simmering in front of him. I had smelled these dishes thousands of times before, and my memory of them was always of revulsion and feelings of being trapped. Much like the familiar sight of the neighboring house, so brightly lit it usually depressed the hell out of me. I had stared at that house over the course of innumerable dinners, asking myself why it was so ugly. And why if it was so obviously ugly, did the Ambroses continue to live in their house, which was built by the same contractors and is virtually identical? But more important, why was I, knowing this, perpetually stuck in the Ambroses' kitchen, bored and irritated by the way Brooke and her mother swooned when they said how "us girls," as they liked to call themselves, had waited for "you boys" to come home? That night I stopped asking myself those questions. None of those things bothered me anymore.

I just sat there, admiring Brooke's chest while halfway listening to her talk about how she would love to go to Greece with me, since I spoke Spanish (I won't even speculate as to how she came to this conclusion) and sailed, so we'd have no problem at all touring the islands in a boat. It was all perfectly pleasant sounding as I mentally went over the following days' appointments in my head, counting miles, negotiating routes, and constructing fake associations in my head. Brooke's tits moved. She turned to her father and suggested that he buy the senior associates at his office Bladeworks knives for their holiday gift.

Naturally my heart started pounding at the thought of such a huge sale (I figured he'd order nine or ten sets), and her father's large eyes shifted over to me. Without hesitation (though I had to dig down deep to find the courage to do it) I said, "Brooke. It's really nice of you to think of me, but I think that would be inappropriate."

I could tell Mr. Ambrose agreed, but he pushed the issue. "Why?"

I didn't want to tell him that not only had I made a resolution at the beginning of the summer not to sell to his family (or the family business, for that matter) but also I felt it was impossible for me to even consider the option, since Brooke had brought it up and not her father. I had come to teetering on the verge of viewing Brooke almost entirely as an object—an attractive one—but still barely human, and I felt so strongly at that moment that if I gave in to this offer, if I pursued this lead that she had dangled out in front of me, that I would be reducing her further, into a tool to sell more knives. It was totally obvious to me that the only reason Ed Ambrose would ever consider buying Bladeworks knives for his company's holiday gift was because I was his daughter's boyfriend. And, as I've said before, I liked him and respected him and still wanted him to respect me. Hell, I even wanted to respect myself. I still, in some very vague way—like maybe even some completely imaginary way—had a shred of self-decency left. I simply couldn't use Brooke like that. As much as I wanted to make some easy money and garner more points in the summer sales competition, I couldn't. And, of course, I couldn't tell them any of this. All I said was, "I think Waterford crystal sugar bowls might be a better gift."

Mr. Ambrose smiled at me, a genuine smile, and said, "Maybe you're right." Then he hit me with the punch line: "After all, I'm sure with how hard you've been working you wouldn't need the sale anyway. Last year, I spent around fifteen thousand dollars on our office gifts." Christ! What did I do? I'm sure the answer is very obvious to you: for once I did the right thing.

The next five days were busy. Not only was I trying to sell like crazy, I was also working on the catalog so that I could have a sample for the next convention. It wasn't the actual work that was difficult so much as working with Toby. I fault myself as much as him, though, because I could not communicate with him. It was obvious that the sample catalog would not be ready in time, but I did not want to let Toby have a break, so I stayed on top of him and pushed him to work as hard as possible, which took up a lot of valuable selling time. I did discover a very funny thing about Toby's dad, however.

One of the nights when I stopped by to work with Toby, he came to the door and said his father wanted to see me. Ty was in the basement wearing a karate headband singing karaoke with a light show, and his entire family was watching. He saw me, winked, sang the rest of the song (I mean, he sang his fucking heart out), and then instead of asking if I wanted to have a turn, which I was terrified he would do, he told me to wait and watch him do a duet with his wife. It was a rehearsed performance, choreography and everything. I asked Toby if this was something his dad did often. He cringed, nodded, and said, "More than you could imagine." Ty's wife did a hell of a job, though. Half of "Up Where We Belong" never sounded so good.

I did have one secret weapon. The cookware. It was expensive and more than doubled my potential selling power. It also greatly tested my selling skill. The product was shit. Although Bladeworks knives are not the very best knives in the world for every person, they are very good knives and for many people—because they don't need sharpening—they are the ideal knives. The cookware, however, I simply could not get to work.

The cookware set was basically like any other collection of pots, except the Bladeworks pots were supposed to have the extra benefit of allowing the user to cook at low temperatures without using cooking oils. The idea being that if you cook at a low enough temperature you won't burn what you're cooking and you don't need the oil. But how do you cook something if the pan doesn't get hot enough? Bladeworks says there are two ways: through even distribution of heat and by the creation of a pressure seal.

The Bladeworks pots are stainless steel on the outside, but they had a three-layer aluminum core. Stainless steel is hard and relatively easy to clean, but it doesn't conduct heat well. The aluminum is supposed to take care of that. As a side note, the best pots are coated on the bottom with copper and are extremely expensive—but that's neither here nor there.

The seal works in this way: the rim of the pan and the lip of the cover are beveled so that they create an airtight seal—the cover (the male piece) fitting perfectly into the pan (the female piece). Okay, this is simple enough, but when you heat something it expands (the air in the pot included) and will continue to expand so long as you keep raising the temperature. You might have noticed that if you cover a pot of water and let it boil, the water (as it expands and becomes a gas) will shoot out of the sides of the pan in the form of steam and cause the cover to rattle.

If you turn down the heat on the boiling pot, the gas inside the pot (steam) will condense again into water. The air molecules bouncing off of one another will also contract and, though still bouncing off one another, will do so from a shorter distance. If you use Bladeworks's patented pot lid to cover the vacuum created by lowering the heat, the vacuum will create a seal between the cooling pan and the lid, thereby trapping the heat (even though it's cooling—or more important, cooler than it was) and cooking whatever you have in the pot at a lower temperature but at a greater pressure.

I tested the pan by cooking a carrot using this method. Actually, I added a little extra water to be on the safe side, and let her rip. After the specified cooking time, the once-orange six-inch carrot had been turned into a piping hot, tiny dark brown cracked rod.

Whatever moisture, color, and vitamins the carrot once had seeped out in a puddle and took the form of a giant carrot (it actually looked more like a giant turnip), except no liquid remained in the puddle. The water had evaporated, leaving a gritty orange tattoo, like the chalk outline of a dead body, silhouetted around the bullet-shaped former vegetable, which was so thoroughly—I won't even say "stuck" because it's not accurate—fused to the stainless steel pan that to this very day, I can still see a brown mark where it once sat.

Up until the end of the push, I was in a constant state of physical motion and mental plotting. I would go through my routine, beginning with my stumbling and stuttering confused entrance and ending in complete control of the client, the authority on everything that involved cooking products. I wasn't entirely conscious of affecting this transformation. This is not to say that I was like a drone.

Knife selling is very interactive. You are watching and reading a person's reactions to what you are saying. I never stopped doing this. In fact, I got better at it. It was part of me. I wouldn't say that my ability to read and react to people had become completely instinctual—it was more like it had become a sixth sense. I didn't need to see a person cringe or listen to them say they didn't like something. I knew it before that happened. I expected it and altered whatever I was doing to use their mood to my advantage.

So what was I thinking about when I wasn't thinking about knife selling? I was thinking about knife selling. I was thinking about the next customer and the customer after that. How I was going to get to their house on time. The best route. Traffic conditions for that day. The lies I would tell if I was late. The catalog. Whether bribing Toby would make him work harder. Maybe I should just hire someone else to do it. Who would I hire? What would it cost? What would Ty Nakamori do if he found out? How am I going to connect myself to Arlene Fineberg, my four o'clock appointment? Her son went to Lasher with Stacey Wright. He played football in high school and hockey at BHA when he was younger. I played at BHA. Her sister works with Debbie Reynolds. She's in a book club with Luanne Battlen. They're reading *Snow Falling on Cedars*. Should I pretend I've read it? What the fuck am I going to say in my speech?

The speech. Bud French had called me to ask if I would make the closing speech of the second push-week convention. He explained to me that as the summer nears its end, sales tend to drop off after the second push week. He wanted me to deliver a speech that might encourage the salespeople to continue selling at their current rate or higher for the remaining three weeks of the summer session. For Bladeworks, August is three weeks long. In truth, it's actually shorter. There are only seventeen selling days from the end of the push week until the final end of the summer celebration in Myrtle Beach, where the winner of the summer selling competition is announced. I told Bud that I'd give the speech.

When I wasn't actively in a knife sale, my mind was still focused on the greater goal of selling. I was constantly on the verge of getting into accidents while driving. I forgot to eat. I couldn't fall asleep. And I was virtually incapable of having conversations that didn't involve selling, the catalog, or my speech.

You might imagine that Brooke did not appreciate this too much, but she did. I wasn't listening to her anymore, so I didn't disagree with anything she said. I agreed to everything. I don't even know what exactly occurred between us during that time. All that exists in my memory are sounds. Her baby voice falsetto and yearning, like a spider monkey calling out for its mother's shriveled teat.

One pleasant benefit of my monomania, which I didn't realize had occurred until it came back like cancer, was that I had stopped thinking about Isabelle. Or I thought about her less. For five amazing days I didn't wake up in the morning angry that she hadn't thanked me for the package I sent her, or hoping that at any moment she might call.

The morning after I arrived back in Michigan, I was hurrying out the door and trying to chug a cup of coffee when my mother walked into the kitchen. She wore a nightgown and a smile. Fancy followed her in.

"Good morning, Jay. I thought I was going to see you last night, but you weren't here when I got in and then I left and didn't come home until late last night. What were you doing?"

"I don't know. Nothing. With Brooke. I don't know."

"If you were with Brooke, you should remember."

"Jesus. I guess I was. Mom?"

"Yes."

"I was wondering something." I dumped the rest of my coffee into the sink.

"What?"

"Do you think Dad is charming?"

"Not when he drinks." She pulled Fancy's bowl out of the cupboard. "I used to think that your father was the most charming man alive." She tapped her nail on the counter.

"What about me?"

"Of course I think you're charming." She took a while to say this and sadly I knew she was lying.

"Huh." I started walking away.

"Wait. Jay, maybe you could just sit and have breakfast with me?"

"I would, but I have to go."

"You're so much like your father."

"Thanks." I walked out.

She called after me. "That wasn't a compliment!"

I had the perfect sale. It was my last appointment of the push week. I rolled up almost an hour late to a modest house in Birmingham. Mrs. Trumeter was angry and ready to leave. I calmed her down by apologizing and lying. Since I had yet to replace the undersized spare tire, or the "doughnut," on the Escort, she easily believed that I popped a flat on the way. I told her a humorous story about how when the tire blew I freaked out, jerked my car off the road, and almost crashed into an above-ground swimming pool. I went on about how an entire family was watching from their deck and helped me change the flat. They even made me take a hamburger for the road. "It's cooking on my dashboard." This got her laughing.

We entered Mrs. Trumeter's kitchen and she told me what had become my favorite thing to hear: "I will not and cannot buy anything." Then she added, "I'm remodeling my kitchen, so right now I'm spending every cent we have on that." Mrs. Trumeter motioned to a set of plans laid out on a nearby counter. Construction had begun that very day. The sink had been pulled out. "The carpenter just left. Can't I just sign something to show that you were here? You know, so you can get your scholarship points and you don't have to do your presentation?"

I also loved when people said this, because it gave me an opportunity to seize the moral high ground. I lowered my head as if I were extremely tempted by her offer and said, "I'd really love to do that. Trust me. I'm supertired. But I'd feel bad about"—I practically whispered—"lying."

She huffed. "You're absolutely right. Where do you want to do this?"

"This table is just fine. Do you mind if I stand?"

She pushed the sink parts to one side of a round antique breakfast table and sat down to watch the Jay show. The pennies had their usual effect.

I don't know what it was. Maybe it was just that I was humored by how quickly these women switch from being on the verge of tossing me out to laughing and fingering the knives, and making little comments like, "Oh . . . I've got to have that." Maybe it was that this was my last sale before a long drive, which I always looked forward to. I don't know. But I was in an extremely good mood and thought I'd toy around with Mrs. Trumeter a little at the end of the presentation.

Just before I finished, Mrs. Trumeter actually climbed out of her seat and stood next to me. She pointed out the place where the knife block could go in her kitchen and where she planned to hang her pans over her oven. I stopped midway through the price comparison, leaving a gargantuan number hanging in the air. I folded my knives up, slipped my pan into my bag, and thanked Mrs. Trumeter for her time.

"What do you mean?"

"You said you weren't going to buy any knives."

"To hell with what I said! Tell me what the things cost. If they're at least ten times as good as Henckels and those pans, which I just love, are anywhere close to what copper-plated ones cost, you must be talking about ten thousand dollars?"

I waited and winced. She raised her clenched fists up under her chin. I stared at her, my face devoid of any expression, "Not even close to that. The Supreme Kitchen Set, which includes all of the gourmet knives plus The Professional Chef Cookware Set costs . . . I don't know the exact figure, but it's a little over three thousand dollars."

She signed. "Oh. Good. I was worried they'd be just unbelievably expensive. When can I get them?"

I filled out the form, recommended she opt for the five-month payment plan, and threw in a vegetable peeler. I actually laughed when I told her I was giving it to her. "This will seem so silly, because you've bought so much, but I just wanted to give you something to thank you."

She thanked me, walked me to the door, and said, "Now you can have your hamburger." I laughed and left.

I laughed at Mrs. Trumeter in my car for two blocks. Then I called Stuart, still laughing. "I just had another three-thousand-dollar sale."

"Bullshit."

"A total stranger. Right off the bat she told me she couldn't buy the knives, that she was pressed for money—"

"They always say that."

"Yeah, I know, but I could see her goddamn renovations. It was hilarious."

Stuart made a sound like he was chewing on something and didn't know whether to swallow or puke. He switched topics. "You're nuts, Hauser."

"That puts me at around fourteen thousand."

"That's great."

"Yeah. I'm a little pissed about fucking up the dates, though."

"Don't be. Fourteen thousand dollars in four and a half days is insane."

"Well, there was still seven hundred from Orange, so it's more like thirteen thousand."

"Whatever. It's unbelievable. Even better than the first push."

"I guess." I drove along a little farther and asked something that had been on my mind for a while: "Stuey, you obviously knew that I was outselling everybody for the first push, right?"

"Yeah. I knew. To me and Chuck you were already a legend. Shit, anyone who saw your numbers knew."

"Why did you lie to me about it?"

"Well, as a general rule I want to challenge people, but with you in particular I knew that if you had any idea of how good you were at selling you would have quit."

As I drove I thought about when I first found out that Stuart was going to be a branch manager. It was after a winter workout session. We were in the all-you-can-eat cafeteria. Anyone who wanted to gain weight was there. Bigger, faster, stronger—coach Shrier's motto. I hated it, but I'd sit there stuffing myself until I could barely breathe. *SportsCenter* was always on the TV. Everybody watched it but me. Even the girls. The room was about 185 degrees, even in the dead of winter, and we were sitting there in the deadest, blackest part.

Stuart was holding a notebook close to his chest. Keating was grabbing at it and Stuart couldn't stop giggling. "No. I'm not going to show it to you."

Panolini cracked, "Your balls. Why not? You're always showing Keating your balls."

"Stuart's selling knives this summer. I wanna see what he's got in there." I looked up from my spaghetti, gasping and fearing I might heave across the table. Keating went on. "You got knives in there, Stuart?"

Stuart laughed and said very sarcastically, "I have knives in this folder. Is that a brain you have in your head, or is it just more of your greasy hair?"

"C'mon, man. My head keeps sweating like crazy."

Woodsy had to clarify something. "Stuart's not selling knives this summer. He did that last summer. This summer he's managing an office."

Keating made a grab at the folder. "How do you know that?"

"Stuart visited me in Alpharetta over Thanksgiving. He gave my mother a set as a thank-you present."

Keating again, "That's not all he gave her!"

"Fuck you."

Stuart snatched a rib off his own plate and fired it into Keating's cup.

"Dude. You dick. Get me another water."

When Keating went to swipe the glass in front of Stuart's tray, Stu fired another rib into his own drink and giggled and batted at Keating like a queen.

I remember one summer when I was eight years old, I had seen a Bladeworks salesman come to my house and try to sell to my mother. I remember him standing at our breakfast table lit up like a burning matchstick.

He cut the penny. I was impressed. He charmed the hell out of my mother, and I thought for sure she was going to buy the knives. He made them look so necessary. But she didn't buy them. She told me after he left that she thought they were too expensive. I've thought about this many times, trying to figure out exactly why my mother didn't buy. I've always thought that it was somehow her fault. That somehow she'd been too cheap or too scared or too something. But now I've figured it out. He fucked up the price comparison.

When I heard Stuart was managing the office I thought that selling knives was something I could do well. I didn't say anything to him for several months.

One afternoon he and I were limping up the hill toward the green. It was during spring ball and the leaves and the grass were bright green. "So what's this knife-selling deal?"

"What? You mean the office I'm managing?"

"Yeah."

"What about it?"

"How does it work?"

"I hire knife salesmen, teach them to sell, and then they make a lot of money."

"Is it the same presentation where a guy comes to your house and cuts a penny?"

"That's the one. Why?"

"I think I can do it."

Stuart stopped. "No. It's not for you. You wouldn't like it."

"I'm not saying that I'd like it. I just think I can do it."

"Why?"

"I don't know. I just think I can."

Stuart shook his head. "Weren't you and Panolini talking about salmon fishing in Alaska this summer?"

"We were, but Panolini's going to work for his goddamn girlfriend at some summer camp."

Stuart took a few more of his pigeon-toed steps. "I don't think you're the kind of guy who would feel comfortable calling people you know and asking them to buy things from you."

I dropped the conversation, but I kept thinking about it. I asked Isabelle for her opinion. She, as I've already pointed out, didn't think I was charming enough to do it. That sealed the deal. I forced Stuart to teach me how to sell knives.

I called Stuart back. "Hey, it's Jay. I just have to drive home, pick up my stuff, and then I'm heading down. I want to ask you one more question. Remember how you didn't want me to sell knives when I first asked you about it at Dartmouth?"

"Yeah." He laughed.

"Were you doing the same thing then as when you lied to get me to sell more?"

"You mean, did I discourage you from selling because I wanted you to sell?"

"Yeah."

"No. I didn't want to have to train you. I thought it'd be a waste of time. I didn't think you'd be a good salesman. Clearly, I was wrong."

"Who the hell did you think would have made a good salesman?"

"At Dartmouth?"

"Yeah."

"Isabelle."

I almost swerved off the road. "Isabelle?! She's a complete snob."

"I know. But she's a country club–type snob. Sometimes those types are great salespeople. She's cute. She's always funny and fun and she's got that thing about her. She'd be great. I don't know what else to say. But hell, she's not doing it. You are."

"Did you ask her to sell?"

There was a long pause. "I might have mentioned it."

"That little bitch! What did she tell you when you asked her?"

"She laughed in my face. We were drunk at Herrot one night. She probably wouldn't even remember it."

"Stuey, what are you talking about? She's a chicken. She's always running away from shit. Goddamn her!"

"Jay, you're so in love with that girl it's weird that you don't admit it. Why don't you just date her?"

"I have a fucking girlfriend! And I got to get off the phone before I run over an old lady or something. I wish there was a squirrel around here that I could hit."

"You're kidding, right?

"Of course I'm kidding."

"One more thing, dude. Did you write your speech yet?"

"No. I'm working on it. I figured out the title, though."

"Yeah." Stuart laughed again. "I know. Chuck told me."

"It's a good one. Don't worry, I'll write the speech on the way down."

"How are you going to write and drive?"

"Very carefully."

I got home and quickly started tossing together the stuff I would need for the weekend, thinking about whether Stuart had asked Isabelle before or after she told me I wasn't charming enough to sell. If he had asked her before she might have been fucking with me or trying to humiliate me in some weird way. If it was after, then why did she say no?

Maybe it was a competitive thing. Why did she laugh at it? Maybe, *if it was a competitive thing,* that's why she didn't write me back—because I was doing well and she wasn't. But I didn't mention anything about selling in my brief note. My head was spinning. I was totally lost when the phone rang.

"Hello?"

"Hello, may I speak to Jay Hauser please?"

"Yes, this is Jay."

"Hi, Jay, this is Nancy Trumeter." My perfect sale.

"Hi. How are you?"

"I'm fine. Jay, listen, my husband just got home and he's making me cancel my order."

"Oh . . ."

"Yes. I got really carried away, I'm sorry. We just can't afford it right now."

"That's okay. I told you it's okay if you didn't want to buy anything."

"I know, Jay, but I'm going to have to cancel the order."

"Okay. Did you tell your husband about the five-month payment plan?"

"I did. But we just can't buy them right now."

"Would you like me to hold on to the order, and when you're ready to buy them you can call me?"

"No. I think it's best if we just cancel the order right now."

"All right. Did you want to cancel the whole order or did you just want to cancel part of it? If you just bought the knives it'd be only about two hundred and fifty dollars a month."

"I think it's best if we cancel the whole order."

"Would you like me to come over and show your husband what I showed you?"

"No, Jay. I think I just want to cancel the order right now."

"Are you sure?"

"Yes."

"Okay. I'll tear up the order form right now. If you'd like I can bring it to you so you'd have it."

"No. That's all right. I've already canceled my credit card."

"Okay. I'm sorry. I'd still like to thank you for helping me with my scholarship."

"You're welcome."

"Well, if you change your mind you can always call me."

"Okay."

"All right. Have a nice night, Mrs. Trumeter."

"You too. Wait, I think my husband wants to speak to you."

I heard the husband yelling, "Gimmie that phone! I want to wring that little fucker's neck!"

Then she said, "Never mind. I better not put him on. Bye." And hung up.

Naturally, I was furious. That goddamn bitch. I called Stuart. He asked if there was any way I thought I could resurrect the sale. Mrs. Trumeter caught me off guard. I'd never had anyone cancel an order before. In fact, the only person who did not buy knives from me was my aunt Tina, and she knew that my grandparents would buy them for her.

Stuart said that the next time someone tried to cancel an order that large I should offer to call my manager and ask him to extend the payment plan to ten months and see if I could get the knives at a reduced price, if they still wanted them. Why not call Mrs. Trumeter back and try?

Mrs. Trumeter was eating when I called to present her with the option. The entire time I was speaking she had to hush her husband going bananas in the background. Then when I finished explaining about the ten-month plan she said, "But I thought you already tore up the order form?"

"Yes. I did. I would have to come by and fill out another one."

"No. Jay. I shouldn't have ordered any knives in the first place. Do I have to call the police about this?"

Her husband shouted, "Police! I'll kill that—"

"Of course not."

"Please don't call back. Ever. Or I will call the police."

Now I was doubly furious. I pulled out my list of referrals and scoured it for anyone who might be able to see me that night, before I drove down to Cincinnati. Did I know any of these people well? Was there a known night owl on the list? A free spirit? A good friend of my mother's who I hadn't called yet because she was an alcoholic and most likely had a crush on me? Suzanne Tammersol! I found her name. Shit. I'd already sold to her.

There had to be some way. There had to be someone. There simply had to be. Maybe I should just forget about the referral system, walk out of my mother's house, and go door to door.

I called three candidates, but they weren't home. It was a Friday night. A beautifully warm summer night and anyone who accepts calls after eight was probably at dinner, or a barbecue or a party. I thought about the outdoor restaurants I knew in the area. They probably had laws about soliciting. Or maybe I could find someone at home, with guests. I could prowl, driving slowly with the windows down, listening to hedges and sidewalks for the sounds of backyard laughter, cocktail chitchat, and faint world music.

Stuart called. I was hunched over the list with a pen in my mouth, the telephone handset squeezed between my shoulder and my ear, the base of the phone in my lap. I jerked back, startled.

"What are you doing?"

"Trying to find a fucking appointment."

"Tonight? It's almost ten."

"I know."

"Don't. It's okay. You sold nine thousand five hundred dollars in four and a half days. You did great. Just let it go and come down here."

"Okay. I'm just going to go through this list one more time and then I'll be on my way."

22

The skinny kid from Charleston stood at the podium. His hair, sun bleached and floppy. His accent, classic southern fried fuck face.

"Thank y'all soooo much. You don't know how much this means to me. I've worked soooo hard the past ten days. I . . ."

I fought through the crowd to the back of the ballroom. All of the faces pointed behind me.

I had come in second place for the push. I lost by twenty-eight hundred dollars. My perfect sale would have won it for me. I cursed myself for answering the phone. There was no answering machine on that line. Only a fax. I wouldn't have found out that the order had been canceled until after the push, when Coulter or my mother answered Mrs. Trumeter's relentless calls, or later when the purchase was processed and the credit card came up declined. Maybe she hadn't actually canceled her credit card. Probably not. Fuck. I should have packed faster and gotten the hell out of Dodge before the phone rang.

Susanne Beatle, the little bitch from Nashville, won third place with nine thousand dollars in sales. She applauded like crazy when I stepped forward to claim the number two slot, screaming the kid from Charleston's name.

I slipped out the back door just as "Eye of the Tiger" began to play. A trio of salespeople were standing out on the patio smoking cigarettes. I sloughed off to the side and tried to hang by myself, but the trio made their way over to me. Two guys and one girl. Both of the guys wore loose baggy clothing and the girl wore a summer dress.

"Hey, man. Good job."

"Thanks."

"Wanna light?"

"I've got one. Thanks."

"I'm Terrance Carter. That's Mell and Tony. We sell out of Chattanooga."

"Hi. Jay. I sell out of Covington, Kentucky."

"We know."

"What happened, man? We all thought you were going to win it."

I shrugged. "Don't know."

"Dude! You should have won!"

"I would have liked to."

Summer dress, "Too bad you didn't. You're our favorite."

"Thanks."

"Do you know the kid that won?"

"No."

"He's supposed to be fuckin' good."

"I'm sure."

"I hear he works part-time at a restaurant and when he's serving meals he asks the diners there if they want to help with his scholarship."

"Oh . . ."

"Yeah. Fuckin' genius right?"

"Yeah."

"Where you at now?"

I knew the figure but I said, "I'm not sure. A fair amount."

"You hear that? Jay Hauser doesn't even know how much he's sold."

"Bullshit. He knows."

"No. I really don't. Nice to meet you."

The ballroom was emptying out. I cut in front of the horde and headed straight for the escalator. Jay Bennish, the manager from Atlanta, strode up quickly and stepped onto the moving platform beside me. He gripped my shoulder and shook my hand. "Jay. Congratulations on second place. I know you probably wanted to win, but second place on your second push is something to be proud of. Ten thousand dollars in ten days is phenomenal."

I wanted to tell him it was ten thousand in five days, but I didn't. "I'm happy."

"You should be. You're a hell of a salesman."

"Thanks."

"You know that, don't you? Don't forget it."

"I won't."

"I mean it, Jay. Keep working. Keep pushing. You can get back up there." I didn't respond. He looked around. "Let me tell you something."

We stepped off the escalator and he took me aside. He leaned toward me with his wet bug eyes. He reached out and shook my hand again, pulling it against his body so that I could feel his firm gut pressed against the back of my wrist. "Don't let this bother you."

I stared at the freak. "I won't."

"Don't. That's all I'm saying." He shook my hand for the third time. "Keep up the good fight, champ."

I yanked my hand away, wiped his sweat off on my pant leg, said "Thanks," and walked toward the lobby.

As I passed the bar I saw Stuart there, standing next to Chuck and surrounded by a bunch of other managers. I was fairly god-damn pissed at myself and at these assholes who seemed to think I'd lost my touch. I wanted a little bit of goddamn encouragement from somebody who knew that had it not been for answering the phone and for the five days that I missed I would have easily won the goddamn push. I nodded at Stuart, but he didn't seem to see me, so I walked over.

"Stuey."

"Yo. What's up?"

"Not much."

"Congratulations on second place. You should have had first."

"Yeah. Hey, you want to sit down and grab a drink?"

"Sure. I, ahhh . . ." Stuart looked at the rest of the managers. "Just wait a couple of minutes, we're having a talk here. Just managers."

"Managers?"

"Yeah. We're talking about something."

"Oh."

"Wait a sec. I won't be long."

"No. It's okay. I got to work on my speech."

"Yeah. That's a good idea. You really don't want to fuck that up."

"What do you mean?"

"Just don't fuck it up."

"You think I'm going to fuck it up?"

"No. Just do it well. You know. It's a big deal."

Chuck turned around. He had beer foam on his lips. "Hauser. Did I just hear you say you hadn't finished your speech?"

"I'm working on it."

"Okay." He patted his lips with the back of his hand. "You just tell me if you don't feel up to it. I can easily get up on that stage to-morrow and say something."

"No. That's all right."

As I walked away I heard Chokewater, the manager with the lisp who was one of Stuart's former rivals, say, "What the hell's he been doin' for the past two weeks?"

Stuart, "Selling knives."

Then Chuck said, "Not like before. Fuckin' one-hit wonder!" They all laughed.

The pizza I ordered was half eaten and half cold when Skeeter knocked on my door.

"Hey, man."

"Howdy."

"Come in."

Skeeter stepped inside.

"You want some pizza?"

"No, thanks. Already ate with the rest of the office."

I noticed a pin on the lapel of his new blazer. "What's that for?"

He lifted the lapel off his chest and looked at it. He smiled up at me. "My fifteen-thousand-dollar pin. I'm the second highest sales-man in the office. Second to you."

"Congratulations."

"Thanks. Ya got a beer?"

"No. Sorry. What's up?"

"Oh. Nothing much. That kid from Charleston's having a party in his room. I wanted to see if you wanted to come."

"That's all right. I gotta work on my speech."

"Cool." Skeeter looked around the room.

"What happened to Julie?"

"Julie. Shit. She quit about a week ago. Git this." Skeet sat in one of the two chairs at the small table where I'd been working on my speech. I cranked back in the seat across from him. "Nobody knew it, but she'd been pregnant the entire time she'd been working for Apex."

"Even when we were in Cumberland lakes?" I thought about the night we spent lying awake, staring at each other.

"Yup. She'd been knocked up during the school year by some basketball player at University of Cincinnati." He laughed to himself. "Stuart was impressed by that."

"Was the kid a starter?"

"Yip. But I don't think he's gonna take responsibility, if you know what I mean. She didn't want to quit, but she had to take a job as a secretary in a dental office—for them health benefits."

"Fuck."

"I'll say she was fucked good and is good and fucked now."

"She's actually going to keep the baby?"

"You know how these Baptist girls are . . ."

"I didn't know she was Baptist."

"I don't know how much of one she is either, but her parents are real religious." Skeeter lit a smoke. "Remember that kid, Judd, who was braggin' all the way down to the Cumberland lakes?"

"Yeah. Yellow hair, fat. Kind of pasty."

"That's the one. Guess what he was doin'?"

"Huh?"

"Faking sales forms. Chuck caught 'm. He'd stopped goin' to appointments. He'd just fill out the sales form with made-up people and made-up credit card numbers and turn 'm in."

"How did he figure he was going to get away with that?"

"Dunno." I pushed a plastic cup with a half-inch of Cherry Coke in it toward Skeeter.

"Thanks." He tapped his ash. "When Chuck confronted him, Judd went ape-shit. He just would not admit to faking the forms and blamed everyone: his clients, fellow salesmen, Apex executives, the people in the goddamn mailroom. He even accused Chuck in front of the whole office of sabotaging him. Shit. Chuck had to call the police to get 'm out of there."

"That's crazy. Why'd you think he did it?"

"Dunno that either. Be part of the team, I guess. Braggin' rights?" Skeeter looked out the sliding glass doors at the glowing white patio and the black skyline. "Funny thing is, after stormin' out and tellin' everybody to fuck off and go to hell and all that, he came back and begged Chuck to talk to him. Chuck finally agreed. He let 'm in and listened to Judd sob for about an hour just for the chance to sell again."

"What'd Chuck say?"

"Impossible. You can't cheat and get back in. No way. Ain't pos- sible." Skeeter exhaled a long blue lungful that rolled upward across the room and then dropped his cigarette into the plastic cup. A puff of cherry-smelling smoke shot into my nostrils. "Now every couple of days Judd parks outside the office for an hour or so and watches them work through that storefront window."

I lit a smoke. "What do you make of it?"

Skeeter shrugged and rubbed the tips of his fingers together. "Nothin'. Suppose I might do the same thing if I didn't have nothin' else goin' on." Skeeter picked up a piece of paper from the desk and let out a big laugh. "This is your speech?! Goddamn!" He read, "'Good evening ladies and gentlemen.' And that's it!"

I had trouble falling asleep. The skyline beyond the patio that had been so dark while the lights of my room were on brightened to a gray fog. A red light pulsed somewhere in the distance.

The plastic cup that Skeeter had been ashing into was on the bedside table—at arm's length, filled with ash and cigarette butts. It reeked. My speech lay next to it. I hadn't written much since Skeeter left. All I really had was the title. It was a damn good title.

I tried to wrap my brain around the idea that in the big picture, winning the second push was not all that important. What really mattered was the race to win the summer season. There were maybe ten people who could realistically win. Acuña was one of them. I was one of them. The little bitch from Nashville was one of them. They would both be there tomorrow, listening to my speech.

The following morning I was sitting at the far end of a table as part of a panel that would answer questions after a lecture given by Reid Tallenger, a former knife-selling legend. Reid was at the podium. Tables were set up, onstage, in a half moon around him. I was stage left.

Simultaneously and in a different ballroom, a different knife-selling legend, Jorge Acuña, was giving a demonstration of his sales technique. The demonstration was in Spanish, and basically everyone at the sales conference was divided into those who spoke Spanish and those who did not. I wanted to attend Acuña's demonstration, since I spoke a little Spanish and I would have liked to steal what I could from his technique, but since I was supposed to be part of Reid Tallenger's panel, I couldn't.

Reid looked at least fifteen years older than the rest of us, had sold knives year-round for the past ten years, and still claimed he was "trying to win a scholarship." He was tall, thin, handsome, and dressed in a boyish manner—khakis, sport coat, and a prep school–type tie. His haircut looked exactly like the haircut Liam Gallagher, the lead singer of Oasis, wore. He looked a little bit like Liam too, in that they both had sunken features, cruel eyes, and continually sported facial expressions that would lead one to believe that they were sucking on hard candies made of cat shit.

When Reid introduced himself, he said that he'd made more

than eight hundred thousand dollars selling knives and as soon as he made more than one million he would stop selling and become a manager. Although this figure was impressive and I wanted to hear what he was going to say, I still had to work on my speech. So as soon as he introduced himself I pulled it out and discreetly began to write.

I was fairly engrossed in this task, so I didn't know what Reid was saying until he got around to talking about technique and something caught my ear. "I've been hearing some unsettling rumors that there's someone out there who's been teaching new, or I should say, different and possibly detrimental alterations to the demonstration. Now, I've been selling knives for a long time and I haven't deviated one bit from the sales pitch I was originally taught. Of course, I'll throw in a joke or two of my own, you know, add a little flavor, but I'm going to urge you to stick to what you've been taught. One of the rumors is that this person says it's a good idea to stand while giving your pitch." He was looking right at me, grinning. He let everyone know exactly whom he was talking about. "Imagine I'm six feet tall and you're sitting down and I'm waving a knife in your face." He swiped a knife back and forth over the podium a few times. "See, that's not a good idea, is it? And another thing . . . I don't know what kind of neighborhood y'all come from, but where I come from, if you start talking about what people are doin' and their friends and what they're doin' then whoever you're talkin' to is gonna look at you funny. The connection a salesman makes with a customer is one-on-one personal. Don't bring anybody else into it." He let out a laugh and shook his head, like what he was about to say was just beyond comprehension. "Acting silly is doggone unprofessional. If something falls out of your pocket during a presentation you look like you don't know what you're doing. Would you buy knives from a young kid who came into your house, bumbling around like a clown, dropping pennies all over the place? Where's the respect? The poise? You must immediately take command of the situation and demand the customer's respect. *Respectfully,* mind you . . ." I looked out at the crowd. The kid from Charleston was sitting high in his seat, his knife-selling trophy on the table in front of him. His smile pert. His head nodding in agreement. Stuey did not look so chipper. He held his chin down and his eyes slid slowly back and forth: Reid to me. Skeeter looked devastated. Chuck looked like he agreed with Reid.

"Naming your knives is just goofy. Who here thinks they know better than all of the Bladeworks employees who've worked for years before him?" He looked around. "C'mon. I want to see some hands go up, because I know that there's someone here who thinks that he does. Nobody here thinks they know more about knife selling than all the people who have sold before him? Then I guess these rumors are untrue, 'cause I sure don't think I know better than all the people who've come before me. I've heard some of these names. Get this one—the Bob Vila Knife. We are selling high-quality cutlery, not fix-it-yourself home videos. If you don't like the product you're selling and want to try to hide it or change it, you shouldn't be selling it in the first place! When you make your price comparison you should not scare your customer into believing that he cannot afford Bladeworks. Hell, I've got a little bit of money, but if somebody parked a Ferrari in my driveway, I'm not gonna buy it no matter how cheaply he tries to sell it to me. I'd think there was something wrong with the vehicle! Do not personalize a sale. Millions of dollars have been made with the Deluxe Kitchen Set. It is counterproductive to criticize Bladeworks or Apex in any way. Really, I can't believe the kind of stuff I've been hearing. It just don't make no sense. God." He shook his head. "This last thing that I've heard is just plain-out dumb. Always, always offer the customer twenty percent of their purchase in free product. Wouldn't you be more inclined to buy a great product if you got an even better deal on it?"

Reid hung his head and then looked up. "Maybe someone's pullin' a gag on me. Or maybe we all don't come from the kind of place where this kind of behavior is acceptable. Maybe in the North, they're a little bit different. Ooops, did I just say the North? I thought we were selling out of the Southeastern division. Anyone around here a northerner?" Again, he looked at me. "I thought not. Or maybe the answer is that these rumors are untrue, because all the things that this person promises will happen if you sell by his technique never happened in the first place."

While the first few jibes at my selling style got laughs, his lecture continued on such a bitter note that it began to poison the conference. The ballroom felt seeped in gloom and vibrated in its nauseating neon light. The faces in the crowd looked green, sick, and angry. As for me, I was resting my head in my hand, leaning on the table with my right elbow. Whoever had been sitting to my left had gotten up in the middle of the lecture and left, so I had my feet up on his seat and my body reclined back and over the table. I was smiling, droopy eyed, and appeared to be doodling on the back of my speech. I'm sure I looked like I was either on the verge of passing out or like I couldn't have cared less about what I was hearing. I was, in fact, dying for the question-and-answer session to begin so I could defend myself.

"Okay, so now why don't we open it up and myself and the panel can answer some of your questions."

I shot my hand into the air and said, "Reid, if I could just—"

"Hold on a second, Jay." It was Bud French, running onstage behind me. "I'm going to have to interrupt you guys for a moment."

Reid stepped aside. Bud took command of the podium, sucking in large pockets of air. He was really excited about something. "Hold on a sec. I just want to make sure—" Just then the doors to the ballroom opened and all of the members of Team Puerto Rico and the other Spanish speakers except Acuña walked in. "Good. Everybody's here . . . You know, the damnedest things happen in this business. Some things just make your heart want to jump out of your chest. And I'm very proud to say that one of these things just happened downstairs." He held his hand up over his eyes and looked out at the control booth toward the back of the room. "Connie? Are you ready with the tape?" Bud stepped away, and a screen descended from above the stage.

The video was of Jorge doing his presentation. The person playing the role of the customer was his girlfriend—a hot Puerto Rican with platinum blond hair and dark brown skin. I couldn't understand what he was saying, but I believe he was transitioning from the price comparison to the close when he got down on one knee, reached into his pocket, and whipped out a ring. He started crying and asked: *"¿Casate conmigo?"*

The girl started bawling, *"Sí! Sí!"* The room (in the tape) exploded in Spanish cheers. The ballroom also exploded in cheers, except now most were in English.

The screen rose back up to the ceiling and Bud stood, looking out at the crowd. "Jorge and Camilla, congratulations! Why don't you just come on in here!"

Jorge, hand in hand with his fiancée, swept into the room and together they began bowing and blowing kisses like crazy. I was still dying to defend myself, but after applauding Jorge and Camilla for another five goddamn minutes, Bud said, "All right, as much as I'm sure we'd all like to have our question-and-answer period, we're running a little behind schedule. So why don't we all break for lunch and be sure to be back here in two hours for our closing ceremony, which I'm sure is going to be great."

I didn't understand what had happened. Why did everybody hate me so much? All I had done was come in second place. For the past five days, I had been making one thousand dollars a day. Nobody else had done that. The kid from Charleston wasn't even in the 50 percent commission bracket. Acuña had come in tenth place for the push. Reid had come in seventh. Once again, in five days, I had sold more than entire branches! How could these people not recognize that I was the knife-selling master?

In retrospect, I probably should have just left the conference and let them all go fuck themselves, but I couldn't. There was some part of me, some big part of me, that had to prove that I could fix it—or at least try. The conference up until that point had sucked. No one was having fun. Chuck had turned on me. Stuey had turned on me, it seemed. My goddamn fans had turned on me.

All I knew was that I had one chance to prove myself, and that was to deliver an impressive speech. One that remained unwritten. I had two hours to do it. I raced up to my room and sat down at the tiny table, smoking cigarette after cigarette, scribbling furiously.

23

I stood offstage watching Bud's glowing yellow mustache move in and out on his upper lip. I was terrified—almost panicked. My heart was beating hard. Bud reminded me of Coach O'Mally, and somehow the idea of being on the practice field seemed like an unbelievably tempting escape. "Usually the honor of giving the closing speech at this sales conference is reserved for executives like myself or salespeople with years of experience, but this summer we're going to break from tradition and have a relatively new knife salesman talk to you." (He laughed, but I could tell he had his doubts.) "There isn't much to say about this young man that you don't already know. He set the first-week push all-time record by a mind-blowing three thousand two hundred and eleven dollars. He lives in Michigan and sells out of the Covington, Kentucky, branch of the Ohio River Valley division."

"Cinci-Slicers!"

"Within the very brief seven weeks that he's been selling knives he has made just shy of twenty thousand dollars and has risen to the rank of the number one Apex salesman in the world. His closest competitor, Jorge Acuña, is nine thousand dollars behind him in sales for this summer. Just to put this into perspective for you, there are fifty thousand Apex salespeople worldwide. He has done all this at just nineteen years of age. Ladies and gentlemen, please welcome Jay Hauser."

I walked out, shook Bud's hand, and stood at the podium, waiting for the mild cheering to die down. I loosened my tie and pawed through my pockets, searching for my speech. There were around three thousand salespeople looking up at me. I was very nervous. I finally found my speech in my back pocket. My mouth was dry and when I spoke my voice died. "I—" I coughed. "I would like to congratulate Jorge and Camilla on their engagement." Jorge nodded at me, and smiled, not out of gratitude, but because hardly anybody else was clapping with me. I was tanking. I breathed out and tried to relax. I gripped the podium.

I had the speech memorized, so having it in front of me at the podium was a handicap. I was trying to find words on the page that I already knew—almost as if I were looking for an excuse not to say them. I lowered my eyes and was shocked to see that my handwriting was completely illegible. So I just looked up and said the first line, even though I couldn't decipher it. It came out angry. "I don't know what your plans are for the next three weeks. But I'll tell you what I'm going to do." I turned slowly and pointed at the giant white and black banner hanging behind me. It read, KICK ASS IN AUGUST. That was the title of my speech.

I glared out at the crowd. "I'm going to kick ass in August." There was a big applause. I felt a rush of adrenaline. My confidence was building. "Yeah." I grinned cool and slow. "I'm gonna kick some fuckin' ass in August. And let me tell you why. The first reason is that this fall . . . Dinner is on me. I've been mooching off of my friends for a long time. But this year I'm going to have my own apartment. One of my roommates is in the crowd with you right now. Stuart Parsi." Stuey whistled, nervously. "And Stuart, when we get back to school there's going to be a few changes. Our buddies are going to be luxuriating on a leather couch. A WRAPAROUND leather couch." They laughed at the way I said *wraparound,* like it was the coolest thing ever.

I took my time, letting the audience warm. "And when they watch movies, they're going to be enjoying a crystal-clear image radiating from a giant TV. They'll be listening to surround sound, probably drunk on Jameson."

Someone shouted, "Fuck yeah!", blasting a cloud of Reid's poison out the back door.

"Whoever said that," I paused and then smiled. "Can come by anytime."

The crowd roared with laughter. I looked out at Stuey. He was rocking back and forth, jutting his head out, like some dude at a heavy-metal concert waiting for a guitar solo to rip.

"AND call me crazy if you want, but I'm kind of partial to Oriental rugs and maybe I can find a moose head to hang on the wall. In my bedroom, though, I'm going to keep it simple. Silk sheets, a king-size bed, and a Bose alarm clock CD player radio, which will never wake me up, but only put me to sleep. And since Stuart's kind of a slob, I'm thinking that we'll need a maid. But that's only a small part of why I'm going to kick ass in August. One thing I've been thinking about lately is how incredibly fortunate we all are to have the opportunity to work for Apex." The audience settled, listening quietly. "And as much as I look forward to outfitting my apartment in the fall, what I have learned, or I should say, what *we* have learned and what we will learn through Apex, will far outweigh the monetary gains that we will accrue over the summer. Tenacity, for one. A work ethic. I used to be lazy. It is a wonder that I have actually worked a single day this summer. But I have. And am extremely grateful to have done it. Most important, I think that what Apex teaches us is how to overcome fear. Reid Tallenger." I paused. I won't say that Reid looked scared, it was more like worry mixed with guilt. "Reid told us this morning that his goal is to make over one million dollars selling knives. Just think for a second about what that means. Reid will have sold over two million dollars' worth of knives. Imagine the courage that must have taken. Every sale, every presentation, is a chance for rejection. I wish I had the kind of courage that Reid has. This August for me is an opportunity to gain more of it."

There was a low murmur in the ballroom, like an agreement, followed by a welling of emotion. The moral high ground was mine. "I remember Bud French's story about how he started selling knives." I was grinning so everybody got the joke. "About how Apex kept him out of jail." I laughed—the crowd did too. Bud waved at me. "Mine is pretty simple—my friend was running an office and I wanted to work for him. He trusted that I could do the work and he took the time to train me and has helped and supported me this entire summer. I have not thanked Stuart for it until this very moment. Like me, I am sure that whether we have said it or not, we all feel the same way about our managers. Thankfully, we have these next three weeks in August to show them our gratitude. This August, I'm going to kick ass for Stuart." I nodded at Stuart.

"There are many other reasons why I'm going to keep working hard for the next three weeks, but I'm just going to tell you one more. My senior year in high school I was on a football team that made it to the state championship two years in a row. The first year we were up by thirty-six points at halftime and lost by sixteen when the game ended. It was a record-setting comeback by the other team. The second time we made it there, we were ahead at half-time again. We went to the locker room, and one of our coaches came in all worked up. He told us how ten years earlier on that very day his brother was on a different football team at halftime and was ahead in a state championship game. He reached in his pocket, pulled out a ring, and held it up for us to see."

I raised my hand, fingers pinched together, as if I were holding a ring.

"And he said, 'This is the ring that my brother was given when he won that game. It was what he wanted since he was a very little boy. Two days after he won this ring, he was killed in a car accident.' Our coach, Coach Mac, proceeded to tell us that he kept that ring with him at all times, in his pocket, to remember his brother, whom he loved deeply. But to Coach Mac that ring was a symbol of the one thing that would help him to cope with the loss of his brother. And it was NOT that he had won a football game. It was that, to him, the ring meant that his brother had lived with no regrets." I paused. "No regrets. Every moment of every day is like halftime and you are ahead. You are fortunate for what you have done, for what you have worked for, but you still have the second half to complete the game. And it does not matter if you win or lose, as long as you have no regrets. I don't want to have any regrets this summer. I AM GOING TO KICK ASS IN AUGUST."

Connie played the music I had chosen exactly as I had instructed her, low at first and then louder as I walked across the stage. I felt the ground shake as the audience recognized the intro to Guns N' Roses' "Paradise City." They leapt up out of thier seats and started slamming their feet down on the floor. It was the second knife-selling conference where I had looked down from that stage to see Stuart crying in a sea of young hustlers. I jumped off the raised platform, just as Axl Rose sang "Oh won't you please take me home?" I passed through a mob of people trying to get at me, and hugged Stuart.

Stuart grabbed my head and shouted into my ear above the blaring music and screaming crowd, "That was fucking historic, dude. I don't think you believe a word of what you said, but you are one charismatic motherfucker." A mosh pit erupted around us when the second verse began.

My body was buzzing with adrenaline. I had saved the sales conference. I had defied all expectations and laid to rest any doubt whatsoever about my ability as a salesman, because I had sold the audience. I wished Isabelle had been there to see it.

When I finished packing I walked out onto the balcony hanging off the side of my room to smoke a cigarette. My room was on the sixth floor and faced Atlanta. I couldn't see the city, only a yellow and brown mass sitting on the horizon. It was some sort of pollution. I watched it swirling, around and around, like a wreath, twisting and turning on a bald head. Hotlanta. Hot damn.

24

Stuart had a dinner that night with the other managers as he did at the first conference. Tammy, Skeeter, and I were going to Alpharetta to spend the night at Woodsy's house. I was waiting for them in the lobby when I spotted Chuck Schick and John Patterson, another manager, sitting in soft leather seats around a table outside of the bar. They were eating peanuts out of a metal bowl and looking at each other and laughing. They were sharing some private joke. They had been wearing suits over the course of the conference and now both were wearing jeans and golf shirts. Both of their golf shirts were tucked into their pants and both wore leather belts, but whereas John wore leather dress shoes, Chuck wore leather dress sandals.

Patterson, trying hard to stop laughing, said, "Hauser, you want a drink?"

"I'll have a Jack and Ginger."

"May I see your ID?" I showed the waitress my fake. "Okay."

Patterson slipped twenty dollars onto her tray and winked at her. Chuck coughed out a peanut shard into his hand. I watched him rub it into his napkin.

"Hey, what do you guys think about a personalized catalog? I'm having one put together. Basically, you build a template that allows you to swap in isolated pieces of text and images, like a photo of the salesman who sent it. The photo would be on the cover, of course."

"What would be the point of that?" Chuck rocked back in his seat, and he fired a few peanuts up into his mouth. "A lot of salesmen send out catalogs with notes attached. It seems to work well." A peanut sailed past Chuck's ear. "Damn."

"There'd still be a note attached but the concept that I'm talking about would increase that personal connection and make the recipient more likely to buy."

John sucked at his teeth. "Sounds like a hell of an idea."

"Well, I'm making one, but I want to make them for a lot of people. Maybe get a percentage of their sales. They'd be professional quality. I'm experimenting with mattes, sheens, and stuff like that."

John shot a quick breath through his nose. Chuck picked up the metal bowl, now empty, and waved it at the waitress. "When I have the sample catalog ready I'm going to run it by Bud French. It should be ready by the time we go to Myrtle Beach."

Patterson stared at me for a long time. "You send me a copy of this catalog when you finish it."

"Take digital photographs of your salespeople before they leave for school and I will."

Chuck asked, "What's a digital photograph?"

"It's a photograph that you take with a digital camera. Anyway, if you can't find one I can scan celluloid photographs, but it'd be a lot simpler if you could just send me a CD with the images on it."

Chuck said, "Right. I think I can do that with regular photos at them machines at Wal-Mart."

"You still have to develop your film, and that costs money and you don't know what your photos are going to look like until then, but however you want to do it."

"Hauser," Patterson said, "Bud French wanted us to talk to you. There's going to be an opening for a manager in the Nashville office next summer. It's a great area. Cherry."

This was sort of a shock to me. "Let me think about it. I hadn't thought past this summer."

Chuck laughed. "You think you're going to win it?"

"Absolutely. Even if I sell ten thousand dollars in August, there's no way Acuña can catch up to me."

Stuart walked over. "How's it goin', fellas?"

Chuck leaned back. "Parsi, you ever hear of a digital camera before?"

"Yeah." He high-fived me and took a seat. "You need to borrow one?" I noticed he had on the same dress sandals as Chuck.

"Who ate all the goddamn peanuts?!"

What I was seeing looked like television fuzz, except it all kept speeding past from left to right. Occasionally a white stripe would worm its way through the frame. Yellow light reflected off the embankment whipping past, left to right. Slowly the fuzz began to stop. I could see the grass on the hillside clearly now. I heard the tires squeak. The passenger door in the front seat opened. The top of Tammy's head passed quickly through my field of view. Then I heard her puking.

I felt Skeeter straighten up in the seat next to me and try to look out the window. "Is she all right?"

"Yeah. She's just puking." Woodsy was sitting in the driver's seat. "Too much beer."

Tammy heaved. "No. Huuuhha." Gasp. "The margaritas did it. Huuuhhhhaa."

Woodsy started laughing. Tammy wiped her mouth, facing into the backseat of the car.

"Sorry guys." She looked in at me. "Jay, you okay?"

I wasn't that drunk. I just didn't want to move. The car rocked when Tammy got back in the passenger-side seat. The weeds and the grass and rocks and all the things I could see started moving left to right again and then I couldn't make anything out. Just the fuzz, the white break-dancing lines and the yellow flashes. I closed my eyes and fell asleep.

25

I got back to my mother's house midafternoon the follow-ing day, ate lunch, studied my list of names, and spent the evening setting up appointments. When I finished making calls I was poking around Coulter's room, looking for a book to read while I was on the can, when I found something rather humorous. Slipped on the shelf next to a stack of books was a Polo ad torn out from a magazine with a male model that looked exactly like Coulter. He had curly blond hair, the same sort of chiseled features with girlie lips, and very blue eyes. My mother had written on the page: "Maybe a way to make some money while you're in school? Think about it. It'll be our secret."

I laughed at the photo. When Coulter and I were growing up our family used to get stopped all the time by people telling my mother how cute her children were and how beautiful Coulter was. This happened at swim meets, every time we flew, waiting to be picked up at school, in grocery stores. All the time. I wondered how many times people stopped my mother when she was with just Coulter and not the older, uglier brother. Constantly, I'm sure. Coulter really was a beautiful kid.

Clearly, my mother had left this for Coulter when I wasn't around, and instead of throwing it away, he stuck it in the shelf. Maybe as a reminder to think about it? Maybe he was already modeling? Impossible. I thought about making fun of Coulter for it, but then changed my mind. I figured my mother didn't want me to know that she had left a note for Coulter and not me, so I put the ad back and found something else to read.

Later, Brooke's father called and said that since it was almost Brooke's birthday (I'd totally forgotten) he'd been thinking of little surprises for her and happened to discover one of her favorite singers (Natalie Imbruglia) was playing at Pine Knob. He bought tickets for the concert and thought that I should take her and reveal the surprise. I really didn't want to commit to hearing Brooke screeching the lyrics "You're a little late, I'm already torn!" But since I'd hadn't planned anything yet and there would have to be a plan I told him I thought it was a great idea, which it was. He told me to come by his office and pick up the tickets.

"Jay, you know I'm quite fond of you and I'm very proud of the way that you've comported yourself this summer, with your job. Both Mrs. Ambrose and I are—" Something on his desk caught his eye. I couldn't tell what. He continued. "You have to trust me that Brooke grew up in a house where I worked quite a bit and was often gone, so I know she understands the way it is with men who want to be providers." There was something forced in what he was saying. Not rehearsed but more like he knew I needed to know this or someone had told him I did. I couldn't tell exactly what. I sensed it.

"I want you to know that if things continue the way they are going between you and Brooke and you have a continued interest in business, which from the look of it I expect you do, you might think about coming to work at PW&A." That was the name of his company—Pratt, Whitney & Ambrose. "I love my daughter. She is the only child I've got. And I've come to care about you very much. We have a program that starts in the summer before your junior year where you could intern for the company. It's a very competitive program. If you do well, we would invite you back the following year." He opened a small black box on his desk, looked inside it, and then shut it. "The point is this. I can help you. After my parents passed away and I moved from Grosse Pointe to Bloomfield Hills, I didn't have anyone looking out for me when I was young, so I know how it is. And I wouldn't want you and Brooke to have to go through that."

I didn't really know how to respond to this. I had been offered jobs before, but not from my girlfriend's father.

"I really do believe in you. You're a charming young man who will succeed at anything he chooses in life. I'm sure of it."

Nobody had ever said anything so nice to me. I said, "Thank you."

He nodded, let out a laugh, and then slapped his hand down. "You're welcome." He reached out for the box. He looked at me, sideways. He waited a second, then he slowly creaked it open halfway. I sort of leaned over and tried to casually glance inside. He instantly snapped it shut. "Consistency, Jay. Be consistent in how you act. It will save you a hell of a lot of grief later on in life, particularly if you decide to marry."

Just then the phone in his office started blinking. He picked it up, listened to it for a second, muttered something, and put it back down. "Hold on a second." He left me standing in his office. I listened to the central air groan. My heart was beating surprisingly fast. I waited until he was out of the room and I opened the box. In it was a moldy chocolate éclair.

I ate dinner with my mother and Coulter at the dining room table.

"I spoke to your uncle John today." John was my mother's brother. He was older than her and a super successful businessman. "He asked all about you. I told him that you were working so hard you were going to be like him one day."

I looked up to John, so this made me feel kind of good and I thought about saying something, but I saw that Coulter got a little jealous when my mother said this. Coulter idolized John and wanted to be a big-time business guy himself one day. I just wanted to impress Isabelle, so I let it drop. Then I remembered something. "How much time does John spend in Charleston?"

"Oh . . . I think he's there half of the year at least."

"Well, I might be somewhat near there later in the summer."

"If you are you really must call John and Elaine. I would be extremely disappointed if you didn't."

I noticed the voodoo doll I'd given Coulter propped up on one of the crescent tables that flanked the door to the kitchen.

"Coulter, why is your voodoo doll out here and not in your room?" Fancy's snout rested on my thigh. I lifted her snout off my leg, kissed her on the lips, gave her half a piece of pork tenderloin, and then returned her snout to its position. She jerked away and barked at me.

My mother said, "When you were little you could always kiss a dog or a cat on the lips, but you hated kissing people."

"Things change. Coulter, why isn't the voodoo doll in your room?"

"I—it scared me, so I gave it to Mom."

I laughed. "C'mon. It's a nice-looking voodoo doll."

"You told me you told the guy in the store to cast a spell on Sherianne. That's weird."

"Speaking of Sherianne." My mother finished chewing a piece of lettuce. I was on the verge of snapping. Not that I cared how my mother felt about her, but I just didn't want to hear another goddamn lecture. "She came by yesterday. To drop off your mail. She told me she was sad that you hadn't gone to see her except to sell her knives. I actually felt sorry for her."

"You're kidding me."

"No. I know what it's like, to be left."

"Yeah . . . I probably should stop by to say hello . . . Was there a lot of mail?"

"Yes. It was too heavy for me to lift."

"I wonder what it is."

"Looked like a lot of magazines."

Fancy started barking again. "Are you looking forward to your trip with Brooke?"

"No. Not really."

"Why in heavens aren't you?"

"I don't know. To hell with vacations, for one. And I know Brooke's going to want to ride horses and all that and I'm not exactly thrilled to see her teetering around on top of some horse talking about fudge."

My mother and Coulter both laughed. She asked, "Then why are you going?"

"Brooke's forcing me into it." I thought about Brooke's dad offering me a job and began to wonder if Brooke had anything to do with it.

Suddenly my mom asked, "Do you think you'll marry her? Everyone in town wants you two to marry, but I think it's a bad idea. I think you need to get away from here."

"Yeah, well."

There was a long lull in the conversation.

After a while Coulter said, "Jay . . . No. Forget it, I don't even want to ask."

"No, what?"

"I was thinking about going to see a movie tonight."

"Dude. I'm sorry. I've got . . ."

After dinner, I picked up the brick of mail wrapped tightly in twine, carried it to Courtney's room, cut it open, and let it all spill out onto the bed. I tossed all the nonfootball mail from Dartmouth immediately and set aside the football stuff to read later. There were several invitations to graduation parties long past. I noticed one from Danny Breck. I had played lacrosse with Danny. He was a year younger than me and somehow I had forgotten to put his mother's name on my call list. I added it and then discovered something that almost made me pass out.

Three letters from Isabelle. I tore into the first. "Hi Jay! Thank you so much for the champagne, wine, and cigarettes. You can trust that I will not let my ass get too hard here. And yes, these will help. Thank you so much. I wish you were here. Well, sort of, only because it's good to make new friends and have new experiences. Does that sound corny? To you, probably . . . How are you? Your note was so short. Why haven't you called? Have you sold any knives? I bet you have. Please get in touch with me. The best time to reach me is either late at night, after I've finished my shift, early in the morning, or during the day, between three and five. I have so much to tell you. I hope you're well. Love, Isabelle."

The next one read, "Jay . . . ? Nice response. Why haven't you called? Are you staying at Sherianne's? You put her address on the box you sent me." Damn. I fucked up. "I thought you were staying at your mother's. Anyway, things are good. There are some boys here that like me. How could they resist? I know that probably drives you crazy. One of them is okay. I've been riding a lot. I take the horses out on the weekend and I love it. You would die if you saw some of the stuff I've been doing. I go so fast through the canyons. No one can keep up. Not even the boys. Call! Love, Isabelle."

The third letter: "To the jerk who will not write me back, What is your problem? Maybe your retarded girlfriend killed you or kidnapped you. I have a lot of nice things to say, but I'm not going to write any of them because I am mad. I have included a picture of me in this letter to show you how hot I am. I have lost a lot of weight. You can guess how." (Isabelle confessed to me that at various points in her life she had resorted to bulimia to lose weight.) I looked at her photograph. She looked hot, thin, and tan. Her hair was almost entirely blond now. The photograph was taken in a bar, with a mountain view. There was a girl standing next to her. They both looked drunk and trampy. It kind of pissed me off that she was making herself puke again. She did look good, though. I've got to give her that. I continued reading. "The girl in the picture with me is Sally. She turned me onto it again. Fuck you for not calling and for forgetting my birthday FUCKER! Just kidding, but you did forget my birthday. I was sure you would call. Where in God's name are you? I miss you. Love, I.S."

I lay on the bed for a while, nearly out of breath. I sat up, reread the letters several times, studied Isabelle's photo, and thought about what to do. It was eight o'clock Colorado time. She was probably working, but even on the off chance that I did get through to her I didn't have time to talk. I wondered if I should call at all. I'd been so pissed at her all summer for not writing me that it was hard to shake off that feeling and figure out how to respond. I didn't want to do anything rash. She wrote me three times. Three times without ever hearing back from me. What the hell did that mean? Did it mean anything? Fuck. I wanted to think about it but I didn't have time.

I drove the Escort over to the Nakamoris'. Toby showed me what he had done for the catalog. He asked about payment. I tossed him fifty bucks and left.

Brooke called. She told me to call her as soon as I woke up and that she could come the following morning and pick me up with breakfast already made so that we could eat in her car on the way up north. We were taking her car because Brooke wanted to bring bikes and they wouldn't fit into the trunk of my father's BMW. She asked if she could see me, but I said I was too tired and going home.

I drove to the lake that I often visited. I had a couple warm beers in the trunk. I could hear a warm breeze buzzing through the chain-link fence behind me. Many of the houses across the lake were lit up on the outside, but dark inside, except a few, where I could see the lights left on in the kitchen or a TV flashing colors across the surface of the lake.

The flicker reminded me of the candelabra in our old house glowing and dripping wax and how it reflected in the polished wood of our dining room table. One time Elsa got up on the table. My dad shouted, "Get that goddamn cat off the table!" Elsa flinched and dropped her tail down over the flaming candlesticks. There was a quick flash of red and the cat shot off the table like a rocket, her tail smoking.

The wax in the candelabra would overflow and the white beads would roll down the curved cups as far as they could before cooling and freezing in place. It would take many dinners before the wax would reach the tabletop.

Often when my dad was away or sometimes when he wasn't, my mother would ask Coulter to give her a back rub in her bed. But it wasn't really a back rub. She liked to have him tickle her back. She would lie on her stomach and Coulter would sit next to her and run his fingertips slowly up her back, across her bare shoulders to her neck, and then sweep down her spine and do it over again.

My mother loved it so much that she would pay Coulter a dollar to do this. I asked if I could do it and get paid a dollar too. She let me try. I remember the way the room smelled—her perfume and very clean sheets. There was a very high steeple ceiling in her bedroom, with a ceiling fan. When I finished giving my mother the back rub she told me that she didn't like the way I did it and so I never did it again. I was nine years old.

I threw a rock into the blackest part of the lake. I heard it hit the water, but I didn't see a splash. I waited and a few seconds later tiny waves rippled across a band of the flickering silver film. I wanted to go swimming, but didn't. Something was bugging the hell out of me. It wasn't Isabelle. It wasn't Brooke. I sat there trying to figure it out for a long time.

When Brooke and I passed the Grayling exit on I-75, I thought about how much I'd like to forget about Mackinac and go to my family's cottage on Torch Lake. Brooke wouldn't go there, though.

She came to Torch Lake the previous summer with my father, Sherianne, and me during the two weeks that my grandparents stayed there. Brooke had baked a bunch of cookies as a thank-you for them. When we got there Brooke took the cookies to my grandmother.

Brooke smiled through her long black hair, which swung from the sides of her face as she held up the glass cooking pan. "Here are some chocolate chip cookies. Thank you so much for having me."

"Brrreeee," my grandmother said, carefully pronouncing the incorrect name. "I have made lemon bars. Why don't you go back and put those in the car?" My grandmother turned abruptly and walked back inside the cottage.

Obediently, Brooke hobbled back to the car and placed the pan in the backseat. She closed the door and started sobbing. She would not stop for hours. Afterward, she said that she had never in her life felt so entirely unwelcome. My grandmother, of course, would not apologize, nor would anybody even dare suggest that she might want to—myself included, so Brooke spent the rest of her time at the cottage hiding from my grandmother and crying whenever she was left alone.

Brooke smiled at me sweetly. I drove on a little farther. "Hey," I said as seriously as possible. "I think my grandmother is at the cottage. Got any cookies handy?" I stared laughing hysterically. Brooke turned up the song playing on her mix.

No cars are allowed on Mackinac Island. Brooke had brought seven bags for our three-day trip. I was standing in a parking lot waiting for the ferry when I discovered this. "Brooke. How are we going to get our bags and our bikes onto the ferry, off of the ferry, and over to the hotel?"

Brooke was laughing—God knows why. "I don't know. I didn't know I brought so much."

"What's that bag?"

"It has all of my shampoos and everything."

I picked up the bag. "Wait, this is a goddamn hanging bag. You have a hanging bag for your shampoo?"

"Well. It's not just shampoo. It's my soaps and my moisturizers." She was still laughing.

"I don't understand what's so hilarious here."

"It's just. I don't know. It's just funny. You *knew* I had that bag." I gripped my hair and tugged it back. I had noticed the bag hanging in her bathroom in her house, but I thought it was a permanent fixture, like a sink. I didn't explain this. I guess she was laughing so hard because she was trying to show me how girlie she was or something, but I could see the ferry approaching in the distance and didn't really want to hang out in the parking lot for another hour.

"Okay. We can hang the bags off each side of the handlebars of our bikes. I'm going to go buy our tickets." I bought our outbound tickets, plus tickets for the 10 A.M. ferry returning on Wednesday.

I could see a rain cloud moving toward Mackinac. It was moving at about the same rate as the ferry. I started hoping that it would catch up to us and soak the ferry. Then I started having this fantasy about how the rain cloud was a huge storm—and we were back in the old days when ships sunk in the Great Lakes all the time. The speedboat coming up to our stern was a pirate vessel. That Brooke was a strumpet I'd stolen from the pirates. They were chasin' us down, tryin' to catch us before we got to the old fort . . .

"When are you going to quit that?"

"Wanna puff?"

She shook her head. "Gross."

I looked back at the storm. I wished to hell that it would beat us to the island. I put my arm around Brooke's shoulder and pulled her close to me. "When it starts coming down, we're gonna have to run. We're gonna have to fucking run! Or we'll be caught—like a wagon train in an Injin barbecue! Whaddya think of that, my little dime-store floozy?"

She nuzzled up to my neck. "I love the way you smell."

The rain did not beat us, but we didn't beat it by much either. The storm's shadow swept down the hill, wiping out the blinding sun at our backs. The wind began to gust, hard, through the main street. I accidentally nudged an obese woman in front of me as I exited the ferry. She turned around and glared at me, making a pig face. "Watch it, buddy."

"Sorry." She turned back and I nudged her again.

"Hey!"

"I slipped, sorry."

"Don't do it again."

"Okay."

She turned back around, and this time I shoved Brooke into her. When the lady snapped back around, I pretended like I didn't know Brooke.

"What the hell are you doing?"

"What?"

"You keep bumping into me."

"It was her!"

"Jay!"

"Who? I have no idea who the hell Jay is." I turned to the fat lady. "What's going on here?"

We had reached the end of the gangway; the lady grunted, and waddled over to a guy who made her look skinny, pointed at us, and started bitching. I walked over to the right, where the ferry workers were unloading our bikes.

"Jay. What has gotten into you?"

"Haven't you ever been to middle school?"

"Yes."

"Then you should know better."

"What?"

"Shut up and kiss me." She kissed me, slow and sexy. "Let's make tracks, baby."

We pedaled our bikes on Main Street, the cold wind blowing up the back of my shirt and chilling my ass. I could hear the rain hitting the pavement behind me. Brooke was ahead of me. "This is it." She wheeled her bike to the left, up a driveway, and stopped under an awning. I followed her. The rain grazed my ankles. I jumped straight up off of my bike and let it crash into a rosebush.

Brooke had made the reservation, but I wanted to pay. I wanted to spend some (hell, any) of the money I'd made that summer—badly. I handed the clerk my credit card and asked if we had the nicest room in the hotel.

"We like to consider ourselves a bed-and-breakfast, but no, currently you do not. All of our rooms are very nice, but there is a suite available on the third floor that boasts a street-side view of the harbor, dressing room, walk-in closet—"

"We'll take it."

Brooke said, "Jay, we should split it."

"No. This is my treat. You've been dying to take this trip and by God I want to give it to you."

"The room is four hundred and ninety-five dollars."

I stuck my hand out. "May I have the key now, please? My buns are slightly frozen." I heard Brooke snicker.

"Of course." The clerk handed me the key.

I tackled Brooke from behind and fucked her on the bear rug beside the bed. I came. I pushed myself up off of her, peeled my shirt off, and hucked it to the floor. I made a little hop and hurled myself crosswise onto the bed, my pants still around my ankles.

"Turn on the fucking heat, please." I felt a draft on the back of my bare legs. "Oh. And you might want to close the door."

Brooke screamed and I fell into a deep sleep.

It was very dark in the room when I woke up. Brooke's blue moonlit face was propped up on her hands, six inches from my lips. Her electric blue eyes, now even bluer, painted by the same light illuminating her face, were transfixed on mine.

"What time is it?"

"Ten-thirty?"

"Jesus. I must have been tired."

I noticed the salty light blue riverbeds running down Brooke's cheeks.

"I was crying because I've been thinking about how much I love you."

"How long have you been awake?"

"I don't know. I slept for a few hours." A tear appeared in the corner of her right eye. "That's a lie. I haven't slept at all."

I touched the tear with my finger and it dissolved into my skin. I told Brooke I loved her. She told me she loved me one hundred times more. She fell asleep. As soon as her eyes fluttered shut, my heart began to race, as if injected with liquid terror.

I saw the future as clearly as I saw the dried moonlit tear on Brooke's cheek. I was caught in a trap, and if I didn't cut myself out of it I was going to be waking up to this same scene thousands of times in my life. In some supposedly beautiful place where I didn't want to be with a beautiful woman who loved me no matter what— I could literally do anything to Brooke and she would still love me in her crazed fanatical way. But did I love her?

I got up and sat in a big leather chair by the window. I was naked and cold. I wrapped myself in the itchy blanket under my ass. I stared out the window at the cold wet cobblestone street and realized that the blue light, which moments earlier I had mistaken for semiprecious moonlight, was in fact beaming down from the bed-and-breakfast's fluorescent sign hanging above our window. I could read it reflected backward in the puddles dotting the street. Goddamn, I thought. I have to get back home so I can sell more knives.

Noon. After Brooke had eaten her breakfast and I had drunk my coffee, we went for a bike ride. We made it halfway around the island when I noticed another large gray and white cloud approaching the side of the island from which we had just come.

2:15. After showering and having sex and warming up from being caught in the rain, Brooke said that even though it was drizzling she would like to go horseback riding. I wanted to get out of the room, so I agreed to take her on the dreaded ride.

5:30. Brooke and I had been standing under the awning of a toilet shack for the past forty-five minutes, holding the reins of our horses. We spotted the shack from the trail after the drizzle turned into a downpour.

6:45. Brooke wanted to stop by the Grand Hotel and look at the longest wooden porch in the world. I refused to step onto it. I watched her taking pictures of an old couple drinking coffee. I could hear her goddamn baby voice shrieking, "You're so cute! I just want to squeeze you!"

9:00 was the time we had reservations at the dining room of the Peninsula Hotel. When we arrived, five minutes late, the dining

224

room was completely empty save the waitstaff, hostess, and jazz pianist. Brooke looked hot and a bit like a hooker in a lace dress with no slip underneath that she'd worn to my high school prom one year earlier. I was already very drunk and wearing the same suit I wore in New Orleans the night I fucked Beth. I tried to rub out a cum stain on the sly with my napkin, under the table. When I tried to pay, Brooke insisted that she pay, since I was paying for everything else and she wanted the dinner to be her treat. The bill, by the way, was a doozy.

11:22. I came on Brooke for the last time. I stumbled out of bed backward and caught myself before crushing the small table beside the chair that I'd been sitting in the previous evening. I picked up the bottle of Maker's Mark that I'd bought at the liquor store on the way home from dinner and swigged it, staring at Brooke's ass facing me on the bed. Brooke turned around and told me to "be careful not to drink too much." I took another hard swig and told her to set the alarm for nine-thirty because I didn't want to miss the ferry. I swigged again. She fiddled with the alarm clock.

"Goddamn it!"

Brooke jerked awake. "What?"

"You set the clock but didn't turn the fuckin' alarm on. It's nine forty-seven. We gotta go!" I whipped off the sheet. Brooke's naked body writhed in the cold.

She moaned.

I leapt out of bed, jumped into my pants, and grabbed my shirt. "I'm going to check out!"

I ran out the door and heard her plead, "Wait. Jay . . ."

"Pack!" I shouted as I rocketed down the steps.

I fired my card across the desk at the same woman who'd checked us in. "We're going to miss our ferry."

"You're already checked out."

"What do you mean? It's automatic or something?"

"Your friend staying with you came down at six o'clock this morning. She said you'd be leaving at noon and insisted that I accept payment on her credit card."

"But I want to pay."

"I've already run her card. You will be receiving a wake-up call at eleven-thirty and"—she reached into her desk drawer and pulled out two ferry tickets—"she asked that Samuel, my gardener, pick these up for you."

She handed them to me along with my credit card and smiled.

I barged back into the room. Brooke was on her knees, packing. "Brooke, I told you I wanted to pay."

"Please, it's my gift!"

"So what, you got up at six, changed all our plans, and then forced that bitch into taking your credit card?"

"I thought you'd want to sleep in. You were so drunk last night."

"Listen, it's a nice thought, but I've got to get my ass home. I have a meeting at four o'clock. I seem to remember you saying something about having to go to work . . ."

"Not until eight."

"We'll, you're gonna be early. Let's go."

I heard her sandals snapping against the stairs behind me. I yanked my bike from the rack. "C'mon. Hurry." I slung the bags down onto the handlebars, took a few quick pedals, descended the driveway, turned sharply to my right, screamed, "Let's go!" and hauled ass toward the ferry station.

The entire way, I had been shouting encouragements over my shoulder. "C'mon, champ! Only four more blocks. You're a big girl, pedal like one!" I was doing it to make up for my general nastiness earlier in the morning. Unfortunately, there was no one behind me to benefit from them. I didn't realize this until I reached the ferry station a few minutes early.

I pedaled back as quickly as I could and finally saw her, carrying her bags and pushing her bike. Her legs and arms were bloody. Her face was drenched in sweat, and she was crying again.

Here's what happened. As I sped ahead of her down the drive, shouting "Let's go!", she, in an effort to catch up, pedaled harder than she should have. Her left foot slipped off the pedal as she made the turn and she jerked the handlebars to the right. When the handlebars dipped right, the bag hanging from that side fell off. The weight of the bags on the left side then whipped the handlebars to the left, midturn. Brooke tried to steady herself by slamming her feet on the ground and pushing back on the flailing handlebars, which only resulted (after her sandals ripped off her feet) in the back of her legs getting locked between the ground and the pedals of the bike as her momentum continued to move forward. The bike was trapped both under her chest and behind her legs as she went skidding sideways across the street at the foot of the drive.

A family on vacation witnessed the accident. After they checked to see that Brooke was okay and helped her gather her belongings and broken sandals they told her that she should never, ever, talk to me again. Apparently, I could be heard shouting my encouragements from quite a ways away.

I could hear the vacuum cleaner from the patio. The door was open. I stepped inside. Revelacion, my mother's maid, looked up at me and smiled. Revelacion was Jamaican and very dark.

"Helllla. Jaaaaii, you been away, ya?"

"Yeah. I was up north."

"Nooooo. I mean, you been away studjin."

"I was at school for the year, but I've been home for a while too. Working a lot."

"Yesssss. I kno'bout yer werkin. D'niess."

"Pardon me."

"D'niess!"

"The knives?"

"Yeh. Y'mom tell me 'bout d'niess."

"Cool."

"Y'got a'ting odder den niess?"

"What?"

"Odder den niess."

"Revelacion, I'm really not understanding you."

She held up her finger. "Yer modder be home soon. A'right?"

"Okay." I carried my bag around to Courtney's room.

I can't remember a time when we didn't have a maid. For a while, every maid I knew was named Louise. The maid we had the longest, while I was growing up, was named Louise. "Weesy," my grandparents' maid, was named Louise. Both of those Louises were black, and my best friend's maid, also named Louise, was white but spoke like a black person.

I was really sad when the first Louise quit, because it was my fault that she left. I had set a trip wire for Coulter, in his room, by running a piece of fishing line from his bed to his dresser and forgot about it. Louise discovered the trip wire before Coulter did and almost broke her neck. She was vacuuming when it got her.

Growing up there was always a steady stream of carpenters, painters, landscapers, lawn mowers, dog groomers, decorators, electric fence fixers, tree planters, tree surgeons, and electricians flowing through and around our houses. I hardly ever came home from school when there wasn't someone doing something. It was comforting in some weird way. Often I worried that one day whatever work was being done would be completed and the workers would not come again. The work was never finished.

When my father left, my mother could no longer afford to employ everyone. Anyway, finding Revelacion working reminded me of the way it used to feel when I came home, and I liked that.

I was in the kitchen when I heard the clanging of my mother's keys. Her car key chain was Coulter's silver teething ring, which made a very distinctive jingle when she moved it. The next thing I heard were Fancy's toenails ticking on the tile floor as she ran down the hallway, rounded the corner, and came up to me begging for food.

My mother followed, sporting a pair of large yellow sunglasses that looked like the kind you'd wear at the shooting range. She set her purse down. "Oh, please don't make such a mess while Revelacion is here. She just cleaned the kitchen."

"Sorry. I was starving."

"How was your weekend?"

"Dismal. As I predicted, Brooke forced me into taking a horse ride with her."

"Did she fall off?"

"About seventeen times."

"What are you trying to make?"

"A crab Louis sandwich."

"You use chili sauce instead of ketchup." She moved toward the fridge. "Why don't you keep me company while I make you lunch?"

I closed my appointment book and we chatted while she worked. My mother also made a salad with baby lettuce, pine nuts, and crumbled blue cheese. She sat with me while I ate the lunch and had a quarter of my sandwich. She asked me if I remembered how I used to help her cook dinner when I was a child.

The lunch was filling and I felt like taking a nap afterward, but I had things to do, so I went over my appointments for the rest of the week, compared that list to my call list, cross-referenced names, and looked for ways to build connections. Then I started thinking about how to use the rest of my day. Maybe I could set up more appointments, make more calls. The rest of the week and the early part of the following week were pretty well booked. Maybe I should start making calls to confirm the appointments.

I was thinking about all this when my mother led Revelacion into the kitchen. "Jay. Revelacion has something to ask you."

"Sure. What?"

"Wha'j'got odder den niess?"

"Sorry, say again."

"Wha'j'got to sell odder den niess?"

"Oh. Well. There's some cookware and ummmm . . . A vegetable peeler. Some spoons. Why?"

"I wanna buy somteen."

"What? No. Revelacion, you can't. Really. You don't have to."

My mother was standing beside her. "Jay. Revelacion wants to buy something from you. Why don't you show her what you have?"

"I'm happy to do it, but Revelacion, this stuff is kind of expensive, I don't think you should—"

"Jay. I pay Revelacion good money. She can spend it however she likes."

"C'mon. Mom. I know how much you pay her." My mother paid Revelacion sixty dollars a day.

"It's good money."

"I . . . Mom. I don't . . . I can't do it."

"If Revelacion wants to buy something you should sell it to her. She knows she doesn't have to buy anything, but if she wants to it's her decision."

"Revelacion. Are you sure you want to buy something?"

"Yessss."

"Let me get my things."

I got my bag of knives and came back. "Now, Revelacion. You really don't have to buy any of these knives. In fact, when I'm done selling this summer you can have this whole set if you'd like."

"No. I don't wan' d'neiss."

"Why don't you want the knives?"

"Because I'm afraid m'son will stab somebody wid'm."

"Wait. Revelacion. You're afraid your son will stab somebody?"

"Yeh . . . He's no good. He probably try to stab me." She smiled wide as hell. I was confused. I looked at my mother. She was giggling.

"Okay. So you can't buy any knives because your son will stab you. How about a pot? But I'm telling you, the cheapest one we have is one hundred and fifty dollars."

"Dat's too much. What about dis?" She walked over to my mother's counter and pointed to a block of knives. "I like dis. How much is dis?"

"That particular set of knives costs just under six hundred dollars."

"No. Just dis." She tapped the block.

"The block?"

"Yessssss."

"Revelacion, forgive me for asking, but why would you want a block of knives if you're not going to put knives into it?"

"I like d'look. What odder tings you got?"

I stared down at my gear. "Hmmmm. Things that don't cut. There's the spoon. The fork has sharp surfaces. The peeler?"

Revelacion walked over and stared at the items on display. She picked up the turning fork, felt the points, and put it down. Then she picked up the spoon, made scooping movements in the air, placed it on the counter next to the block, and said, "How much fer dat?"

"The block is ninety-nine dollars. The spoon is twenty-five. That's one hundred and twenty-four. If you buy the block and the spoon I can give you this excellent vegetable peeler for free."

"Okay. I buy it. Kin I pay in cash or do I need a check?"

Coulter came home.

"I've got to tell you something."

He followed me into his room and I closed the door. "What's up?"

"You won't believe what just happened."

"What?"

"I just sold Revelacion a knife block and a spoon."

"What?"

"She wouldn't buy knives because she was afraid that her son would stab her with them."

"Jay, tell me you did not really just sell Revelacion knives."

"Like I said, I didn't sell her knives, just the block and the spoon."

Coulter started laughing. "You can't let Revelacion buy anything from you. She can't afford it."

"My God, I know. Mom practically forced me into it."

"You've got to make her cancel the order."

"I can't."

"Why not?"

"That would be rude."

"Jay, Revelacion does not need a knife block and a spoon. How much did it cost?"

"One hundred and twenty-five dollars. I threw in a vegetable peeler—for free."

Coulter started laughing uncontrollably. "Oh my God. Did you just say you threw in a vegetable peeler?"

"Yeah. It's a twenty-dollar item."

"Oh my God." Coulter started shaking his head, still laughing to himself. Then he looked at me. "Jay. I'm going to demand that you do something for me."

"What is it?"

"Just say yes."

"What? I'm not going to force Revelacion to cancel the order, if that's what you want."

"No. That's not it. Just say yes."

"Tell me what it is."

"You have got to come up north with me."

"When?"

"Right now. I'm going right now. Wex and Anneke are flying in tonight. So is Uncle Jay. I think Dad may go up too."

I thought about this. Wex was our cousin. His name was actually Jay, like his father, "Uncle Jay," and me, of course. Anneke was Wex's wife. We're a pretty close family and I hadn't seen them since Christmas, so it was pretty tempting to go up. Plus, I missed the hell out of the lake. "I'd love to, but I've got appointments all set up for tomorrow."

"No. You have to change them. I have not hung out with you once this summer. All you've been doing is selling your damn knives, which you promised you'd give me a percentage of if I gave you names."

"C'mon. *That was a lie.*"

"Please, you have to come up north. I haven't asked you to do anything in a fricking long time, but I'm just asking you this one thing. Please be my brother and just come up north with me and stay the night. You can come back early in the morning if you want."

"Dude. I just got back from Mackinac. It was a four-hour drive."

"It's only three and a half to the cottage. Just drive with me. If you want to turn around and come back as soon as we get there, I won't stop you, but you haven't spent any time with me this summer. You haven't seen Wex and Anneke or Uncle Jay since Christmas and you haven't even been to the cottage yet this summer. You have to come."

"Coulter . . . Come on . . ." Frankly, it was okay if I missed one more day of knife selling. I still had a healthy lead over Acuña, and if I busted my ass when I got back there was no way he could stop me from winning the summer season. Before we hit the road I called and moved all of my appointments to the following week. It was complicated and a pain in my ass persuading customers not to cancel, but to my credit, I didn't lose a single client. I was able to reschedule them all.

Coulter and I stopped by the Nakamoris' house on the way. I had to check on Toby's progress and I wanted to show Coulter what we'd been up to. I gave Toby more instructions, paid him some money, and we left.

I pointed the Beamer at the on-ramp. Coulter was silent. I could tell he had something on his mind. I asked, "What'd you think?"

"I think it's weird."

"It's supposed to seem like a kid made it."

"No, the whole thing. Ty Nakamori. His son. It's all weird."

"What do you mean?"

"The whole situation. It creeps me out."

"What's creepy about it?"

"You're paying some sixteen-year-old kid to fake a catalog and his dad's in on it."

"I'll admit, it's not typical but I don't see anything creepy about it."

"I asked Dad about Ty Nakamori. He said a lot of people are asking questions about the way he does business."

"How does Dad know about him?"

"He just does."

Coulter was staring out of the window, jaw clenched, lips pursed and frosted white.

"What bug crawled up your ass?"

"I don't like what you're doing."

"I'm not doing anything."

"Okay."

We drove on in silence for a while until Coulter asked, "And what was that weird music coming from the Nakamoris' basement?"

"That was just Ty singing karaoke." We both did not stop laughing for a while.

27

When we got to the cottage I was sweaty and nauseated from all of the cigarettes I'd smoked. Wex and Anneke weren't there yet. I unlocked the door, put the key back in the light fixture, and stepped into the cottage.

Torch Lake is visible from the car as you're driving along the Alden Highway, from Lake Street, from across the street where you park, and, obviously, walking up to the cottage, but there's nothing like walking through the cottage to get to it. It's like taking your time opening the last Christmas present. Walk to the left, past the staircase, and smell the cedar from the sports closet beneath it and turn into the living room. A big bay window frames the lake like a postcard. Through the smaller window to the right of the back door the swing and the slab dock beyond it are visible, stretching out into the shallow water along the eastern shore.

The cottage typically smells a little stuffy from the trapped air because it usually hasn't been used in a couple of weeks, but the smell is also familiar, like the first hint of something beloved. Across the pink carpet is the back door, and when opened the air blowing across the lake rushes past, both warm and cool, instantly fills the house, and then empties out the front door, which was left open. If someone else comes along, he will normally walk to the kitchen, which is on the street side, and open that door, so the air that's trapped on that side of the house will flow out. And the cottage will feel exactly the way it always did.

Coulter and I walked out to the end of the dock. We were still wearing our shoes, which is another thing to eliminate in order to get the full effect, but it's better to feel the soft wooden slats flexing under your shoes and then feel them bending under your bare feet, so you feel how much better it is. Anyway, I always walk right out to the end, get down on one knee, and dip my hand in.

It was August and the lake was warmer than usual. "I wanna swim this second and not a second later."

"Me too."

"All right. Let's put our suits on."

Unlike most lakes, Torch has a sandy bottom, hard packed and granular under your feet. The water is clear, so when you look down off the end of the dock you see the yellow of the sand. Farther out, it becomes light blue, and because the lake is extremely deep, there are various shades of blue that turn purple in the deepest places.

After I got in, I walked out a little farther, pretending like I was in some deep state of contemplation, and tried to tackle Coulter. Of course, he was thinking the same thing and before I knew it I was underwater and everything slowed down to a chilly, crystal-clear drift and then I came up and took another breath and then dove back, stretching slowly away from the dock and out into something that is so comfortable and perfect that I closed my eyes and let myself sink until my shoulder touched the sandy bed beneath me. The feeling is so nice and relaxing that I sometimes think that the lake is daring me to fall asleep. That time I did not try it.

Coulter and I swam and then quickly began checking to see that everything was more or less in order. The Ski Nautique was gassed up and the battery to the lift charged. I called Dewitt's Marina to see if the Evilo was running. It was. The mast on the Hobie Cat had been stepped, but the sails had not been rigged. All of the windsurfing boards were down by the lake. The sails were in the garage. We brought those down. The Sunfish was rigged. Nobody really used it anymore, but my father liked to rig it early in the summer and take it out for a spin (probably to justify owning it). His huge mass boogying through waves on such a tiny sailboat looked funny. His thin, shiny hair whipped from side to side when he jibed.

We had more or less just finished getting all of this crap taken care of when Wex and Anneke arrived.

The tip of my slalom ski dug into the water outside the wake. I flew out of the binding and rotated head over heels through the air. The back of my head hit the surface of the water, then my body. I skipped six feet in the air, hit the surface a second time, rolled across it two or three times, and sunk. When the boat came around to pick me up, everyone was laughing.

It was getting dark. The sky was pink. I hobbled up onto the fantail of the boat.

Wex, "Coulter, you want one more?"

"Why not? Anneke, you mind if I go or do you want to go again?"

"I'm not going again." She was still laughing. "I think I got hurt from Jay's fall."

Coulter stepped out on the fantail and did a bizarre little dance to psych himself up to go in again. Coulter was always coming up with delay tactics right before jumping in the cold water in the middle of the lake. He started saying, "God. I love it up here. Look at the sky. And those birds—"

Wex, "Coulter, look at the water—perfectly flat but with a slight hash. If you're not going to go right now, I'm going." Wex stood up and started to take off his T-shirt—like he was going to ski first.

"Fine." Coulter jumped in. Anneke passed me a towel. Wex turned the boat back on, dragged the rope over to Coulter, made the line taut, and pulled him out.

After skiing, we showered and got ready for dinner. We ate on the back patio.

Coulter, Wex, and I sat outside after dinner and drank a bottle of a very strong beer called La Fin du Monde. I felt tired and sore from my fall, but good and sleepy. The air was calm and the lake reflected the few gray clouds in the sky that were lit by the moon and some of the brighter stars. The rest was black.

Wex asked, "Jay, what are you going to do?"

"I got to go back tomorrow. It's too late to change my appointments. I don't know. Maybe if I get up early I can make some calls in the morning, but if I'm going to win the sales push I gotta get back and sell the shit out of those knives."

Sleep. There's something about sleep at the cottage too that is very particular. It's a deep, cold sleep, where there is warmth inside of you and as you dream and the night speeds ahead, you shrink and constrict, collapsing inside yourself, trying to find that warm center.

There was no possible way I was going to make my first two appointments the next morning. I called and tried to reschedule for a second time, but the customers were understandably annoyed and would not set aside more of their time after I had already wasted two hours of it. I didn't bother to call the rest of the appointments I had that day. I charged out the back door.

There was no wind. The sun was bright and hot. Anneke wore a giant hat and a sarong. Wex and Coulter were out on the dock tying the Evilo to it. Both were shirtless and sweaty. Anneke asked, "When are you leaving? Are you going to wait to see Uncle Jay?"

"Probably." I walked down the steps, ran down the length of the dock, and tackled Coulter off the end of it.

We had just gotten back from Elk Lake when Uncle Jay came walking out toward us, slightly hunched over, head tilted forward, wearing his Speedo, and stepped up on the ladder. Coulter said, "Uncle Jay, don't do it."

He waved his hand, said, "Don't distract me," and dove, all six five of him, into two and a half feet of water. The miraculous thing about the dive is that he actually dives straight down and not out like off a racing block.

Jin, Uncle Jay's wife, and Xander, Wex's half brother, came down the steps moments later. Xan, not knowing any better, was wearing the same swimsuit his father wore. We kissed Jin hello. Uncle Jay ordered Xan to get in the water, and after Xan did Uncle Jay asked, "Has anyone swum through the boiler yet?"

The boiler was from a school that had been moved across the lake in the 1940s. Whoever moved the school decided that the easiest way to get the boiler to the other side of the lake was to drag it across during the winter while the lake was frozen. The boiler broke through the ice about a quarter of a mile off the end of the slab dock in fifteen feet of water. The iron, several inches thick and coated with some sort of underwater mold, is soft. There were a few fish in the boiler. Some stayed when I pulled myself through. The seaweed inside brushed against my ankles as I kicked toward the surface.

Right before we were about to have dinner the phone rang.

Uncle Jay answered eating a carrot. "Jay! Brooke's on the phone."

I took the receiver and leaned over the small table beside the staircase where we kept the phone. It was an uncomfortable position, but my skin was still warm from the outdoor shower, so I felt good. "Hello?"

"It's me. How are you?"

"Fine. How are you?"

"Fine. I didn't know you were going to your cottage."

"Yeah . . . Coulter kind of forced me to come up with him."

"Why didn't you call me?"

"I can't hear you."

"Why didn't you call me?"

"I called yesterday. No one answered."

"Why didn't you leave a message?"

"I did." Of course I didn't leave a message because I didn't call. "Anyway, how would you have known I was up here if I didn't leave a message?"

"I called your mother and she told me. I left a bunch of messages on your cell phone."

"It doesn't really work up here."

"Aren't you supposed to be working?"

"Yeah." I was getting mad. The entire summer Brooke had been begging me not to work so hard and now she was using the knife selling to get me to come home. "I've got appointments next week."

"So you're going to come home after the weekend?"

"I don't know."

"What do you mean you don't know?"

"All I need to do is sell ten thousand dollars' worth of knives to win the summer season. I just have to figure out a way to do it."

"If you come back you can do it."

"I know." My neck was beginning to ache from leaning over the table. "You still there?"

"Yes. I'm in bed."

"Are you crying?"

She sniffed and let out a long, hard breath.

"Brooke, I don't like that you are upset all the time."

"I know . . . I think we need to have a talk. It's just that . . . It's just that I think it might be best if we take some time. And I think that all we need to do is just talk about it . . ." She rambled on. Listening to her, I realized that she was repeating something that she had practiced or at least prepared. Her mother probably helped her.

Wex said to me, "Dinner's almost served."

"I'll be there in a minute." When I lifted the phone back up to my ear, I could hear Brooke's voice, but I couldn't listen to the words. All I could do was recognize her monkey sounds attacking me through the slats in the earpiece. I waited for the sounds to stop, straining to stand in that bent-over position. I watched sweat droplets land on the table below me. Finally there was silence. "Okay, great. Can I call you right after dinner?"

"Yes. But just tell me if you agree with me."

"I agree."

"Then you think we can make it work if we really try?"

"What are you talking about?"

"If you agree with me then we can make it work."

"I'm confused here. What's not working? You're just pissed that I'm at the cottage and didn't call you for a day. My neck is really fucking hurting here . . ."

"Jay . . . I . . . It's a sense that I have. Can we talk about this more?"

"Yes."

"When?"

245

"I told you, after I have dinner with my family."

"Okay. But will you call, please? I'm going to sit by the phone."

"What the hell are you talking about, waiting by the phone? It's right next to your bed."

"I know." She giggled. I had to hold myself back from shattering the handset on the desk.

"Please, I'll call."

"When?"

I clenched my jaw and forced myself not to scream. "I don't know." I paused, meting out my words. *"However long dinner takes."*

"I'm not moving. Promise you'll call."

"I promise. Gotta go."

"I love you. Wait. Promise one more time."

I staggered backward. I was afraid I might faint. I leaned back against the door to the coat closet and spread my arms out, steadying myself while I tried to catch my breath. When I came to, Uncle Jay was staring at me, with a carrot sticking out of his mouth. One foot in the dining room. One foot in the foyer. The veins in his legs bulged. He wore short shorts, no shoes, and a ratty T-shirt. He stood perfectly still, like he'd just caught me smoking or something.

He pulled the carrot out. His jaws moved, chewing. He swallowed. He looked like he might say something important, some observation or advice, but he didn't say anything to me, he just stepped back into the room and said, "Jin. Jay will be having wine."

I didn't call Brooke back that night or the next day or the day after that. Brooke and clients were calling me nonstop. I let the appointments go. Time passed. I swam and I skied and didn't think about anything.

After Uncle Jay flew back to New York, my dad came up with his even newer girlfriend, Ruth, who had replaced the woman who looked like a smoked mackerel. They were supposed to stay for a week but had to go back down-state when my dad accidentally rammed Ruth with the Hobie Cat and injured her hip.

When I was young I was very sleepy. Always sleepy. I liked cold gray days where you could practically fall asleep anywhere.

I don't know how old I was, maybe five or six, but whenever my mother would leave for a weekend or whatever I would sob and beg her not to go. In the house where we used to live when I was that age, the door to my parents' bedroom was right down the hall from mine. Just past Molly's. There was one time when I knew she was leaving. I found out the evening before. I cried and pleaded with her, and when she went to bed I followed her to her room. She closed her door and I sat down outside of it and kept crying.

She woke me up in the morning. I could hear my father in their bedroom, banging around and bitching. "This is ridiculous. I don't know what the hell's wrong with him. Nearly tripped over the son of a bitch and broke my goddamn neck . . ." I was still in the hall-way outside her door. She was sitting on her knees across from me, brushing my hair across my forehead. She had her bags packed and everything and was heavily perfumed. She just whispered to me and told me over and over not to worry, that she loved me and wasn't going to leave.

I had just woken up on the living room floor of the cottage when I remembered this. I stared at the wall. It was clean and white and I kept trying to hold that feeling inside of me. Something had gone wrong. I don't know when or what had happened to me, but somehow I had become a tremendous asshole. I didn't want to be one. I did not want to be a sleazy, hustling, condescending, petty manipulator who knew how to beat people and did it for no other reason than to show them that he could. I almost cried when I realized my nice feelings were slipping away.

Coulter answered the phone. It was Stuart.

"Yo. Stuey. What's up?"

"What are you doing?"

"What do you mean? I just took a nap."

"Just took a nap?"

"Yeah."

"Jay. I understand you're on vacation and all and I'm glad, because I think you need one, but the summer sales competition is getting past you. You lost your lead. If you want to win, you gotta get out there and sell knives. A lot of knives and fast. It's that simple. You are not going to win if you don't."

"Stuey . . ." I was still a little groggy. "I'll probably head back soon, but listen, if I don't go back, I know how I can win. I have an idea." And then I said as hopefully as possible, "Just trust me, dude."

"What idea?"

"I don't want to get into it. It's just an idea is all, but I'm telling you. I can do it. Don't worry. I got it handled."

"Jay—" Stuart started rambling about how he wanted to believe me but he couldn't and I was barely listening and getting irritated. Because it all came down to the one thing I'd been told at the beginning of the summer—I knew how to win. Stuart did not. I might not have looked like a winner or acted like one, but I knew how to fucking do it. You had to beat people and be willing to do the thing that the fucking guy next to you doesn't think of or isn't capable of or fast enough or mean enough to do. It's something I had figured out and this asshole on the other end didn't see it and it pissed me off. Where the fuck had he been all summer? I let him shoot his tongue for a while longer and then cut him off—politely, 'cause in the end, all I wanted was for people to trust me to know what I was capable of.

"Stuart. I want you to listen to me. I know how to win this thing. I can do it. It's not something I necessarily want to do but I can do it. I know how. You have got to trust me."

The other end of the phone was silent for a while. "I'd rather you just be honest with me. If you're not going to work anymore, just tell me. You did a great job this summer. Just tell me so I know."

"Stuart. Maybe your girlfriend's got her legs wrapped around your fucking ears, but you're not listening to me. Believe me. I will win."

"Tell me how. Tell me your plan."

"No. I don't want to." And I really didn't want to tell him. This was the truth. I hated myself for thinking it and still hoped that I'd have some other alternative, but either way I was 100 percent certain I could win the sales competition. Period. "I'm going to ask you one more time. Do you trust me? Do you believe I can win?"

"Not unless you get your ass home right now."

"Fuck you." I hung up and unplugged the phone. Wex came running down the stairs and said that the lake was perfectly flat and if we did not go skiing at that exact moment we would never forgive ourselves.

28

My time at the cottage was full of subtle surprises for me. Some were so subtle that I hardly even noticed I was surprised until the surprise passed and then years later I discovered the source of the strange and almost undetectable feeling. Others are not so subtle. One nearly knocked me on my ass—literally. It came as I was skiing past the cottage. I saw her standing on the end of the dock. Her right hand was up over her eyes, blocking the sun.

Her bag at her feet. The gold bracelet. The tight-fitting blue T-shirt. White capri pants. Her thin ankles. Skin tanned. Hair nearly blond from the sun. I could see her earrings glowing, but I couldn't see her face. But it didn't matter because I could practically smell her— making my stomach spasm and my balls tingle. You can guess who it was. Isabelle had arrived.

How she got there is fairly simple but needs some explanation. Basically, I woke up one morning with a boner. I'd had a dream about her in which I was chasing her all around Dartmouth. She wanted me to chase her and she was laughing and goading me on the whole time. Eventually, I cornered her outside a fraternity, pinned her against the wall, pulled her sweatpants one third of the way down, and I woke up.

It was weird how much the dream made me feel like I'd seen her. Made me feel like she wanted me to chase her. I mulled over our relationship and questioned some of Isabelle's peculiar behavior toward me. I questioned whether it might have been her slowly seducing me. Many instances seemed like they may have been. I started to believe that she did in fact want me to chase her down. It was highly possible, and in that moment it seemed undeniable.

But did I want to chase Isabelle? I felt like I did, but I wasn't sure, so I took out her letters and stared at her picture for a while, trying to figure out what the hell was going on in my brain. Everyone else was in town buying coffee and the *New York Times*. The sun was still low in the sky and the room was dim but the photo felt warm in my hand. Her chest was damp and shiny and every little speck of light glinting off her seemed to lead down, between her breasts, run across her stomach, roll over her belly button, and . . . Her skirt blocked my eyes from going any farther. I bent the photo so I couldn't see the slutty-looking girl or the hump they were hanging out with and jerked off. I finished, laid on my back, and thought.

My head was clear. I wasn't just being horny. It wasn't the dream, either. It was Isabelle. It was true. I loved her. I wanted her. It didn't matter that she wasn't hot enough.

So, that was one part of how she got there. The other part was that in observing Wex and Anneke I saw something that I'd never seen before in my life. I saw two people who were in a relationship be genuinely nice to each other. This was one of the subtler surprises.

A couple hours after I jerked off to the photograph I called a travel agent in Detroit and bought Isabelle a plane ticket to Traverse City. I had the agent FedEx it to her in Colorado with a note attached. "Isabelle. Got your letters—late. Was at my mother's house. Happy birthday. Here's a ticket to Traverse City with an open-ended return. I'm at the cottage with my family. Come if you can. Take a cab from the airport. I'll reimburse you when you get here. Don't call. I'm not answering the phone. Afraid it might be Brooke. Will be here for a few more days at least. You can leave whenever. Hope to see you soon. Yours, Jay. P.S. If you don't come it's no big deal. Just call Pam at Complete Travel. Will pay changing fee if there is one."

After I got off the phone with the travel agent, it occurred to me that she probably wouldn't come. I had no idea when her job ended or if she had plans for afterward. And when she didn't call after she received the FedEx I assumed she must've had plans or work. Now, I know I told her not to call, but I only did it because I thought it sounded cool and never thought that she would actually jump on a plane to fly two thousand miles away after simply receiving a ticket accompanied by such a vague note. She did. It was surprising. And that's why I almost wiped out after spotting her.

I regained my balance and signaled Wex to loop around to the dock and drop me off. He made a wide turn and headed back for the shore, cutting it as close as he could without digging the prop in the sand and then swung the boat hard to the right, slinging me across the wake at a high speed. I came very close to hitting the dock and would have had I not leaned back and kicked the ski to my right, sending up a clean, crisp spray in her direction. She clapped as I slipped out of the ski.

I looked up at her darkened face. She was still blocking the sun with her hand.

"Hey."

"Nice ski. That looked too good to be you."

I took off my life vest and chucked it on the dock. "Happy birthday."

"Thanks for the ticket."

"I'm surprised you came."

"Me too."

"Wanna swim?"

"I need to put on my suit first."

I climbed up the ladder and wiped the water off my face. She asked, "Are you going to give me a hug or something? I've been here for a while." I took her by the shoulders, leaned in, and gave her the obligatory peck on the cheek. Before I could back away, she touched my arm. I didn't flinch. Her fingers felt surprisingly warm and soft on my wet skin. She glanced up at me. Her face, uncomfortably close, relaxed in my shadow. I looked into her eyes and tried to read what she was thinking. But I couldn't see anything in them—not even my reflection. I only saw what looked like plates of frozen Windex, shattered and shot through the center. I could have died inside those eyes. I wanted to dive into her, to find their home. I wanted to kiss her and I probably could have, but I didn't. I was too scared. I just stood there staring at her, feeling my wet shorts sucking away from my legs and crotch, until the boat rumbled up behind me. The motor cut out, I jumped into the water, and glided the boat manually into its slip.

After she said hello and all that I carried her bag into the house and showed her the bedroom on the first floor. "You can have this room if you want. It has its own bathroom."

She glanced into the room. In addition to the full bathroom there were double beds, a walk-in closet, and a vanity. She hummed and glanced out the window to the lake. "This is nice, but I might feel a little weird down here by myself. Can I see the room upstairs?"

The pink room looked over the backyard, Lake Street, and the hill behind it. Isabelle walked in. She made some weird faces. Touched the bed and opened an empty drawer. She glanced inside—at nothing—and frowned. "Where are you staying?"

Shit balls. It had been a while since I'd cleaned up.

"You don't want to see it. It's messy."

"Show me. Is this it?"

"No."

"Bullshit. I can see Coulter's shirt on his bed and that's obviously Wex and Anneke's room. It smells like her perfume."

"It's mine."

"Funny." Isabelle darted down the hall and pushed the door open.

Without even really looking at the room, she grabbed her bag out of my hand and said, "I want to stay here."

"Why?"

"I want to be able to see the lake." The room did have an excellent view.

"Jesus. Let me clean up first . . ."

"No. It's okay. Let me dress and let's go for a swim."

"No. Come on. Change in the pink room. Let me clean this up and we'll swim in a minute." Naturally, I wanted to get Isabelle out of the room for a quick sec because I had something I wanted to stash. "C'mon." I grabbed her and tried to pull her out into the hallway, but the little rat slipped out of my grasp like she had Vaseline skin.

"No. Let me change here. I . . ." Isabelle jumped onto the bed. "What is this?" She slithered over to the bedside table and picked up the photograph. "Is this the picture I sent you?" She paused and shot me an evil grin. "Next to a cum rag?"

We waded out from the dock. I was still laughing. I watched the water level rise up her body. She raised her arms and waited for the water to barely touch the bottom of her bikini before going under. She was not a great swimmer. She was one of these types who every time they stick their head in the water and pull it out they've got that expression on their face like they're shocked that they got wet. I found this hilarious and watched Isabelle splashing around. After a while she got cold and sort of wrapped herself in my arms and floated in my lap. The sun was making its run for the horizon. I wanted to kiss her, but she never turned around to face me, so I didn't.

While Isabelle used the outdoor shower, I used the one in the first-floor bedroom and masturbated wildly. We ate dinner with everyone and Isabelle was quite possibly the most charming I'd ever seen her—rattling off jokes and quips and asking about a million questions. I, as usual, acted a little strange and remained more or less silent. When dinner was over we went for a walk. Isabelle asked why there weren't more stars so far away from any big city. I told her it was because of the ambient light from the cottages and streetlamps, so we walked out onto the dock and lay down.

It was packed with stars. I pretended to know the constellations. She was impressed. A white dot tore a line across the sky. "Make a wish."

Isabelle rolled onto her side and looked at me. We stared at each other for a while. I was terrified. She closed her eyes. Her lips slowly spread open just enough for me to see a thin streak of wet enamel shining back at me. Her face was beautifully smooth. I forgot about how badly I wanted to kiss her. I simply admired her.

The exact moment the thought occurred to me that I had a chance to make a move, her eyelids snapped open. "Let's go upstairs."

Isabelle had made the bed while I was in the shower. She slipped under the top sheet in a T-shirt and jogging shorts. "Okay. I don't want you touching me or anything."

"Then stay on your side of the bed."

I crawled in on my side and shut off the light. She wiggled around. Her hip brushed against my hand, disappeared, and then settled back so it was barely resting on my knuckles. You could have driven a spike though my hand and I would not have moved it a millimeter. The pressure increased. As gently as I could I slid my other hand across my chest, turned onto my side, and slowly ran my fingers down her back.

"Jay."

"Yeah."

"You could have kissed me when we were down on the dock. I think. There was about a moment when I wanted you to, but the moment is gone." I rolled onto my back. She went on. "We're friends. I think, right now, we should stay friends."

"Right now?"

"It's just how I feel right now. I might feel different tomorrow . . . But I doubt it."

Love is a horror. There's nothing pleasant about it. It's pain and torture and loss and worry and sickness and insanity and dread and there's no stop to it until the love ends or mellows and then it's no fun. Afterward, you're nothing but a guy armed with a tremendous experience and the hope that the next time you'll know better and so you will do better, but you can't. You can't because there's nothing more powerful and consuming than the first girl who cuts your heart out and gobbles it up like a vampire bitch in a bad B movie.

That didn't happen to me with Isabelle. Something worse happened.

In the morning she made a confession to me. "I think while I was in Colorado I was thinking that maybe we should try dating. I don't know why. I guess I came to the conclusion because I was thinking about you all the time and I wasn't really thinking about anybody else. But the problem is . . . I don't know if I'm attracted to you." A long moment went by. "Are you going to say anything?"

"No."

"Why not?"

"Either you're attracted to me or you're not."

"I guess you're right. I think I am. I just want to see. Okay?"

"Whatever."

"Are you upset?"

"No."

"Then what are you?"

"Hungry."

We ate breakfast and went for a ski. Isabelle wore a bikini that she was afraid would come off if she fell hard. As soon as she got up, I was praying for this to happen. Of course, it didn't. She got scared and dropped the rope. I gave her some tips—all geared toward a good, hard, aggressive ski that would naturally be followed by a tremendous wipeout. She didn't bite, but for her first time slaloming she did well and was proud of herself and after we'd all had enough skiing for the morning we drove around the lake. Isabelle lay splayed out on the bow next to me, smiling. The wind blew her hair across her face gently. She leaned toward me. "I love watching you ski." She stared at me and said, "I've never seen you smile like that before."

We took a nap. When we awoke, the wind had picked up, so we went for a sail on the Hobie Cat. Isabelle got on my nerves when she started giving me instructions on how to come about, so I purposefully tipped us over. That shut her up until we righted the boat and she demanded to take the tiller. I gave it to her. She was terrified—for about a second—until she got the hang of it and took us ripping at breakneck speed across the lake. The boat was way up on one pontoon, so I hiked out on the trapeze and the entire time was genuinely afraid that she might dig the tip of the leeward pontoon into the water and pitchpole the boat, which could have sent her flying into some cables, but I didn't say anything. I wonder if she appreciated my silence. Probably not. We made it back to the cottage safely and she did not stop bragging about her sailing ability until she took her shower before dinner.

Then she sang some song. I wish I could remember it. I do remember thinking that if I wasn't careful I might never sell another knife again that summer. I really loved being near Isabelle. I loved it so much.

She dried herself and slowly dressed in front of me. It took her about an hour to perfume her neck and put on her jewelry, which she did completely naked. I did not speak or move. I just lay on the bed, paralyzed by my boner. I remember noticing a squirrel on the roof eating an acorn. It was facing our window. I got the distinct feeling that if the squirrel and I had swapped places—if there was a giant squirrel in the bed and a tiny Jay on the roof, staring inside, dying for a touch, a look, a nod, anything—it wouldn't have made any difference to Isabelle. She couldn't care less—as long as there was a pair of eyes pointed in her direction.

After she finished putting on her clothes, she looked at me as if I'd just magically appeared on the bed, asked me if I liked her shoes, and walked out of the room. The door clicked shut. I silently slid the bolt home and unbuttoned my pants. I started masturbating, then stopped.

Four hours later, I felt a little dizzy walking out on the dock—still drunk. The air was cold on my body. The wooden slats bent underneath Isabelle's feet behind me. I stood at the ladder.

"Okay."

"They're all in bed."

I dropped the towel. The breeze swirled around my bare ass and penis.

"Turn around."

I turned. Isabelle looked me over. "Okay. You can get in now."

I climbed down the ladder and swam around. She watched me, arms crossed on the end of the dock.

When I climbed out of the water, my cock was half hard. Isabelle was practically standing on top of my towel. I picked it up. She didn't move. I was close enough to her that if I was fully erect my penis would have been poking her in the stomach, but I wasn't. I started walking back up to the cottage.

"What's wrong?"

"Nothing."

"Let's see what happens when we get up to the room."

"I know what's going to happen."

"What?"

"Nothing."

This humiliation lasted one more day.

The following morning Isabelle and I went on a road trip. Her big idea was that she felt like all of the other people at the cottage were making her feel uncomfortable and self-conscious. We took Wex's rental car. It was a convertible and the day was bright and sunny so I just drove around, trying to find increasingly remote areas while she sat next to me, tanning in her bikini. We had a late lunch in Harbor Springs. Neither of us ate much. We just watched each other. Isabelle told me she thought I was the smartest person she knew and then a moment later reminded me she grew up on a horse farm. I bought a bottle of vodka. We headed for the Upper Peninsula.

I had no destination in mind. I don't know where we were headed or what we saw other than a lot of green shit. Trees were whipping around and the wind was slapping me in my face. "Why did you laugh at Stuart when he asked you to sell knives?"

"What do you mean?"

"When Stuart asked you to sell knives. Why didn't you do it?"

"He asked me to sell knives?"

"Yeah."

"When?"

"You were at Herrot. I don't know when. Sometime in the spring."

"Huh. I vaguely remember hanging out with Stuart one night, but I think I blacked out. I blacked out a lot this spring. Why do you ask?"

"You told me I wasn't charming enough to sell knives."

Isabelle laughed. "I remember that."

"That's why I did it this summer."

Isabelle took this in like a compliment, pursing her mangled lips in the sun and staring off at whatever was around us. She turned in her seat, kicked off her sandals, and put her feet in my lap. Below the waist I boiled. Above it I tried to be as cool as the wind blowing past me.

We stayed in a teepee. We were the only people in this huge campsite full of teepees. There was no place nearby to have dinner, so we didn't eat. I drank most of the vodka. Again, Isabelle changed in front of me. This time it was quick. I had hung a flashlight from a strap dangling from the roof of the teepee. It didn't give off much light. Her skin looked brown. We'd only brought one sleeping bag.

I sat across from Isabelle on the grass floor, swigging away at the bottle while she stripped, sat naked, and dressed. She was talking aloud. "I don't know what I feel. I don't know if I feel anything. I don't know. I've a problem. I think I have a problem." Her face was red. She looked like she might cry and started taking off her clothes one more time.

"Why don't you just stop that fucking crazy bullshit and come over here and kiss me?"

She looked stunned. "I told you how I feel."

"I'm not sure if I believe it."

"I told you that I don't know if I'm ready yet or if it's right. *Now*," she said, like she was punishing me, "I don't know at all."

I was tired. "Isabelle. I love you. It's obvious. It's also obvious that there's something seriously wrong here."

"What's that?"

"Whatever it is that you're doing."

"I've never felt sexually comfortable before. I'm not going to have sex with anyone again unless I feel comfortable."

"We don't have to fuck. Just give me a kiss."

"If you put it like that I'd rather you just fuck me." Isabelle snatched the bottle out of my hand and drank some of it. I snatched it back.

"So what's this all about? You're sitting here taking your clothes off in front of me so that you can see or feel or whatever if you're attracted to me or if you're comfortable around me or with me sexually or what? I don't understand it."

"I'm not sure if I do either. I think you mind-fucked me."

"Mind-fucked you?"

"You've brainwashed me somehow."

"Jesus. Isabelle. This is really going in the wrong direction here. I just want you to know that I love you. That's it. It's fucking simple."

"Well, I don't know if I'm attracted to you. You can be charm—" It was that goddamn word that got me.

"Charm! You know what charm is? *Charm* is a fucking cocktail napkin. It's . . . It's . . . It's what an idiot wears to work when he wants his friends to think he's funny—a funny tie. It's a wink at a bar. It's nothing."

"I was going to compliment you."

"I don't want the fucking compliment. I know I can be charming and I know it's meaningless. I want a fucking kiss. I want something. I want this bullshit to end. You're always talking about charm and confidence and those ass-licking turkeys from D.C. or wherever the fuck you come from, but you know what? You don't have an ounce of confidence. You'll fly to Michigan to see me. You'll do your goddamn belly dance in front of me, make me swim around naked for you like some fruit, or worse—a dog. But you don't have the tiniest amount of bravery. It's a risk—sure, you kiss me. You try it out. See what it's like. You don't like it. Okay. That's it. But going through these hoops. This insanity—for what? A better bet? A safer guess. What the fuck? It's stupid. Or maybe it's not. The only sense I can make out of it is that you're a coward."

"I'm just scared."

"I know. It's okay. *I love you.* Do you know what that means? Do you know that for the entire summer—shit, for the past year—I have been slowly falling more and more deeply in love with you? You are a fool if you don't love me. Actually, I take that back, because it's blatantly obvious that you do on some level. No, it's not foolishness, it's weakness if you don't accept some goddamn part of this."

Isabelle looked at me—trying to comprehend what I was saying. I don't know why, probably because I was so drunk that I thought this rant of mine was working, that somehow I had her on the line and that I just needed one more hard yank to land her in the boat.

So I said what had been on my mind. "When I first met you I wasn't attracted to you either, but as I've fallen more and more in love with you I have become insanely attracted to you. Impossibly attracted to you. I think that you are beautiful beyond comprehension. Beyond explanation! And so I've realized that despite all the shit I've thought about girls and *you!* . . . That it doesn't matter." She was confused. I don't blame her.

"What doesn't matter?"

"That objectively you're not hot enough for me."

263

She ran out of the teepee.

I drank the rest of the bottle of vodka and smoked a cigarette. I hadn't finished the smoke when the teepee started shaking, like a bear was grabbing it. I figured it was just Isabelle pitching a fit so I crawled out. No one was there. Everything was gray and windy. A storm was rapidly approaching from the south.

I looked around for Isabelle but couldn't see her, so I started walking through the giant maze of teepees. Maybe she was in one. I didn't know. I began calling out for her. Obviously, she could see the storm. Maybe she couldn't hear me. The wind steadily picked up and dirt was swirling all around me. It actually stung my skin. It was hard to see. I had to shield my eyes from the flying debris with my hand. Then I saw her, a yellow streak sprinting down the road beside the campsite toward the highway. I chased after her. It took me a while to catch her. She was pretty quick. I had to physically stop her. She was out of breath and her lips and eyes burned hot.

She just stood there, panting and glaring at me when the storm got us. There was a lot of lightning, and in a flash the ground was laced with rivers of mud. More than anything else the rain persuaded her to come back to the teepee for shelter. Isabelle slept in the sleeping bag. I slept on a soaking patch of grass, using a blazer I found in the trunk of Wex's car as a blanket and a pair of Isabelle's jogging shoes wrapped up in a T-shirt as a pillow.

The next morning was gray, cold, and drizzling. Using my cell phone she confirmed a seat on a flight out of Traverse City that afternoon. I stopped at the cottage so she could grab her stuff. Fortunately no one was there. We didn't speak until we got to the airport.

We stood beside the car. Isabelle was holding her bag.

"I'm sorry for what happened last night. If there's anything I can do to convince you to stay, I'll do it."

"No. You can't. I just don't feel comfortable around you anymore."

"Why?"

"I don't know."

"Maybe if you got naked one more time you could figure it out."

Isabelle laughed, but not hard. She thought about something and said, "You should give up. I don't think I'm ever going to love you."

I'd had enough. "You better get on your plane. I want to get out of here."

"Wait. Jay. I don't know what's wrong with me." I started to walk around to the driver-side door. She jumped in my way. "Just one more second. Jay. I think I love you. Sometimes I feel like I do. Sometimes I feel like there is absolutely nobody in the world who understands me like you do. And when I imagine my life without you—I get scared. Genuinely, it terrifies me."

"Then maybe you should get used to the feeling."

"Jay. I'm sorry I said that, I think I can love you. I just don't know. I need time. I need . . . I don't know what I need. All I know is I need you to be understanding."

"Of what? That you're fucking crazy? Trust me. I got it."

"No. It's not that at all. I told you, you have to be patient." Then, quick as lightning, Isabelle grabbed my face and tried to kiss me, but I was too tall. I leaned back. She started crying.

"Please. Get away from my car."

Isabelle turned and started walking toward the terminal. I listened to thirty yards of sobbing and left.

The storm that I had seen the night before was to be the first spray at the head of a long front. I smoked and drove. A wet brown leaf was stuck underneath my left windshield wiper. It kept waving back and forth in front of my face.

I thought of what I had to do. Winning the summer sales competition was job number one, and I had a good idea of how I was going to do it. Football—easy. I was definitely going to play. Start. Win. I thought about the fuckers on the team and how much I was going to enjoy hurting them. School. I hated Dartmouth. I really did, but I was going to go back and graduate summa cum laude. Because it was easy. Ivy League schools are hard to get into but that is where it ends. As long as you don't waste your four years away on bad beer, ugly girls with eating disorders, and endless rounds of pong you'd have to be a fool not to get out of there with at least honors. And I would pledge Delta Theta Chi. For two reasons. One: it was Isabelle's favorite fraternity. I hoped to ruin that. Two: Fuck Woodsy. They wouldn't let him in. Who cares? That cock-sucking bandit had been leeching off my cool from the moment I strolled into the football locker room. My catalog? If it wasn't ready I was going to physically harm Toby Nakamori. Or let his father karate-chop him. I paid Toby enough money. Neither his level of intelligence nor his age would serve as excuses or reasons for me to overlook his failures. Lastly, Brooke. I would get her back—hell, I wasn't even sure if I had lost her. I would marry her, which is exactly what she wanted. And I would continue to cheat on her, fucking her too as long as she remained attractive. But I wouldn't divorce her. That was weak. I would just shut her up and crush her. I would crush her into something so thin and insignificant that her spirit would evaporate in a quick hot puff and her existence would be reduced to nothing more than wallpaper.

Coulter was on the phone when I walked in. Wex was walking down the stairs in his socks and underwear, eating a bowl of ice cream. "Where's Isabelle?"

"Grandmother got sick."

"I got a favor to ask."

"Huh?" I was looking around for some of my Apex materials that I'd left by the phone two weeks earlier.

"I thought you might like to drive my Mustang to Michigan. Maybe take Isabelle with you. I'll pay you to do it."

"I got football preseason."

"Okay."

"Do you know where all that shit I left here went?"

"Look in the sports closet."

I turned to Coulter. "Get off the phone."

I checked my watch. I needed to make two calls. One I hoped would be brief. The other I hoped might be longer.

Coulter put the phone to his ear. "Mom. I've got to call you back. I love you."

Brooke picked up. I put on my salesman voice—my best Coulter imitation ever. "Hey, you . . ." She was cagey at first, but with a few jokes and some quasi-serious lecturing I was able to get her warmed up, talking, quickly yapping, and most important, distracted enough to subtly find out if her father knew that I hadn't called her in about ten days. Turns out Brooke was too embarrassed to say anything to anyone. After hearing this, I made a vague plan to see her in the near future. I explained to her how the problems with our relationship were her fault, largely because she was imagining problems where there were none and ended the conversation by gently reprimanding her for "torturing herself." She apologized and promised to be "good."

The next person I had to call was Brooke's father. "Hi, Mr. Ambrose, this is Jay Hauser."

"Hi, Jay! How's Torch Lake?"

"It's great. I miss Brooke like the dickens, but you know, I haven't spent time with my family all summer, and so as much as I hate to be away from her, it's nice to see them too. Listen, I've got just a few days until I end my summer job and I was thinking that before I hang up my spurs, I would check with you and see if you were, in fact, actually interested in giving Bladeworks knives as your company's holiday gift. I really don't need you to buy these knives or think that you should, I just thought that if you were interested, while I'm still a salesman, I could give you as good a deal as possible."

"Oh . . . That's a thought. What were you thinking about, which knives?"

"Well, I wish I could show you them in person—you know, this opportunity didn't actually occur to me until it started raining and we had to stop skiing. But if you can get online and take a look at . . ."

Wex, Anneke, and Coulter were sitting at the table, looking at the lake. Coulter wouldn't look at me.

"I just won."

Late that night when I was very drunk, I fished the photograph Isabelle had sent me out of the drawer where I had stashed it. I held it up to my lips. "Fuck you, you pathetic, nasty bitch." I spit in her face and laid it on the bed beside me, figuring I would jack off on it and then burn it in the morning. I passed out instead.

29

The weather never improved and I never relaxed. I had a lot to do at the cottage. There were many voice mails. I called every person back, including the irate clients I had blown off, and apologized to all of them. I sent one lady, who I had rescheduled three times, flowers. I booked my flight to Myrtle Beach for the end-of-summer celebration, and then booked a second flight to Hanover. I called Coach O'Mally, told him I was going to play, and gave him the date and time I was arriving in Hanover.

I made Toby Nakamori FedEx me three sample catalogs and a floppy disk with the templates on it. To his credit, the catalog was goddamn good. It had the exact mix of professionalism and personalization that I had hoped for. I mailed him a check for $500.

The Ambrose order came to $14,228. My commission on that phone call was $7,114. It made me a little nervous to be carrying the order form around. But I figured the safest bet was for me to take it with me to Myrtle Beach and turn it in when I arrived. Also since I had not sent the order in to Stuart, no one at Bladeworks knew I had won. It would be a surprise when I revealed it, and I began to think about the best, most dramatic way to turn in the form.

There were other little odds and ends I had to take care of, like figuring out how to get my stuff out of storage, order books, clothes, and other sorts of bullshit like that. I handled all this stuff quickly and effectively. I jogged in the morning and ran sprints in the evenings. I even did some push-ups. In two days, my life was better organized than it had been before. My goals were clearly laid out in front of me and easily attainable. My mind was sharp and quick, my will unbending, and my sympathy for others at an all-time low. I thought I cut a mean figure. Sometimes even going so far as to imagine my feet slicing up the ground as I walked.

The one thing that I didn't get around to doing was jacking off on Isabelle's photo and then incinerating it. I couldn't find it.

The trees outside my mother's house dripped. I could smell fall coming. My head hurt. I had to pee badly. I walked in. My mother was standing inside the door with her arms crossed.

"Jay. I just spoke to your father. He told me you're flying to South Carolina tomorrow and then heading from there to Dartmouth."

"Yeah. Excuse me. I've got to take a leak."

She followed me to the bathroom. "You *are* leaving tomorrow?" I shut the door in her face. I peed so hard I thought I might have injured myself. I washed my hands and splashed water onto my face. When I stepped out of the bathroom she was still standing there.

"Yeah. Mom. I'm sorry." She followed me into the kitchen. "I didn't know what I was doing until the very last minute. Really, I just booked my flights and whatnot the other day. I'm going to have to leave some stuff here. FedEx is going to pick it up on Monday. By the way, do you mind if Brooke comes to dinner? It's okay if you do."

"I can't believe this."

I opened the fridge. Was I hungry or should I wait? "What can't you believe?" I pulled out a block of cheese. I saw Fancy hiding in the dining room.

"That you are going to leave without having spent any time with me this summer."

"Mom. I've been staying with you all summer." I got out a cutting board and a paring knife.

"That's nice. You've been staying here all summer? Like I run a hotel. You haven't been here at all!"

I cut off a wedge. "Fuck. Mom. I've been working. I won, by the way." I popped the cheese into my mouth and smiled.

"Congratulations. Why don't you just leave?"

"I am. Tomorrow."

"No. Why don't you just leave right now?"

"Oh, goddamn, Mom. Would you please lay off of me?"

"No. Jay. This is unfair. You come here and stay in my house. I buy all of these fricking knives from you and you don't even let me know when you're going to school or anything and you spend almost three weeks with your father up north and you don't even call me once!"

"Mom. I was not up there with Dad. I went with Coulter and I didn't know I'd be staying for so long. It just happened. I don't know what to say. And shit, Coulter was there with me! Why don't you bitch at him?"

"Because he called me every day."

"Well, why didn't you ask to speak to me?"

"Because I was waiting to see if you'd ask to speak to me."

"I didn't know he was calling you."

"You never even thought of calling me. I told Coulter not to put you on the phone unless you asked and you didn't."

"So you were testing me. That's cool."

"No. I just wanted to see if my son would call his mother."

"Yeah. You can't call me?"

"No. I can't."

I looked at the cheese on the counter and wanted to pound it flat. Then I looked at my mother. So bitter. "Fuck you."

"What did you say to me?"

"I said 'fuck you.' I don't know what your goddamn problem is, but it's a big one. You have no idea of what you are."

"Why don't you tell me, Hal?" My mother used to call me Hal all the time. For years after my father left her, she would call me by his name when she was mad at me or just mad. I was nine years old when she first started calling me by his name. As a child I could never figure it out, but by then I could.

"I'm not going to tell you what you are. You can figure it out for yourself. But I'll tell you what you do. You love to hurt people. I don't understand why you enjoy it so much, but you take pleasure in putting me through your fucking tests and your bullshit while you sit on your goddamn ass blaming everybody for what's happened to your life and taking no responsibility for it. Why do you think I don't call you?"

"I don't know." She said this through gritted teeth. I stepped toward her.

"Try this. Remember Christmas two years ago when I was waiting at Dad's house all day for Courtney, Coulter, and Molly to show up and kept calling and calling to see where they were and they never showed up and then after Dad left to go to Sherianne's mother's house, you had Coulter tell me not to come over, and I waited and waited and you didn't know it because you were just too happy to sit here fucking torturing me, but I was fucking sobbing for hours and finally when Coulter called me and it was okay for me to come over, you'd had Christmas without me."

"I did not."

"Don't lie to me. Not now!" I stepped forward again, she lurched back. "Molly fucking told me what you did even though it was so blatantly obvious. And she told me how you wouldn't let them leave and made them open up all of their gifts before I got here so that 'I could know what it's like to be left out.' That is exactly what you said to them."

"I'm not listening to this . . . You're a bully just like your father." She tried to get around me, but I shoved her back.

"No! You're going to shut the fuck up and listen to what you did. You fucking tortured me the entire time I was in high school. You kicked me out. You kicked your son out of his fucking home and then bought another house without room for me in it. How could you do that and then try to blame me for living with Dad. I wanted to live here, with you."

I watched her try to accept this but she was just shaking her head indignantly. I went on, "But you know? That's okay. If you didn't want me around, fine. But the sick part of it is that you had the nerve to try to blame ME for what YOU did! You tried to make me feel guilty for your failed marriage. When you figured out that you couldn't hurt Dad, but you needed someone to hurt so badly to make yourself feel better, you chose me. That's why you've called me Hal, since I was fucking nine."

"I never purposefully tried to hurt you."

"Stop lying to me!" I slammed my fist into a cupboard, splitting it down the middle. My mother let out a little shriek. I went on.

"You forced me to go to court and to those fucking social workers who made me convince them I wasn't getting abused. You know what that's like? How humiliating it is to do that? Staring at some poor woman who's listened to your lies? And all I'm trying to do is figure out why I'm there and why they won't believe me when I tell them I hadn't been molested by my father!"

"I was trying to protect you!"

"Bullshit! You didn't give a fuck about me. All you wanted was to have another stab at Dad, and then when that failed you tricked that fucking idiotic judge into sending me to rehab. To rehab! Just so you could get me out of Dad's house for a few weeks. And why would that be so nice for you? Because you thought Dad would give a shit about losing me. Because you thought it would hurt him. It only embarrassed him. But the person who it did hurt was me. And the saddest part is that you can't do any of it yourself. You've got to get a lawyer or that disgusting judge or Courtney to press charges against Dad."

"He attacked her!"

"He did not. I was there. Were you there? Huh?" I had my mother backed up against the wall. "You weren't fucking there because you were out to dinner with one of your goddamn bitch friends who would help you spy on Dad. I don't give a fuck what you do or what you think, but I'm not going to be blamed for this anymore. If you had to live with yourself, with your nagging bullshit and the cruel fucking shit you do, you would have left yourself, but you can't see any of this because you have too much pity for yourself and absolutely no sympathy for anyone else."

My mother was cringing and crying. I hovered over her. She sobbed. "I just wanted you to call."

"Yeah, maybe I did too." I kicked the wall beside her, denting the plaster. I didn't hear Coulter running up from behind me. "Why didn't you fucking call me?"

274

"Get away from her!" he screamed. I turned. Coulter's face was beet red. He grabbed me and jerked me away from my mother. I didn't think. I just punched him as hard as I could in the sternum. The wind shot out of him and he crumpled over. He tried to dive at my legs, but I punched him in the ear and he went down on the tile floor, flat and struggling for breath. I stared down at him. "Don't fucking touch me!"

My mother scrambled up behind me. *Shink.* I heard the knife slip out of the block and turned just in time to dodge the petite slicer that she swung at me. She held the knife with both hands, and as she swung it, partially over the center island, she knocked the clay pot of spoons and whisks onto the floor. It shattered. Fancy was barking and nipping at me. My mother stepped around the side of the island, lunged and swung at me again. The end of the knife sliced through the air four inches from my face. She was really try-ing to cut me. I jumped back and stepped on one of Fancy's paws. Fancy yelped and scrambled out of the room. I backed up as my mother approached. I was breathing too hard to speak. She was screaming something but I couldn't really discern the words, be-cause she was crying so heavily. I continued backing toward the hallway when she tripped over Coulter, stumbled, and then came at me half sprinting, half falling, holding the knife out in front of her like a sword. I leapt to my left. She charged forward, narrowly missed me, and planted the tip of the blade in the wooden cabinet to my right. She lost her grip on the handle and her hands slid down the length of the blade. The tip snapped off and the knife fell to the floor. Her fingers were cut badly, trembling and leaking blood. "Get out of my house!" She said this clearly.

"Calm down."

She grabbed the toaster off of the counter beside the fridge and threw it at me, weakly. It sailed through the air at my chest but stopped abruptly in midair. The toaster was still plugged in. It flew back at her, banged against her knees, dangled for a moment, and then disconnected from the wall socket. Since she was out of weapons and projectiles in her immediate vicinity, I could've grabbed her, but I was too stunned to move. Her eyes were crazily darting all over the place. They found a home. The paring knife I'd been using earlier to cut the cheese. She snatched that baby up and hucked it at my head. I dipped to the right. The paring knife flew past me and into the dining room, where it plinked across the table and dropped to the floor. "Get out."

I backed up a few more steps and she made a mad dash for the rest of the Bladeworks knives on the counter beside the sink. I'm not sure which knife she grabbed. But I heard a big one bounce off the wall adjacent to the dining room, exactly where I'd been standing a moment before. She probably grabbed another one, but I didn't wait to find out. I bolted out the door, past the photo of my mother riding the horse in Africa, jumped into the BMW and kicked the pedal down. Giddyup, bitch.

My father didn't say anything the entire way to the airport. He stopped outside the terminal at the departure level. He put his car in park, grabbed the steering wheel, and stared straight ahead. He was thinking about something to say. The exhaust from a crappy cab rose up in front of the hood. I got out.

I was in such a rush to pee when I had gotten to my mother's house, I hadn't removed my bag from the trunk before going inside. So the only clothes I had were the ones I had taken to the cottage. Since I'd gone up north with clothes for more or less one day there wasn't much in the bag, and I had to borrow one of my father's old blazers, some fresh underwear, socks, and dress shirts. I didn't get around to washing what I had. Most of it was still wet from the lake and had been left in the trunk overnight, making the trunk smell musty and damp. I left my demonstration knives in the BMW, but I'd fortunately remembered to remove the order form for Ed Ambrose's $14,228 purchase. I had it folded and in the breast pocket of the blazer, which, incidentally, fit me nicely. It was a tailored job, cut to my father when he was about my current slimmed-down size.

My father was clearly pissed at me, but I'm sure that there was some part of him that keenly understood my side of the story, which he actually didn't hear from me but could have gleaned from my mother's. She had called him shortly after I left her house. The police were there. Fancy was barking and Coulter was threatening to come over to my father's condominium to kill me. I was driving around smoking cigarettes and trying to figure out what to do. I felt like seeing a friend, but off the top of my head I couldn't think of any friends that I hadn't sold knives to. I didn't want to see Brooke and I couldn't go and sit at any of my lakes because it was still raining. I ended up staying at a motel and I drove to my father's in the morning to drop off his car. I was hoping he'd be at the office. Obviously, he wasn't.

My father sat in his car while I got my bag. I walked around to the driver-side window. "Thanks for the ride."

He looked up at me, pursed his lips, then looked back at the dash. He fiddled with some of the knobs on it. I saw his eyebrows lift, like he was about to say whatever it was he'd been thinking about on the drive—probably some speech—but he stopped himself. Then he shook his head and said, "I'm lucky your mother wasn't so well outfitted with cutlery when we were living together." He laughed, and then said sternly, "I'll see to it that you get all your stuff . . . Unless your mother's already sold it." He dropped his new Mercedes in gear and pulled out.

There is no hell compared to the pedestrian hell of an airport. I waited for an hour watching seemingly retarded people be checked in by worse and caused a miniscene when I finally stepped to the ticket counter, slapped down my ticket and driver's license, and said, "Jay Hauser. Here's my ticket. Here's my ID. How in God's name does it take so long to process that?"

"Sir, there are the elderly and young children that sometimes need extra assistance."

I fairly shouted back, "Well, maybe if you drool and need to wear a diaper you shouldn't be on an airplane!" And then I mumbled, loudly, "Or work for an airline." The flight attendant's pause was so long and awkward that I almost regretted what I said.

Needless to say, I received a thorough spot check at the security line. I was able to exact a pleasant revenge for the wait when the security woman who opened my bag caught a whiff of what was inside of it. She reared up like a cobra. I smiled as her hands rifled through my mildewed clothes and then shivered in horror when I spied Isabelle's face leering up at me. Her photo had somehow been tossed in my bag! Fortunately it was quickly slapped back into hiding by a dirty sock. The woman coolly returned the favor I had given her when she said "have a pleasant flight" with breath so venomous it made my eyes tear. I purchased a pair of tortoiseshell Ray-Bans and made my way to the gate. I realized that the sunglasses were the first purchase I had made for myself all summer.

I had a few drinks on the way down to Myrtle Beach. The flight attendant didn't even ask to see my ID, which I thought was cool. I attributed it to the blazer.

There was a van waiting, with several other knife salesmen in it, to take me to the resort. I could smell my bag reeking. I lit up a cigarette, further pissing off everyone in the van.

The key to my condo wasn't there because Skeeter already had gotten it. Apex was paying for my accommodation this time, which I thought was pretty sweet. I'm sure Skeeter was psyched too. I got the spare key and piled back in the van, which sped me past the golf course to the other side of the resort where there were several rows of condominiums next to the beach.

Skeeter was taking a nap in his bathing suit. He woke up as soon as I walked in, then staggered across the floor, shook my hand, and flopped back onto the couch. The condo was on the second story. The drapes were fluttering, blown toward Skeeter by the offshore breeze. The ocean looked silver and the haze above it a grimy yellow. I put my shades in one of my coat pockets. The haze turned to a blinding white. I opted for a glass of whiskey and Coke. I finished the first and immediately poured another one.

"So. What's going on, man?"

"Nothin'."

"What's this deal all about?"

"Dunno. I'm sure they sent you a schedule in the mail."

I picked it up. *Friday. Arrive. Check in. Six o'clock push competition for August. Sunday. The end-of-the-summer banquet.* This was where the number one knife salesman would be announced and given his scholarship. *Check out.*

The condo that we had was nicer than I expected. There was a living room, a kitchen, and two bedrooms. I tossed my blazer over a chair in the kitchen and noticed the Ambrose order form poking out of the breast pocket. I toyed with the idea of telling Skeeter about it but thought it'd be better to let him share in the surprise.

"When did you get here?"

"Couple of hours ago."

Skeeter pointed to a closet. "That's the owner's closet. There's Boogie boards in there an' shit. There's one in there for you too. Just got to be careful for them riptides." Skeeter looked me over. "Whatcha been doing?"

"Been water-skiing a lot."

He smiled. "You kick ass in August?"

I fixed another drink and thought I'd better be careful not to get too drunk.

I said, "I want to swim a little before we have to go to another one of these damn push deals."

"I'll be right here. Gonna make myself a margi. You sure you don't want one?"

"Why not?"

I called the central office and asked to be connected to Bud French's condo. When Bud answered I told him that I had an idea about a catalog that I wanted to try and that I'd like to set up a time to come by the next day to show him. He sounded groggy on the phone, like I'd woken him up. He told me to come by before noon. I apologized for waking him and hung up. The next call I had to make was to my uncle John Harrison and his wife, Elaine. He lived in Charleston, which was an hour away, and from what my mother said before I went to the cottage, I thought maybe they'd like to see me. It'd been a few years since I'd visited them. They were surprised to hear from me, told me that normally calling on such short notice was a bad idea, but that fortunately they were free, and we could meet at some point midway for dinner the following evening.

The ocean sobered me up a little. My tan, which had faded slightly during the rainy last few days at the cottage, snapped back after just two hours in the sun, and as I inspected myself in the mirror, steaming from my shower, I thought I looked golden. This probably had to do more with the light fixture in the bathroom than anything else, because being so fair, I never really tanned, but rather got pink and flushed with a slight brownish base, like an albino who'd been slapped all over his face and body until he began to bruise. Nonetheless, I felt good and felt like I looked good. I even liked the bloodred around my blue corneas from the salt water and the booze.

I brushed my now-white hair tightly against my head and slicked the sides back. I dressed in the bathroom, wearing a white dress shirt and pair of bluish pants I'd found at my father's house. I had no tie, so I left the collar open. I put my sunglasses on, checked myself once more in the mirror, opened the door to my bedroom, crossed it, entered the living room, and made myself another drink. I thought Skeeter would be ready, but he'd fallen asleep while I was in the shower, so I had to wake him up and wait for him to shower and dress.

It felt good to walk, but because I was wearing my shades I couldn't see very well and stumbled a few times as we picked our way through the maze of condos and golf course, passing a plastic bottle filled with Jack Daniel's back and forth and smoking cigarettes.

Walking out of the darkness and into the bright light shining down onto the entrance of the clubhouse did not have a sobering effect. I felt like I'd been walking through a dim comfortable dream and just stepped into a vibrant nightmare. The air-conditioning leaking out of the clubhouse was cold and wet. I shivered before I entered. I tried to walk past Chuck and Patterson like I didn't see them but I was two feet in front of them and they'd been sort of nodding and jutting their chins at me as soon as I walked in. "Hey. Hey! What's happening? Hauser."

"Howdy."

"You okay?"

"Yeah. Where's Parsi?"

They looked at each other, puzzled. "Jay. Stuart's not coming."

"Oh." I looked around. I didn't say anything for a while. I took a cigarette out and stuck it in my mouth.

Patterson said, "You can't smoke in here."

"Okay." I took the smoke out of my mouth and tried to put it behind my ear, but because of the sunglasses it wouldn't stick there so I put it in my front pocket. Chuck glanced around the room and said, "I'm going to say hi to Bud French." He patted me on the shoulder and said to Patterson, "Take care of this guy for me, will you?"

Chuck sashayed over to Bud, hand out and "heyyyying" him from across the room. Bud was chatting up some young sales-woman. He turned to look at Chuck as if he were annoyed. I glanced around to see if Bud's wife was there. The room seemed empty. I thought we'd be late but we were early.

Patterson started to crack some joke, but I interrupted him. "What's the deal tonight? Where's everybody?"

"They're here. You must be drunk. Apex only invites the top two hundred salesmen to come here this weekend."

I laughed. "Shit. John. I'm an idiot. Just a little tired."

The bartender scrutinized my ID, smirked, handed it back to me, and gave me my Jack and Coke.

I dropped a fiver on the bar and looked around for someone to talk to, but I didn't know anybody beside Chuck and Patterson and Skeeter and I didn't see Skeeter anywhere so I went outside for a cigarette. Susanne Beatle, the little bitch from Nashville, was lean-ing against a small wall to the right of the entrance. I walked over to her.

"Hey, Susanne, gotta light?" She lit my smoke.

She smiled at me and I noticed something different about her, which for a second scared me because I momentarily thought that maybe this girl wasn't, in fact, Susanne. "Wait. Something's different about you."

"I just got braces. That's why I started selling. My teeth were a little crooked."

"Crooked teeth are charming. Fuckin' braces suck, no offense."

"How did you do?"

"When?"

"In August?"

"Oh. Not so hot."

She laughed. "Yeah. Right."

"No. Really. I had two sales."

"Two sales?"

"Yeah."

"Why?"

"Dunno." I looked at her and thought about how good it would feel when I revealed to everyone that one of my two sales was for fourteen thousand dollars. A smile spread across my face.

"You know, I hated you," she said.

I shrugged. "That's cool."

She laughed. "*What* is your deal?"

I looked at her, with my head tilted. Her lips started to part and her braces caught the light beaming down from her left. I heard someone speaking Spanish behind me and turned to see Acuña walking up to the entrance. His hair, as usual, was slick, and Camilla looked goddamn hot, floating along next to him like a long piece of tissue paper dangling from his wrist. He didn't look at me. Behind Acuña was Reid Tallenger and his wife, walking arm in arm, just like Acuña. He smiled at me, inches from Susanne, and winked. I nodded. I looked back at Susanne. She'd pulled away from me a tiny bit and stepped into a different sort of light that made her look particularly small and withered, her cheeks gaunt, her lips thin and dry, and her mouth, containing her tiny little teeth and huge braces, was pushed out like she was wearing an athletic mouth guard. I noticed a faint brown mustache on her upper lip and a stain on the sleeve of her dress. She took back the distance, closed her eyes, and leaned forward, turning her primate mouth up toward mine.

I walked back inside.

I sat at a table with Skeeter and two guys he knew. I didn't bother introducing myself. I slumped into my seat and stared at the piece of Dover sole on my plate. It's flakey white meat, baked and greasy with butter. The vegetables beside it were equally greasy. I wondered how many times I'd been served something with grilled vegetables that showed absolutely no evidence of being grilled at all. I flicked a seed out of one of the pieces of squash with my fork.

I had never seen a live Dover sole, but I think they're supposed to look like flounder, and I've seen one of those before, when I was ten, visiting Lilly Abbot during the summer. We had gone to their family vacation home in Antigua, and one night when there was a full moon, Lilly's cousin Charlie waded out into the shallow water right off the beach to hunt them.

He slid his feet along the sand and watched in the light of the moon for something to flutter, a little brown cloud in the water. On the other side of the bay a lightning storm flickered. Iridescent jellyfish glowed on the surface of the water. Charlie moved slowly, head bent, his left arm poised with a trident spear. The lightning came closer and he mumbled something about getting shut out and then all of the sudden, he silently slammed the spear into the water. He held it there, erect for a moment, whispered something else to himself, and then said, "C'mon. Look."

We already had our pants rolled up and we walked out into the water next to him. The flounder curled slowly and then snapped its body out, like fingers trying to flick something off one's hand. Lilly's cousin turned the flounder over so we could see its white belly, bleeding just a tiny bit where the three spikes poked out of it. Flounders are not supposed to be beautiful-looking fish, but I thought this one was, and the way it moved and opened its mouth, the way its skin changed from scaly black to smooth white seemed so perfect.

I had no drink in front of me and I was too drunk to speak intelligently so I just sat there, staring at the seed I'd flicked out of the slice of squash, and the more I thought about Lilly and the crappy fish and what had happened in New Orleans the more I couldn't stop thinking about how amazingly good some people were at turning something nice into complete crap. It did not escape me that I was someone who had mastered this craft. Then I got an idea—a pretty good one.

Skeeter and his buddies were talking about the prizes that were going to be given out. In a very un-Apex-like way, the gifts were not given out by sales amounts, but by a lottery. The format of the August push was slightly different from the other pushes. Instead of everybody walking up onstage en masse and then sitting down one by one, each salesperson would just walk up when Bud called out their amount and then sit back down. The lottery was going to work this way: when you went up to say how much you sold, Bud would hold out a hat filled with scraps of paper and you closed your eyes and picked your prize.

Anyway, while I was staring at the buttery seed, I got an idea. What if I pretended that I'd only sold the one hundred dollars' worth of stuff that Revelacion bought and then, on Sunday, when Acuña went up to receive his award for winning the summer selling season, I stop him on the walkway and produce the fourteen-thousand-dollar form? I started laughing at the seed. This was a good idea.

I was so goddamn pleased with this idea that I almost forgot to get up when the ceremony began and Bud said, "Now, I doubt that any of you have sold this amount, but out of tradition I'll begin by asking, is there anyone here who's sold less than one hundred and fifty dollars?" He looked around. "Didn't think so. How about—"

"Wait!" I coughed and stood up.

"Jay. Um. I said, one hundred and fifty dollars."

"Yeah." I swiped Skeeter's Jack and Coke from in front of him and swigged it. The drink dribbled onto my white shirt. "Damn." I set down the drink and started walking toward Bud at the podium.

Bud said, "Oookayy."

The small audience watched me, confused. My plan was in effect. The room was very quiet, but my ears were ringing and felt hot. Bud did not stick out his hand, but I shook it anyway. I addressed the room. "Hi. I'm a Cinci-Slicer. I ummm sold one hundred and twenty-five dollars' worth of stuff to my maid, Revelacion . . . I can't remember her last name. Jackson, maybe . . . I don't know . . . Wait. I ummm gave her twenty percent off so I think that's one hundred and five dollars."

Someone in the room started clapping. It was Reid Tallenger. He shouted, "Kick Ass in August!"

No one in the room laughed except me, because I was thinking about how fucking good it was going to be to whip out the Ambrose order form Sunday.

"Pick a prize." Bud stuck out the hat. I pulled out a piece of paper with a number on it. "Sixty-two."

Bud looked at some woman standing behind a table piled high with packages. She had her own microphone. "Sixty-two is a pair of Ray-Ban sunglasses modeled after the ones worn by Will Smith and Tommy Lee Jones in the hit movie *Men in Black*."

A helper brought the sunglasses over to me. "That's funny. I just bought a pair of Ray-Bans. I'm wearing them right now, in case you didn't notice."

Bud coughed. "Congratulations, Jay. I hope you enjoy your extra pair of sunglasses."

"Me too." I walked away from the podium. You can imagine what everyone was thinking. Right as Bud started to carry on with the ceremony I lobbed the box of sunglasses in Susanne Beatle's general direction, shouting "Catch" midflight.

"Hey, man," said Skeeter. "I could have used those." I smiled, but he wasn't kidding.

The ceremony dragged on at a snail's pace, since everyone who sold anything got to pick a prize out of the hat. I kept drinking throughout the entire thing until a waiter told me that he was asked by someone not to serve me anymore. Susanne came and sat with us after a while. Skeeter hadn't received his prize yet and Susanne had, but Skeeter mentioned something about how he wasn't supposed to stand up and receive a prize or some crap like that but I figured it was just 'cause he didn't want any of these lame gifts, so the three of us got up and left.

We walked outside.

I said, "We need more booze. How are we going to get some?"

Susanne, "I've got a car."

"Why didn't you fly down?"

"It wasn't a long drive so I refunded the ticket that Apex bought for me."

Susanne drove a dirty late 1980s Camry or something like it. I bought a bunch of booze. I don't remember what. We drove back to the resort. Susanne wanted to pick something up from her condo. "Who are you staying with?"

"Nobody. There weren't enough girls to put with me so they gave me my own condo."

It was exactly like ours two rows over from the beach. She put her keys down in a dish on the kitchen counter, went to the bathroom, came out a short time later, and said that she'd gotten whatever it was that she'd wanted to pick up.

While she was gone and Skeeter and I were standing there alone in her condo I remembered something. "Hey, man. I totally forgot, but I wanted to congratulate you on finishing in the top two hundred. That's really great."

Skeeter lit a cigarette. "I didn't finish top two hundred."

"You didn't?"

"Nope. Apex didn't send me down here. I paid for myself."

Only half of Skeeter's face was lit by light coming in through a small window beside the door. "You probably think it's kind of stupid to pay to come down here, don't you?"

Back in our condo when Skeeter went to take a leak, Susanne came up on me fast. "It's just so unbelievable that you could come here after selling only a hundred dollars' worth of knives. You must have known how everyone would react when they found out you hardly sold anything." Susanne took a long drink and then stood there, leaning up against the kitchen counter, looking me over. "Was it laziness? Did you get scared?"

I grabbed her around the waist and tried to pull her over to me, but she pushed me away. She held up her finger. There was a ring on it. "I'm married. I usually don't wear my ring when I do anything Apex related, but I thought I should wear it tonight."

"Was that why you wanted to go to your condo?"

"Yes."

The Ambrose order felt like a gun pressing against my rib. I couldn't wait to pull it out. Skeeter stepped out of the bathroom. "Let's go to that party."

31

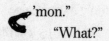'mon."

"What?"

Susanne was kneeling next to me, patting my cheek. I heard the ocean. The air was cool but not cold, and I felt like I had been comfortably asleep for some time. Black clouds were blowing past a big moon. They were really moving very quickly and then the moon was black again.

"C'mon."

"Where? What? I . . ."

"You passed out on the beach. Skeeter and I have been looking for you for over an hour."

"What?" I stood, stumbled, and vaguely remembered having been at some party in another salesman's condo. I might have gotten in a fight—or told someone off. I didn't know. Something bad had happened. I had a difficult time walking. Susanne had to support me. I felt the sand on my feet. My shoes were gone. I gripped at my chest. I wasn't wearing a shirt, but I was still wearing my blazer. I couldn't feel the Ambrose sales form. I shot my hand into the breast pocket. Nothing. I was on the verge of having a heart attack when I stuck my hand in the other breast pocket and yanked it out. I breathed deeply. The form snapped in the wind like a flag. I rammed it back into place.

"My ankle hurts."

"You jumped off the second-story balcony."

"What?"

"Yeah. Skeeter dared you to."

"Oh." Suddenly I had the yen to swim. "Hey, let's go swimming."

"Not now."

"I'm a very good swimmer."

"*I* know. Can you walk on your own?"

"Yeah." I let go of Susanne and straightened up. My neck was sore. "Did I get in a fight or anything like that?"

"Almost. There was this kid, Toffer Perkins. He was joking around about your speech . . . And you didn't like it very much. You told him to go fuck himself and then you told us all that we were idiots, except for Skeeter, and that Sunday you were going to show us all something that would quote, 'blow our brains out of our stupid asses.'"

I laughed. That was a pretty funny remark. "What'd he do?"

"He said you were pathetic."

"Huh. What does he look like, by the way?"

"Oh. He's okay. Brown hair. Tallish."

"So, anyway, when he called me pathetic, what did I say?"

"Nothing. That's when Skeeter dared you to jump over the rail."

"Why in God's name did he dare me to do that?"

"I guess he didn't think you'd do it, but it was like the words weren't fully out of his mouth and you just walked out of the balcony and hopped over. We all ran over to see if you were okay and you were on the ground, lying on your face in the sand, shouting out for someone to bring you the drink that you'd dropped when you jumped over the rail. Thank God Toffer's condo is on the beach."

I grabbed her hand. "Isabelle, please come swimming with me."

"My name is Susanne."

"Susanne. Please. I just need to swim for a second. Please come with me."

"No. Jay. You're still drunk. Besides, you already swam."

"What?"

"After you jumped off the balcony, you demanded to go swimming, so we all went down and watched you. You swam naked. Skeeter has your shirt and shoes."

"How did you lose me?"

"After you finished swimming, you got halfway dressed and we all started walking back to the condo, but you just wandered off."

"Oh. Hey, Isabelle?"

"Susanne."

"Susanne. Why are you so nice to me?"

"I don't know."

In the day I did not feel particularly stellar. My lower lip itched like crazy. It was around two in the afternoon when I woke up. I was taking a long piss when I recalled my conversation with Susanne. My ankle was still sore. I remembered the push ceremony and how I was such a complete idiot when I stood up at the podium with Bud French. Shit. I was supposed to meet him two

hours ago. I dressed as quickly as I could, grabbed the phony catalog materials, and ran out the door.

Everything was white. I felt like I was breathing white. Hot dry
air that choked me clung to my lips coated in spittle. I crashed into
a bush. I dropped the catalog and the floppy disk went flying somewhere. I regained my vision crawling through the bush, collecting
my crap. My brain really was not functioning to its full capacity and
it took me a while to figure out where Bud French's house was and
how to get there.

I jogged past an even crappier Ford Escort than the one I drove
that summer, parked at the base of the walkway that led to the front
door. I climbed the porch steps, panting and sweaty. Bud's house
wasn't on the ocean, but close—across the street from a row of gigantic white plantation-style homes. I looked into the house through
a window beside the door and something caught my eye. A huge
pink bra dribbled off the staircase onto the shiny wood floor. Each
cup was bigger than a pair of men's boxer shorts—a pair of which
lay outside what appeared to be a sitting room to the right. I started
backing away from the porch when I caught a glimpse of Bud looking down the hallway at me, wearing a white cotton robe and holding a drink in his hand. He did not look thrilled to see me.

A black figure stepped out from the kitchen area behind him
and into my view. He pointed back into the room, shouted something, and then turned to me, held up his finger, and mouthed the
words "one minute." I stepped back in front of the door, so as to
not allow myself the opportunity to spy into his house any further. I
waited, awkwardly. Bud poked his head out.

"Hi, Jay. The maid is just finishing up in here, why don't you
meet me around the side of the house?"

"Sure thing."

"Thanks, Jay."

There was no path, but there was a driveway in the back that
led to a short staircase that descended from a door to what ap-

peared to be the kitchen. Beside the staircase was the central air-conditioning unit. I sat on that and smoked a cigarette while I waited. A short time later the door opened. Bud wore a pair of pleated baby blue shorts, a beige soft-collared shirt, a gold bracelet on one wrist, and a large stainless-steel Rolex on the other. His face was red and splotchy. The patch of white chest hairs popping out of his collar glistened like they would on a wet cat.

Bud carried a pair of golf shoes and short, womanly socks. He sat down on the steps and began putting them on.

"I just wanted to show you what I had with this catalog I've been putting together."

"Do you have it with you?" I passed the materials to him. He read the paragraph on the back of the catalog and flipped through the pages. Watching Bud squatting on the steps, sweaty and in his casual golf attire, there was something thuggish about him. All of his slick, albeit corny, style was gone. I noticed that his eyelashes were dark, his trademark blond mustache was really gray but dyed blond, and his breath stank of sausage.

He set the catalog on the step beside him and laid the floppy disk on top of that. "So, what do you want to do with it?"

"Well. I've got a couple of ideas as far as that goes . . . I could handle the collecting of the photographs, print the catalogs, and mail them out myself, or I don't know, what do you think?"

Bud tapped the floppy. "Maybe we could find a way to try it out within the corporate structure."

"You mean, you collect the photos, put it together, print it, and distribute it?"

"Maybe. Perhaps, as far as the legality of it goes, it might be best for you to handle that side. But as far as the idea, I like it. And, you know, as long as it doesn't cost too much, I don't see any harm in trying it out."

"I've already got a printer who'll produce the catalog for hardly anything."

"Okay. What do you want to get out of this?"

"A commission on the sales."

Bud laughed. "Yeah. I figured." Bud rubbed his deeply pock-marked nose. He studied me. "What happened to you last night?"

I flushed. "I . . . I was pretty drunk."

"Why didn't you sell? Were you just busy with this catalog? I don't understand it."

"I . . . Shit. I guess I can tell you, I don't really know what I was thinking, but I . . . Can I trust you?"

"If you want to."

I was nervously crossing my arms and twisting the hair on the side of my head—a habit I have. I wanted to save the surprise for everyone, but somehow I felt like I should probably tell Bud, so that he would at least know what I was up to and I wouldn't fuck up the final banquet too much. "I have this plan."

"What plan?"

"I cooked it up last night while I was drunk. I don't know if it's such a good idea, but I had two sales in August. One to my maid and one really big order."

"How big?"

"Fourteen thousand dollars."

"Ha! I'll be damned. Why didn't you say anything about it last night?"

"I thought it'd be cooler if I revealed this information at the final banquet tomorrow while Acuña was walking up to accept his award. No offense, I mean, maybe he's a friend of yours and all, but I kind of wanted to outshine him and that prick Reid Tallenger . . . You know, I just wanted . . ."

"You wanted to steal the show."

"I guess."

Bud nodded a bunch of times and then shook his head. He stared at me for a moment, looked down, and then shook his head some more. I began to smile. "Jay, I've met a lot of people in this business, a lot of great salesmen and executives, but I don't think I've ever met a single soul who"—he was laughing at himself as he was saying this—"put so much thought into what we do and how we do it. I'm telling you, it's just crazy."

I shrugged. I was feeling nervous and worried that I might've just blown the full effect of my surprise on Bud, which would have been extremely satisfying to see in front of an audience.

Bud stuck out his hand. "Help me up, would you?" His hand felt like a sea cucumber. He laughed again. "I thought I had a flair for the dramatic, but compared to you, I feel like one of those whale song tapes that my wife uses to put her to sleep." He stretched his hands up. "I am not looking forward to this round of golf." Bud bent over, groaning, picked the catalog and the floppy off the step, and belched. "Well, I'm glad you came by. Let's talk later. I'm sure we can work something out."

"Great."

I stepped back. He waddled toward his car, hunched over and taking painful steps. His shorts were up his ass in a huge wedgie. "Wait. Bud. Do you think it's a good idea for me to stop Acuña and pull out my big order during the banquet?"

He grinned at me. "I think it's a great idea." He swung his head back around toward his car and called out, "Let me know if you want me to do anything special; otherwise, I'll just follow your cue."

While walking back to my condo, the Escort that had been parked outside Bud's house pulled up next to me. A large black woman with long fingernails and a bad wig was driving. She was wearing a tank top, and I could see the straps of her pink bra. "Hey, you know how to get outta here? I've been driving around this damn neighborhood forever."

"Sorry, sweetheart."

She cocked an eyebrow at me. "Sweetheart?" She laughed. "Pay me a hundred and fifty bucks and you can call me sweetheart all day long." She looked around over her dash. "C'mon, sugar, you sure you don't know how to get out of here?"

"Hold on." I saw one of the signs along the footpath, went over to it, figured out how to get her out of the compound, and then gave her the directions.

Walking to my condo, I kept scratching my cheek from the corner of my mouth to my chin. It was itching like hell. With my tongue, I could feel a small bump on the edge of my lip, which I figured was a zit. When I got back, I went into the bathroom to check it out in the mirror. It looked like I had two or three little pimples on my lower lip, because they were partially on the skin below the lip but they were also definitely on my lip. I tried to pop one, but there was nothing to pop. It frankly didn't really feel like a zit, but I couldn't figure out what it could have been until . . .

I locked the door. I sat on the toilet. This was not good. This was the very goddamn thing I had been dreading my entire life. I paced back and forth in the bathroom. I checked again. There was no change, except maybe they'd gotten a little bigger and clearer. They were not pimples. They were tiny blisters. I was almost crying and boiling hot. I tore off my shirt and looked again. No doubt about it. They were blisters. This was a cold sore. Somehow, I'd contracted goddamn herpes. I stared into the mirror and at my lip for the next thirty minutes, praying that there would be some sort of change, hoping that I could have been wrong. I leaned my head against the mirror and waited with my eyes closed. I checked again. Same thing. I turned on the sink and washed my face over and over and over with cold water and looked again. Same deal. I sat on the floor of the bathroom with the water running.

I heard Skeeter leave. I stayed on the floor with my arms crossed over my knees and my head resting on them. I prayed and I prayed and I checked again and there was no improvement in the situation.

32

I asked the cabdriver to stay as close to the Intracoastal as he could. I wanted to smell it. I wanted to smell the briny marsh that all life came out of and feel the air that came off of it blowing in the car and onto my face.

As I stepped out from the cab, I had to steady myself on the door. I climbed the steps leading to the restaurant entrance, walked past the hostess, and entered the dining room to my left. The room was surrounded on three sides by windows and jutted out over a small cove. The sun glancing off the water and into the room made the crystal glasses and forks glimmer like crazy. I wanted to put on my sunglasses to fight the glimmer but that would be rude. I had to be goddamn polite. I had to be polite.

My uncle John is an impressive guy. He's six five, has short light hair, and has very sleepy gray eyes. He sits, slightly hunched over, always with his head tilted toward you—always listening, always watching. He has a scar like mine above his upper lip on the same side. Mine is from a dog bite. His is from a motorcycle accident in Paris during World War II. His bottom teeth are crooked and jut out slightly from his lip. His voice is slow. His words bang around in his mouth and come at you off of his teeth. I've never heard a voice like his. He winds his words together—naturally—but there is also something classic about their sound, like he's swallowed a record player.

Although John has fair skin, his age and a ruddy hue have given his face an even color, the color coming from the mixture of myriad scars, broken blood vessels, and time. He has deep-set eyes. High cheekbones. When he listens, he watches you with an unreadable expression. The effect of this is that when conversing with him people are constantly trying to elicit a positive reaction and so they are very careful how they go about it. Around John I've always felt people being careful. It can be very intimidating.

My aunt Elaine on the surface is everything that John is not. She is a classically beautiful woman and would be the first to tell you that a certain amount of plastic surgery has helped her maintain that beauty. Outward appearance is extremely important to Elaine. She does not necessarily demand that you be beautiful—but that you try to be as beautiful as possible. That you go through the same pains that she took when presenting herself. You also must be polite and interesting, but most of all interested.

"May I help you, sir." A waiter or maître d'—I couldn't tell which—was aggressively smiling at me. I shook my head. I felt faint. I didn't want to speak.

"Sir." He nodded toward my right hand. I followed his eye line. My hand was on the back of a chair, the fingers of which were snagged on the red hair of the woman sitting in it. She was tugging her head away. I let go. The woman glared up at me indignantly. "Sir! Perhaps I could help you to your seat."

"I'm looking for my aunt and uncle, John and Elaine Harrison."

"Right this way."

I wiped my face. My stomach hurt. My lip tingled.

John wore a dark blue suit. Elaine wore a white one, her blond hair pulled perfectly back tightly to her head.

"Good to see you."

Elaine touched my hand. "Are you okay, Jay?"

"Yes. I'm fine."

John said, "You look sick, maybe."

I picked up the glass of ice water that was in front of me with two hands and drank half of it. "Actually, I'm a little upset. Do you mind if I tell you why?"

"No. Please."

"My entire life I've been terrified of getting a cold sore, and just a few hours ago, I think I got one." They stared at me blankly. I pointed to my lip.

John squinted. He gritted his teeth and made a noise with his mouth. "They're annoying buggers, but I don't see much point in worrying about them. You've gotten one. It'll be gone soon. Why don't we take a look at the menus?"

I obeyed, trying as hard as I could not to think about the damn thing, and to a degree John was right. Actually he was absolutely right, but I still couldn't quite concentrate on anything else.

Part of the reason why I wanted to see John and Elaine, other than simply to catch up, was that I wanted John to know how well I was doing. I'm sure that this had something to do with my mother and how she hated everything that I did and the fact that I never knew her father, but I wanted in the worst way to be able to prove to John that I was not a waste and that I had been and could be extremely successful at something. Since he was such an extremely successful businessman I thought that telling them about my knife selling would do it.

Typically, when I told someone about my experience with Apex I immediately put forward all of the more dubious elements—my seven steps to selling, the scholarship, the frenzied, cultlike over-hyper push celebrations, and how I manipulated them to my advantage. These anecdotes revealed my skill and cunning, and usually got laughs. John and Elaine hardly snickered. The more and more I talked, John's eyes sharpened, the muscles in his face tensed and shifted forward, a wrinkle descended his forehead. His body continually leaned toward mine to hear my quieting voice; however, the distance between us grew.

I had planned on asking him his opinion of the catalog, but ended up not mentioning it at all. Although John had not said a disapproving word, I found myself defending Apex, their practices, the people involved, and of course, I began defending myself. I kept saying, "It all really wasn't as bad as I've been making it seem to you. You know, I wasn't really manipulating these people."

The worst part was, the more I stared into John's drooping eyes, slowly blinking and revealing nothing, I got worried that John and Elaine thought that I might have set up this dinner in order to get something out of them. The softshelled crabs. A free calamari fritti, which they ate most of. That they could think these things about me really pissed me off. I was not a user. By the time the check came I was virtually incensed. I snatched the leather booklet from the waiter. "Please. I'm going to take this. And could you call a cab for me? I'm going to Myrtle Beach."

"I'll call right now and bring you your receipt."

*   *   *

Outside the restaurant, Elaine said, "We would have liked to bring you down to Secessionville."

"I would have liked that, but tomorrow I have one more thing to do with the knife convention and then I'm flying to Dartmouth."

"Well, we so enjoyed hearing your stories. You're a fine young man. Stay in constant touch, would you?"

"I will." I hugged and kissed Elaine and opened the car door for her. She sat and I closed the door.

"Well." John stuck out his hand. "It was a pleasure as always." I shook John's hand.

"There's one thing I wanted to ask you."

"What's that?"

"Do you think there's anything wrong with what I've been doing?"

He stuck his lips out and shook his head. "No. Not really." He set his hand on the top of his car and looked at me. "I was just thinking while you were telling us about your knife selling that, if I were your age and had the means, I would have spent my summer fly-fishing." He smiled. "But maybe you don't like fly-fishing."

"I don't know how."

"Well, then, I'll have to teach you sometime." He stuck his hand out once more. "I'd love to stay and chat with you, Jay, but my wife is waiting. It was good seeing you and thank you very much for dinner."

The cab pulled up as I was walking back to the restaurant. I felt my lip itch and realized that I had forgotten about my cold sore for a good forty-five minutes at least.

Skeeter had left a note with the address of a party in a nearby condo. I'd go in a minute. I took off my blazer, shirt, and dress shoes and sat down on the edge of the bed. I flopped back with my feet on the floor. I'd just close my eyes for one minute.

I had a disturbing dream. I was in my old pool, swimming in tight circles a few feet below the surface. I could see the roof of the pool house and the legs of people milling around nearby. The chlorine in the water began to burn my skin. My face was covered in cold sores. The legs came over and stood beside the pool, looking down at me. Coulter. My father. My mother. Wex. My uncle Steve. Friends from Dartmouth. Sherianne was wearing a bathrobe. (Isabelle was not there.) They were all talking about how amazing it was that I could hold my breath for so long. They were waiting for me to get out of the pool, because they wanted to swim but were afraid that if they got in the water with me that they would become infected with whatever was on my face. I wanted desperately for somebody to pull me out.

Eventually, Sherianne said she wasn't afraid to swim, so long as she didn't have to touch me. She took off her bathrobe and jumped naked into the pool. Her ass wagged. Her legs and arms pumped pathetically. Her vagina was bright red and her pubic hairs looked like a giant patch of black moss. She sort of dog-paddled above me, half choking and spitting up water as she said, "See! It's okay. Look at me. I'm fine." Suddenly I kicked with both feet and swam up at her. My teeth were made of knives. She shrieked. I shredded her body but did not eat it. Her flesh ripped apart like a soggy birthday cake. Her screams turned into a gentle hiss and then stopped. I climbed out. The pool was like a thick bloody soup, with chunks of Sherianne's soggy birthday cake flesh hanging in it. I smiled, my knife teeth poking out of my crusty face, and everybody ran away screaming.

The clock on the bedside table said it was four in the morning. My body was slick with sweat. My arms were folded across my chest.

I was wide awake and thought about drinking myself to sleep again. I got up and walked into the kitchen. Skeeter's head was tossed back and his legs up on the edge of the couch. The beers and bottles of booze on the counter bored me. I heard the Atlantic Ocean.

I didn't bother putting on my bathing suit. I dropped my towel in the sand. The beach was utterly quiet, save for the waves and the wind. The water was warmer than the air. I needed it on my skin. I'd heard that salt water was good for warts and viruses. I thought it might help get rid of my cold sore, which was no longer itchy but hard and stung slightly when I moved my mouth.

A wave coming to shore nearly knocked me over. I couldn't see it. The foamy water washed past me and brushed against my naked body. I dropped into it. I could feel the riptide pulling me out, but it wasn't that strong and I wasn't worried about getting taken out too far, so I let it pull me and I just kept my head above water and watched the lampposts that lighted the walkways between the condos glow orange and move away from me.

I kept my eyes open as I dove down into the black water. I swam along the bottom, feeling the sand with my fingers. My hand jerked back when I touched a starfish. I let my body drift underwater a little farther. An undertow gently twisted me onto my back. I closed my eyes.

33

"Wake up." I shook Skeeter.

"Wahh . . ."

"Wake up, man. I need to ask you a favor."

"What?" He blinked at me.

"I need you to break into Susanne's apartment and steal her car keys."

"What for?"

"You gotta drive me to the airport. I'm flying to California at six." This was partially untrue—but I'll explain that later.

"What?"

"C'mon, dude. Just get up. We gotta go. It's almost five."

Skeeter lifted his body off the couch. He looked at me and tried to fall back onto it. I grabbed his hand and pulled him to his feet.

"Okay! Okay! I'm up." Skeeter rubbed his face, then whipped his hands away and looked at me with a crazy smile. "Good morning."

Skeeter and I stood below the backside of Susanne's condo—below her balcony. "So, dude. You remember where the keys are?"

"Not really."

"There's a dish on her kitchen counter."

"Why don't we just wake her up and ask if we can borrow her car?"

"Because she might say no. I tried calling every cab company in the phone book and they're all closed. I already paid for my ticket." Again, this was partially a lie. "If I miss my flight I'm not getting out of here."

"Okay." Skeeter inspected the wall. "Here, help me get up that drainpipe. Once I get in, I'll let myself out the front." Skeeter kicked off his flip-flops. I laced my fingers together and held out my hands. I gave him a boost. He latched onto the pipe. Pressing his feet against the wall and pulling on the pipe, he more or less walked and pulled himself hand over hand up onto the balcony. I heard the screen door slide open. He leaned over the balcony, gave me the thumbs-up, and disappeared inside the condo.

Skeeter drove, shirtless. I smoked. He didn't say much. His eyes were red and tired. The sky was turning blue. He was already squinting. "The sun's going to be up on your ride back."

"Yip. Right in my face."

I reached into the breast pocket of my sport coat and handed him my shades. "You can have these."

The terminal came up quickly. "Skeeter, you're the best thing about Apex, you know that?"

Skeeter was shifting around in his seat. "Hey, man. I'm not gonna get out and give you a hug and all, not that I don't want to, but because I really gotta take a goddamn mean piss."

I shook Skeeter's hand and got out. He peeled away. I laughed to myself as I walked up to the terminal entrance, thinking about the surprise Skeeter was going to find in the can when he got home. Before we left, I laid the Ambrose order form in the toilet, like a skin on the water. It didn't entirely fit, so I had to bend the sides of the pages up and press them flat against the round surface of the porcelain bowl. Skeeter was going to rush home, burst into the bathroom, and unleash a hearty stream of urine into a makeshift paper cup that was worth seven thousand dollars in commission.

I didn't bother going to the check-in desk. All flights to Atlanta were sold out. But I'd bought a ticket from Atlanta to LAX at eight-thirty, so I had to get to Atlanta. I still had the paper ticket for my flight to Hanover later that afternoon and used it to get through security.

"A little early?" the security guard said to me.

"Like to beat the rush." This, of course, was a joke, since the Myrtle Beach Airport is tiny. The guard didn't laugh.

He handed me back the ticket and said, "Have a ball, kid."

I bought a baseball hat in a souvenir store and walked down to the gate where the 6:10 flight to Atlanta was about to board. I stood off to the side of the mass of people in golf clothes ready to board. I identified the group of ten or so standby passengers standing beside the check-in desk irritably staring at those who had seats. There were a lot of them, so there was no point for me to even try to fly standby.

I didn't have a seat, a ticket, or a plan of how I was going to get on the flight. But I was going to do it. The flight attendant made the expected announcement. "We are just about to board Delta flight three-seventy-six with service to Atlanta, Georgia. The flight is over-sold and Delta would like to offer anyone with a confirmed seat a first-class round-trip ticket to . . ."

There was still time to make a quick call. It was damn early in New York, but I had no choice. I had to call Wex.

"Hellllo." He sounded like he'd just been kicked in the throat.

"Wex. Hi, this is Jay."

"Jay?"

"Yeah. Dude. I'm sorry to wake you up."

"It's okay. What's going on? Are you all right?"

"Yeah. I'm fine. Listen . . ."

"Wait. Let me get out of bed. I don't want to wake Anneke."

I heard Wex groan and the floor creak as he crossed to the far side of his apartment. "Hey. What's up?"

"I'm so sorry for waking you, but I didn't really know what else to do."

"Yeah."

"I'm in the airport in Myrtle Beach trying to sneak on a flight to Atlanta. I've got a flight from Atlanta to L.A. in a couple hours. I could have called then, but it's a tight connection and I wanted to catch you before I got there."

"What'd you need?"

"Do you still want me to drive your car to Michigan?"

"Yeah. Sure."

"Okay. I'll do it. I'll let you get back to sleep. Just tell me, where do I find it?"

"It's ummmm. In a parking garage on Pico. Number eight-four-eight-two. The keys are under the driver-side doormat. It's un-locked."

"Cool. Thanks, man. I'll try you when I get there."

"Do. It might not start. There's some shit I got to tell you."

"Okay."

Wex yawned. "So, ummmm . . . are you going to drive the car back alone?"

"No." I looked over at the boarding area; people were walking onto the plane. "Isabelle's meeting me there."

"Yeah? How's her grandmother?"

I laughed. "You think you got it bad. I called her about three hours ago."

"You're a gentleman."

"Well . . . If it's any consolation, I bought her a ticket. She's flying in at around five, so I've got to make sure I get on this goddamn flight or else I'm kind of fucked."

"Do you have a seat?"

"No. I'm going to sneak on."

Today, of course, this would be nearly impossible, but back then it seemed to me to be what my father would call a "poor choice." I figured if I got caught I might get hassled a little, maybe arrested, but nothing too bad. I, however, didn't really believe I would make it on the flight. But I had to.

Wex laughed. "Good luck."

"Thanks."

He hung up.

Back at the gate, the flight attendant was calling people up— boarding from the back to the front. I stood there, among the ticket holders. Passengers kept boarding. Seats were filling. The flight attendant called the last few rows forward. A woman with what looked like a shrunken head whined, "Are we next?"

"Just a minute and we'll get to you."

Out of the corner of my eye I noticed an elderly woman struggle to pull herself out of her chair. She had a cane in one hand and a large bag on her lap. No one moved to help her. All the southern gents around her just looked at their tickets or out the window and she jerked forward in her seat but couldn't quite get to her feet. It was sort of painful to watch.

I strode over to the woman. "May I help you, ma'am?"

"Yes, you may."

I took her bag, helped her out of her seat, and handed her the cane.

"Thank you." She fumbled with the cane. "Would you mind walking me to the gate?"

"Not at all." I held on to her bag and offered her my arm. "I was just about to board."

When we got to the short line at the entrance to the jetway, the woman asked to see her bag. I held it open for her. She leaned her cane against her body and while still holding on to my arm fished around inside of it. "Here we go." She pulled out the envelope with her ticket in it and handed it to me. "Why don't you give that to the flight attendant."

"Okay."

When I offered to help this woman out of her seat I did not think that she could help me sneak on the plane, but as we approached the flight attendant the thought distinctly occurred to me. I took the woman's ticket out of the envelope and put my ticket to Hanover underneath it.

"May I have your tickets please?"

I handed the flight attendant our tickets together, the old lady's on top of mine. The shrunken-headed woman was still griping at her. "I'll sue this airline. I'm not afraid to do it."

"Ma'am, we're going to try to board you in just one minute. If we don't get you on this plane we'll get you on another."

"There aren't any more until tomorrow!"

The flight attendant looked at the ticket on top, glanced at mine, and said, "Thank you. Have a nice flight." She smiled. "Next."

I walked the old lady to her seat, stuck my bag in the overhead compartment, and went to the bathroom. I probably would have stayed in the bathroom until the plane took off if I thought that would work, but I was sure that it wouldn't. The plane wouldn't take off with me in there. I had to sit down somewhere. I opened the door and saw one of the flight attendants looking down the aisle, counting empty seats.

The flight attendant was about to start boarding the standby passengers. I didn't think through what would happen next. I just planted my ass next to a very fat middle-aged Hispanic woman, pulled the brim of my hat down over my eyes, curled toward her, and pretended to sleep.

Announcements were made about proper seat assignments. "If you do not have a seat, please get off the plane and we will reseat you on a different flight." Feet kept passing back and forth, slowing by my own. Then the feet stopped. I could hear the flight attendant breathing as she hovered over me, looking at her seating chart. "Sir. Excuse me, sir. May I see your ticket?" I didn't move. "Sir!"

I was practically hugging the Hispanic lady's huge arm. I'm sure I even drooled on it.

"Sir!" This fucking flight attendant was really getting loud. She shook my shoulder. I didn't budge. Finally, I heard her say to the lady next to me, "Ma'am. Is he with you? Does he have a ticket?"

The woman replied in Spanish. As I've told you before, I speak the language—though not perfectly. However, I perfectly understood the woman when she replied, *"¿Sí? Yo tengo mi boleto. Ya te lo mostré."* Which translates to: "Yes? I have my ticket. I already showed it to you."

I have no idea whether the flight attendant misunderstood the woman and assumed we were together or whether she realized that if she wanted me off that plane she was going to have to pry my cold dead fingers off the fat lady's arm. All she did was make a sound like a stabbed goat and stormed off down the aisle. She didn't return until she was pushing a drink cart and I was no longer pretending to sleep. I was in a deep, dreamless sleep. She rammed my knee with the cart. I yanked my leg back, looked up at her, and said, "Jesus, lady!"

She smirked at me. "So, you are alive, after all."

34

The Mustang's engine sounded like the Evilo—deep and throaty. I heard a faint ticking sound bouncing off the walls of the garage. I put the car in reverse, backed out of the spot, stalled, fired it back up again, and rode the clutch all the way until I was on Pico. I bottomed out as I crested the ramp and swerved out onto the street.

I had been swimming in the Atlantic ten hours earlier. I wanted the Pacific salt on me before half a day elapsed. I had the top down. The Mustang felt good when I drove fast.

There were a lot of people walking in the sand and on the boardwalk, but curiously few in the water. None, to be exact. I wondered how it was that so many people could live so close to the water and not swim in it. West Coast assholes, I figured. I took my shirt and shoes off, looked around to see if anybody was watching, and stripped down to my boxers. I left my clothes in a mound about fifteen feet from the water and walked down to it.

It was a beautiful, sunny day. I thought about Isabelle. When I spoke to her on the phone, she was groggy and confused. I told her I'd bought her another open-ended ticket and that I didn't give a damn if she came or not. She kept asking me if I would be understanding and patient. And I kept answering no. Why the hell did she agree to come meet me? I didn't know. I didn't care. I didn't care if she came, tortured me, and left. She could do it a thousand times (and she would). Endless rejection. Endless pain. It did not matter. I was determined to get her to love me.

My natural instinct was to run out into the surf and dive in, but I kind of wanted to savor the moment, so I strolled around in water up to my ankles, still staring out at the sky. What would Coach O'Mally do when I didn't show up? What would Stuart think? Would he blame it on the knife selling? Would he think I'd gone crazy? Woodsy? He'd never know I was tapped at Delta Theta Chi or that I accepted or the fact that I didn't want to betray his friendship had anything (even if it was just the tiniest amount) to do with why I wouldn't go back to Dartmouth. He'd probably leave me eighty-five messages about all the fun I was going to be missing this fall when he pledged and got dinged from the frat.

I wondered if Bud French would ever make the catalog. My dad said he had a version of something like it mailed to him a few years later. He saved it for me, but I never bothered to check it out. Maybe Ty Nakamori printed them, but I doubt it. The last I heard, the karate/karaoke-loving billionaire went broke, wrote a self-help book, had a nervous breakdown, and then moved to Texas to open a megachurch. Apparently, he's known for his wildly entertaining and convincing sermons. I like to imagine him standing at a pulpit, glazed in sweat, screaming into the microphone while holding a pair of kitchen shears in one hand, a gleaming copper penny in the other.

Poor Brooke. After gently reprimanding her for absolutely no reason and then making her promise not to annoy me, I did not call her back. I wouldn't call her for another seven months, when I found out she'd been in a boating accident and I called to see if she was all right. She was still under the impression that we were together and asked if she was "being good." I didn't know that any of this would happen as I stood up to my ankles in the Pacific. All I knew was that I actually did love her, in a way, and that I didn't want to crush her—although, if I ever spoke to her or saw her, the temptation was too great to resist. I decided it was best to leave her alone.

My dad? Would he care? Probably not. He'd find it funny. My mom? I actually knew what my mom thought. I called her that morning, before I called the airline, or Isabelle, and even before I woke up Skeeter. I said to her, "Mom. I'm sorry for waking you but I can't go back to Dartmouth right now. I don't know if I'm ever going back and I think that if I don't do something right now, if I don't make some move, if I don't get the fuck out of here I'm going to have a problem."

"Jay. What are you talking about?"

"I can't keep doing this."

"What?"

"I don't know. I don't know what it is. I just know that I was swimming in the ocean about five minutes ago and . . ." I stopped.

"What? What did you do?"

"I don't know." I was sort of crying on the phone, but quietly, because I was trying not to wake Skeeter. "Mom . . . I just, I almost just drowned."

"Did you just say you tried to drown yourself?"

"No. I didn't really try to drown myself. It's too complicated to get into, but no . . . I just got sucked way out like a mile maybe . . . I was really scared."

"Hold on. I'm sitting up in bed. Fancy! Move. Let me turn on the light . . . Wait. Jay. It's almost five o'clock in the morning. I've got to get my bearings. Now, why did you almost drown yourself?"

"It was nothing, listen . . ."

"No. Jay. Listen to me, I want you to go back to sleep. Don't go swimming anymore tonight. Tomorrow, I want you to call me in the morning and let me know that you're okay and then I want you to get on your flight to Dartmouth or you can come home if you want but I don't want you to do anything rash. Do you hear me?"

"Yeah. I'm fine, but you got to hear me out. I'm not going back to Dartmouth."

"Then what are you going to do?"

"I don't know. I'm going to get out of here."

"Where are you going to go?"

"I know where I want to go, but getting there could be a little dicey."

"Dicey? What are you talking about?"

"Never mind, Mom. That's not why I'm calling. I just wanted to say thank you for letting me stay with you this summer."

"I'm happy to have you."

"No. I really mean it. I don't know how to say it. I guess I just missed you all those years that I was with Dad and Sherianne. I really missed you."

I could hear my mother crying. "It was so hard on me, Jay. I really think I lost my mind. I think something happened. Something snapped in me, Jay. I'm so sorry if I did anything to hurt you. But you've got to understand . . ."

"I know the feeling. It's okay. And even though we didn't spend much time together, I'm glad that I was there with you." There was a long pause.

"Jay. You're a good person. You're a loving person. You don't have to put that pressure on yourself."

I almost got mad, but I didn't. Instead I laughed. "It has nothing to do with pressure. Trust me. I can handle pressure. Listen, Mom. I've got to go. I love you."

"I love you too, Jay. You know that, don't you?"

"I do, Mom. But seriously, I'm kind of in a rush here. I've got to make some calls . . ."

"Please don't hang up, you've got me worried."

"Don't be worried. I was just swimming around and I kind of thought I could fall asleep for a second. So I did."

"You can't, Jay, not in the ocean, for God's sake!"

"Let me tell you, I'm well aware of that now."

"Jay, please just come home. Please come home right now."

"I'm sorry. I can't. I love you. Bye."

So I was thinking about all of this stuff as I slowly waded out into the water. The Pacific was much colder than the Atlantic. I ran my fingers across the surface. A wave rolled toward me, breaking. I dove headfirst into its face. I came out the other side, feeling distinctly unclean. I noticed that I smelled awful. Or maybe it was the water. I couldn't tell. I bodysurfed the next wave as far as I could, and when I stood up a short fat Mexican was shouting at me from the shore.

"Huh?"

He kept shouting, but the wind was coming off the ocean and his words were blown back east. "Hold on! I'll come over to you!"

I walked until I was standing in the wet sand where the waves were washing up. He was standing on dry sand, seemingly very worried about getting his sandals wet, because he kept looking down to make sure he didn't step too close to the foam. "What's up?"

"De beach. Is close. Water ess dirty. It rain last night." He pointed at a sign I had completely disregarded on my way to the ocean. It read, WARNING. AVOID CONTACT WITH THE WATER. ANY CONTACT MAY BE HAZARDOUS TO YOUR HEALTH.

I looked back at the Mexican. He smiled, nodded at me, and then waddled back up the beach toward a group of women who were waiting for him.

I felt something brush up against my foot. I looked down. A condom floated out from between my legs. I watched the foam carry it toward the beach and then it swirled back toward me on the outgoing wave. I lifted my right foot out of the water so it didn't touch me again. It swept out toward the next wave coming in and was taken under. The more I looked at the surface the more I noticed little bits of what could only be sewage, bubbling and churning in the water all around me. My own body wore excellent evidence of this. Brown and green flecks coated my skin. The sun was cooking the stuff on me. The smell now grew stronger—putrid and baking.

I turned back toward the ocean. I was confused. It still looked beautiful. I wanted to be swimming. I wanted the salt water to cleanse me. I wanted to be in the goddamn Pacific Ocean. "Fuck it." I took a few quick strides, dove into the next oncoming wave, and stroked out into the sea of shit.

EpiLoGue

The motivational speakers are right. You can get anything you want. It took me three years of effort and Isabelle a brief stint at a nut home before I got her. We dated for two
years. Had horrible sex. And hated each other passionately.

I don't really know when we broke up. I think it was when she
tried to hook up with a friend of mine after she found a note in my
apartment from a girl who I'd been seeing on the side. I don't

know. But we both moved on and quickly became friends again. Over the years, we've spoken often and seen each other occasionally.

Not long ago we slept together. Isabelle was into it for about ten minutes and then asked me to come. I did. We slept together once more after that. We probably made it twenty minutes before we both decided to stop. That was the last time. There was something nice about it, though. We were friends. I wasn't trying to sell her anything. And she was hot. I really thought she looked hot, lying naked on my bed, a little sweaty, her legs open at her thighs but crossed at her ankles looking at me, thinking God knows what.

ACKnoWLeDGmeNts

I would like to thank Kerri Kolen, Anne Carey, and Tod Culpan Williams, Jr., for their help with this book, as well as my father, Richard Jamison Williams, Jr., for his generous support.